MW00577668

SERVES ME WRIGHT

SERVES ME WRIGHT

K.A. LINDE

ALSO BY K.A. LINDE

The Wright World

WRIGHTS

The Wright Brother

The Wright Boss

The Wright Mistake

The Wright Secret

The Wright Love

The Wright One

A Wright Christmas

WRIGHT VINEYARD

One Wright Stand

Wright with Benefits

Serves Me Wright

Wright Rival

Wright that Got Away

All the Wright Moves

CRUEL

One Cruel Night | Cruel Money

Cruel Fortune | Cruel Legacy

Cruel Promise | Cruel Truth

Cruel Desire | Cruel Marriage

COASTAL CHRONICLES

Hold the Forevers | At First Hate

RECORD SERIES

Off the Record | On the Record | For the Record

Struck from the Record | Broken Record

AVOIDING SERIES

Avoiding Commitment | Avoiding Responsibility

Avoiding Temptation | Avoiding Extras

DIAMOND GIRLS SERIES

Rock Hard | A Girl's Best Friend

In the Rough | Shine Bright | Under Pressure

TAKE ME DUET

Take Me for Granted | Take Me with You

Following Me

FANTASY ROMANCE

BLOOD TYPE SERIES

Blood Type | Blood Match | Blood Cure

ASCENSION SERIES

The Affiliate | The Bound | The Consort

The Society | The Domina

ROYAL HOUSES

House of Dragons | House of Shadows

PART I

THE ARRANGEMENT

1

JENNIFER

*M*y smile was fake. I'd perfected a pleasant exterior as my insides roiled, and I wondered how the hell I was going to escape this guy. Why had I ever agreed to go on a date with him? It had clearly ruined everything.

New rule: don't date anyone you work with.

"Oh, that's nice, Evan," I said, taking a step backward.

Evan moved forward again, swinging his Nikon around as if it hadn't cost him a small fortune. He'd been my second shooter at a dozen weddings all over the country, and it had seemed like a great idea to ask him to shoot the grand opening of Wright Vineyard. That was before I'd agreed to go on a date with him. The worst date of my entire life.

"Maybe after we're done, we can head out for a drink," he suggested.

I bit my lip. I'd decided after our last date that I was going to go cold turkey on guys for ninety days. After a string of horrendous dates—truly horrendous dates—I couldn't stomach it. I wanted the summer all to myself. But saying no was easier said than done when I'd spent my

3

K.A. LINDE

entire life doing what everyone else asked of me. It was time to be more like my best friends, Annie and Sutton. They got what they wanted. I wanted that, too.

"I don't know, Evan."

"Ten o'clock downtown?"

"I..."

"Perfect."

My eyes were wild with alarm at the stupid word that wouldn't escape my lips. How hard was it to say *no* to a guy? *No, I don't want to date you. No, I don't want to sit through another dinner where you talk about yourself. No, I don't want to hear how much better you think you are than me.* Just *no*.

But the word never left my mouth.

"Uh...I don't know. Maybe..."

Evan furrowed his brow and opened his mouth, as if he were going to say something, but then his eyes darted up and over my shoulder. He took a step back in response.

I whipped around and found none other than Julian Wright. My heart stuttered at the sight of him. He was dressed to impress in his typical preppy attire—sharp khakis, a blue button-up, gray blazer, and boat shoes. His dark hair was swept to the side, and his dark eyes were fixed right on me. I'd been attracted to him since the day he'd literally fallen into a pool on top of me. That was three years ago. One date and one perfect kiss later, and I was a goner.

But that was ancient history. We were just friends now.

"Hey," I said with a smile.

"Hey, Jen," he said. "Think I could borrow you and your camera?"

His eyes moved to Evan behind me. His jaw flexed for a moment. The news of our bad date had circulated. He'd probably heard about it.

Damn Annie! I wanted to bury my face in my shirt.

4

"I can go," Evan said quickly.

Julian dismissed him without a word. "Jen?"

"Yeah. Sure. What do you need?"

He gestured for me to precede him, which I did. We headed across the main barn and toward a side exit, which helped us avoid the crowds. Because not only was today the grand opening, but we'd also secured the band Cosmere to play a private concert for us right here in the Wright Vineyard barn. It helped that the lead singer, Campbell, was from Lubbock and his brother, Hollin, was a co-owner with Julian.

We exited the barn, and I took one fleeting look behind me. It was already busy with early-access guests. The high ceiling and ambient lighting made the rustic interior shine. The floors, which used to be dirt, were now a glossy hardwood, and there was a stage set up at the end of the place, just big enough for a band or a wedding party. It had taken them months to get it the way they wanted, and it had all paid off.

"What do you want me to shoot?" I asked Julian.

"Oh, nothing," he said, running a hand back through his dark hair and shooting me an alluring smile. "You looked like you wanted to be anywhere but talking to that guy."

I laughed self-consciously and tucked a strand of my light-brown bob behind my ear. "That is the truth."

"Didn't you recommend him for the job?" He tilted his head to the side.

"I did," I said with a wince as I fell into step beside him.

We took a trail away from the bustle of the barn and toward the cellars. Hundreds of people were already waiting in line before the barn door for the Cosmere show. Thankfully, they'd hired security for the event, and everything seemed to be in order. I was glad that we were taking a different route to the cellars rather than past the crowd. My anxiety couldn't handle that on a good day. After dealing with Evan, today was not that day.

"What happened?"

"Oh God, haven't you heard?"

He shook his head.

I sighed. "Well, we went on a date. He took me to La Sirena." Which was my favorite restaurant in town. I'd thought it was looking up. "Then he spent the entire dinner talking about himself. He got handsy into the third course of tapas."

Julian cringed. "Jesus."

"Yeah. It, uh...dissolved from there."

"So, why is he still coming around? I'm shocked he'd take the job."

"Well, I'm not Annie," I said with a laugh.

Julian arched an eyebrow in question. "You aren't going after my brother?"

I laughed, a genuine one at that. "Dear God, I am most certainly not."

"That's a relief," Julian said.

His dark eyes met mine, and something fluttered in my stomach at the look.

I glanced away. "I mean that I'm not as extroverted."

"No one is as extroverted as Annie," Julian said with a laugh.

"You are."

"Psh! Not even me."

"Well, *I'm* definitely not. So, I guess I didn't make it clear enough to him that I wasn't interested. I honestly think that he thought the date went well."

Julian wrinkled his nose. "Fucker."

I snorted and then immediately covered my mouth. "Oh

my God, don't make me laugh like that."

His eyes found mine, and his own smile was wide and unassuming. "Why not? That snort is the best part of your laugh."

I giggled, tucking my hair behind my ear again. "You're ridiculous."

He was flirting with me. Oh my God, was he flirting with me? I didn't know. Julian Wright was as charming as they came. I'd never met anyone who could woo someone so thoroughly. And I wasn't just saying that because I'd been into him for so long. I knew it wasn't going anywhere and that he couldn't control the charm. But I also couldn't help *hoping* that this was more than his normal charm...and actual flirting.

It seemed unlikely. Just as much as I wasn't dating because of my string of bad dates, coupled with my inability to tell people how I really felt, Julian hadn't been dating the last couple months either. He'd been dating Ashleigh Sinclair for two years when he found out that she was trying to sabotage the winery to get him to work for her father—a real estate mogul here in Lubbock. Their breakup had been swift and brutal, and he hadn't dated since.

"Come on. Let me show you the cellars while we're down here," Julian said, opening the cellar door.

I'd already had a full tour. Ever since Julian and Hollin had offered me a spot as the company wedding photographer, I'd been all in on Wright Vineyard.

For more than three years, I'd been working weddings and elopements as a travel photographer. I went all over the country and the Caribbean. I even shot a wedding in Bali. *Bali.* But it had been hard, being gone every weekend and most weekdays from April to October, especially since I found it impossible to say no to clients. And not every wedding was as much of a dream as the trip to Bali. They were a lot of hard work, and I liked the idea of having a full-time job here in town. Then I got to pick and choose which elopements to photograph. It was an easy way for me to say no to potential brides without saying *no*.

But I couldn't say no to Julian either. Nor did I want to.

So, I stepped into the cellars and breathed in the wine fermentation. It was a particular smell that I was coming to enjoy. Especially with the added benefit of free wine on the job.

Julian was regaling me with stories about the different vintages. I only half-listened. From the moment he'd decided to purchase the winery, he'd been full deep dive into winemaking and running the business. This was his life, and even if I only understood half of it, it was interesting to hear his excitement.

The cellars were at least relatively deserted, and we made it all the way down and around the corner, uninterrupted.

Julian stopped in front of his office. "Well, that completes the tour. Show should be starting soon," he said. "Probably should get you backstage."

I nodded. "Probably."

Despite the fact that I'd said *no guys for ninety days* and I wanted the entire summer to myself, I didn't want to walk away from Julian. It was impossible anyway. Probably stupid to even consider.

Then his eyes rounded in circles as he looked over my shoulder.

I turned to find none other than Ashleigh Sinclair on the property.

"What is *she* doing here?" I whispered.

As far as I knew, all Sinclairs were banned from the

premises.

"I have no idea." Julian reached out and grabbed my hand. I looked back at him in surprise. "I really don't want to find out."

"What?"

But he put a finger to his lips and then tipped his head back. Without a word, he pulled me into his office, decisively shutting the door behind him. The lights were off, and I could hear our breathing in the space as we waited to see if Ashleigh had seen us.

"What are you doing?" I barely breathed.

He hadn't dropped my hand, and he squeezed it. "It's opening day. I just...I don't want to deal with her."

"I thought she wasn't allowed on the property."

His sigh was audible. "She isn't."

"Do you think she saw you?" I whispered.

He didn't respond. We lingered in the silence of that dark space. The heat between us potent. An energy crackling that I'd never felt before. It started at the top of my head and ran all the way to the tips of my toes. I could lean in, and our bodies would touch. I wanted to. Even knowing it was stupid.

We were hiding from his ex. This wasn't...anything.

"I think she's gone," he breathed softly.

I felt him pull away, and then against all odds, the door to the office began to open. I saw a flash of bleached-blonde hair and creamy white skin. Ashleigh *had* seen us.

I heard Julian's quick intake of breath and the two simple words that turned my life upside down, "Forgive me."

His lips crashed down on mine, and there was no longer air left in the world. There was simply this moment as I drowned in him and forgot what it meant to breathe.

2

JENNIFER

I'd kissed Julian Wright once before.

Just once.

At Jensen and Emery's wedding, we'd danced all night, and he kissed me before saying good-night. I hoped it was the start of something special. I'd been wrong.

He'd moved to Lubbock from Vancouver to be with his mom during her cancer diagnosis. It was the third time she'd fought it, and she beat it again. But that year, dealing with her chemotherapy, had been a blur for Julian. And when he'd come out of the haze, he'd found Ashleigh. Not me.

I hadn't been surprised. What had I expected anyway? He was a Wright. They were essentially royalty in our dusty, small town. And he hadn't been treated any differently as a Wright cousin when he moved here. I couldn't believe that he'd even seen me ever so briefly at that wedding.

When he'd found Ashleigh Sinclair, I'd thought that made perfect sense. Her parents were big-time real estate moguls. They owned almost everything downtown and near Texas Tech University. Wright built the town, and the

Sinclairs owned it. That was how it had been for years. Why wouldn't a Wright end up with a Sinclair? And not...some nerdy girl with a camera permanently attached to her face. Some girl who hadn't even gotten into pharmacy school. Someone like...me.

Or at least, that was what all my dark fears said about me. My therapist was working with me on my negative talk and worst-case scenario-ing. I was better than I'd ever been. But not as good as I could be.

As Julian had his lips pressed to mine, I hoped that this time would be different. That he'd see me again. Even though I knew it would never happen.

Julian pulled back just barely. Our lips still hovered together. I could have hung in that second forever. His dark eyes opened to look down into my hazel eyes. Something flashed across his face that I couldn't place. I'd never seen him look at me like that.

I swallowed, wanting nothing more than to stand on my tiptoes and claim his mouth for mine again. But at the end of the day, I'd never be confident enough to do that.

"What is going *on* here?" Ashleigh's voice snapped me out of my reverie.

Julian's jaw tensed at the sound of Ashleigh's high-pitched voice. And that fast, I lost him. If I'd ever had him.

He wrenched back, his face a mask of tightly controlled fury. "Ashleigh..."

I winced at the sound of his voice. I'd never heard him talk like that before. Charming Julian Wright had fled the building. He'd been betrayed by Ashleigh. He hadn't forgiven her, and he wouldn't forget what she'd done. If it were me, I'd be cowering at that voice. But Ashleigh continued to look at him in some form of mock shock.

"I came to see you, and *this* is happening?" she

K.A. LINDE

demanded.

"What are you *doing* here?" he snarled.

"I wanted to see you."

"You're not *allowed* on the premises."

Ashleigh flicked her bright blonde hair off her shoulder. "I came to talk to you about the gala that we'd planned."

Julian tensed. "What about it?"

"I have some final details to go over with you, and I want to coordinate our outfits."

"We're not going together," he said lethally.

Ashleigh fluttered her eyelashes. "We always planned to, love."

"That was before."

"We can get past this..."

My jaw dropped. The audacity of this woman.

"It's time for you to leave, Ashleigh. If you have something to discuss with me, you can send an email," Julian said, crossing his arms over his chest and straightening to his considerable height. "Now, go."

Ashleigh's smile turned purely feline. "But, *babyyy*..."

Her whine grated on my nerves. No one had ever really liked Ashleigh, even when we'd tolerated her for Julian's sake. I still had no idea what he had seen in her as far as personality went. She was a nightmare. But she was gorgeous with long tan legs, thick blonde hair, and bright blue eyes. She always wore the latest fashions and had money coming out of her ears. Maybe it was easier to ignore her personality with all the rest in your face. Maybe for a dude.

"Don't make me call the cops."

"You wouldn't," she hissed.

He narrowed his eyes, as if to say, *Just try me.*

"I'm done with this. If I see you on the property again,

12

I'll have you arrested." He stepped forward, towering over her already-tall frame. "And I'll push to take you to court for everything you did earlier this year, too."

Ashleigh sighed and rolled her eyes. "You're so dramatic."

Part of me wanted to reach out and shake her. She literally didn't see the danger in front of her face. The other part of me wished I had her gall.

Julian looked like he was going to blow his gasket, but she dismissively waved her hand.

"I know this isn't real. There's no way you could go from me to *that*." She pointed at me.

My face turned three shades of red. I swallowed and wished I had a comeback to that. Instead, I felt humiliated by the accuracy.

Julian stepped forward. "Don't fucking talk to her like that."

Ashleigh lifted one shoulder. "Whatever."

She turned on her four-inch stiletto heels and stalked back through the cellar. Julian watched her exit with hyper-vigilance. Not until she was out of the building did he finally relax and slump back against the doorframe.

"Fuck," he said, running his hand down his face. "*Fuck.*"

"You okay?"

He shook his head. His eyes were squeezed shut. Then, they cracked back open and met mine. "I'm so sorry for everything."

"You can't control what she says and does."

"No," he said easily, pushing off of the doorframe. "But I can control what I did."

I flushed and looked down at the ground again. *Here it comes.* All the ways he regretted that kiss. The kiss that I thought had been perfect...even if it was fake.

"You were just telling me that some other guy touched you without your permission, and then what do I do? Kiss you without asking if it's okay."

"It's fine," I said quickly.

"I mean, it was a great kiss."

My head jerked up in surprise. "It was?"

He laughed and shoved his hands into his pockets. "I thought so. If you didn't like it, then I'm doubly sorry."

"No, it wasn't...it was fine," I finished lamely.

"Fine," he said with a nod. "My mother tells me that *fine* never means fine from a woman. So, I'm going to continue to apologize for everything that happened. Kissing you without your permission and everything Ashleigh said. Don't listen to a word out of her mouth. I learned the hard way how much of a poisonous snake she is."

"I'm sorry."

"Not your fault," he said automatically. "Should I continue apologizing?"

I laughed and shook my head. "It's okay. You saved me first. I was happy to do the same."

His smile was electric. "I guess we're even then?"

"We are," I agreed.

"Good. Well, I should probably get our photographer back to the concert before it starts." He gestured for me to step out of his office, and we went back toward the barn.

I bit the inside of my cheek as I second-guessed whether or not I should dive into his business. Curiosity ended up getting the better of me. "Have you been dealing with a lot of Ashleigh?"

He breathed out heavily. "Well, sort of. She didn't take our breakup well. Mostly she's mad that she got caught and thinks that if she pushes enough, I'll bend to her will."

"That doesn't sound like you."

He flashed me a smile. "It doesn't, does it? Stubbornness runs in my family."

"Sure does."

He nudged me. "Hey!"

"What? Sutton is one of my best friends. I've seen Wright stubbornness way up close."

"Yeah. It doesn't matter how much Ashleigh hounds me; we're not getting back together."

"I'd think not after what she did."

"Never pegged you as a grudge-holder, Gibson."

I flushed at the use of my last name. "I'm not. But she didn't just hurt you, she tried to force you into her mold and hurt the winery, too. I'm kind of attached to it, to be honest."

"Me or the vineyard?" he asked, waggling his eyebrows.

I covered my blush with a laugh. "The vineyard!"

"Likely story."

Our eyes met, and we both broke down into laughter. As much as I wanted something with Julian, the main reason I'd never gone for it was because of what was happening right here between us. I was into him, but I valued his friendship more. I wouldn't risk losing this easiness between us to shoot for more.

I pulled my camera up and snapped a picture of him.

"Hey!"

I took another.

"What are you doing?"

"I won't miss getting a real Julian smile."

"Let me see," he said, coming around to stand next to me.

I pulled the back of the camera up and flipped through the pictures I'd taken. This was the one thing I *wasn't* self-conscious about. My pictures were good. I was certain of that. I loved photography, and I did it constantly. All those weddings had really honed my craft. I wasn't like our friend Blaire, who was a legitimate social media influencer with a million followers, but I had a good thirty thousand–plus people following my photography. I'd been featured in wedding magazines and won contests for my work. This was my passion.

"Jesus Christ, Jen," he breathed. "How the fuck do you do this?"

"Talent," I teased.

He nodded his head. "Absolutely. I'm so glad that we convinced you to work here. Couldn't have been easy, giving up all the traveling."

"Well, it was, and it wasn't," I told him. "I like that I can be picky now, and as I said, I'm already attached to the place."

His smile was bright. "Could you send me this one?" He pointed at the picture I'd captured of the real him—charming and laughing Julian Wright. Exactly how I saw him. "I'd like to put it on the website."

"Definitely. That's what I'm here for."

We continued up the walk until we nearly reached the barn. I could hear the concert had already started and winced. I was supposed to be there for that.

We stepped inside to the backstage. It was *loud* from the show. Sutton was standing off to the side, watching the show. A group of the production crew was buzzing around. Hollin was speaking to the new manager, Alejandra. Jordan was sitting at a table with Annie in his lap. And someone else was standing before us that I'd never seen before.

Julian stiffened next to me. His eyes widened.

"Dad?" Julian gasped.

3

JULIAN

*M*y father was standing in front of me.

In Lubbock, Texas.

Not in Vancouver, where he lived and where I'd moved from. This wasn't a call, text, or email, like he'd been trying to reach me and I'd been ignoring him. I hadn't seen him in almost four years. He'd asked us to stay, knowing we never would, and then I'd said good-bye. I'd meant it forever. What was he doing here?

I didn't want to have to deal with this. It was bad enough that I already had to deal with Ashleigh today, but Ashleigh and my father in one day? Fuck.

"Hello, son," my dad said.

Son. I recoiled from that word. The years of idolization and then the complete shattering of everything that I'd worshipped in him.

I pulled myself together. I couldn't be the same person I'd been when my dad fucked up all of our lives. I couldn't cower and hope that Jordan would take care of it. Like he always did. I had to handle it on my own.

I straightened to my considerable height and crossed my arms over my chest. "What are you doing here?"

"Good to see you, too."

"Is it?" I mocked.

Jennifer fidgeted next to me. "I'm just going to..." She pointed at the concert, where she had been hired to take photographs.

My gaze shifted to hers. Fuck, how had I managed to drag her into all of my drama? She shouldn't have had to witness any of it. I was such a mess.

Her hazel eyes were wide with concern and discomfort. Her bottom lip was caught between her teeth. I'd kissed her, and I'd much rather be doing that again than dealing with what was right in front of me. Not that it was going to happen. She'd made it pretty clear that she wasn't interested. And it wasn't like I should be dating right now anyway. Ashleigh was a hurricane, plowing through my life. It wasn't fair to anyone to start dating when she was still rampaging.

"Sure," I said with a nod. "Let me know if you need anything else."

She smiled shyly. The same Jen who had drawn me to her at a pool party right before I fell in on top of her. After I'd moved here, I'd pushed her to date me, but she'd never really been interested. My flirting was relentless, and still...it was hard to tell what Jen was thinking. The opposite of Ashleigh, who wore every emotion on her sleeve.

I shook the past away from my eyes as she gave me a half-wave and disappeared toward the stage. My father was still waiting.

"New girlfriend?" he asked.

I clenched my jaw. "No. She's our photographer."

"The place is nice."

"What are you doing here?" I demanded again.

"I came to see you."

"You saw me. Now, you can go."

My father sighed but held my gaze, unwavering. He'd had more practice in that than I ever had. "Can we go somewhere more private and talk?"

"I'm actually at work, if you haven't noticed. I'm kind of busy."

"Five minutes, Julian."

I ground my teeth together and then nodded, heading for the door without looking back. My father followed me out of the building. I forced down my nerves and rising irritation. He still hadn't fucking answered me. He wouldn't have flown across the entire country just to see me. Not after everything had shattered. Why now?

The door shut behind us, drowning out the noise of Cosmere blasting through the building. A hot summer wind whipped around me, bringing in dust from the nearby cotton fields. Lubbock was small enough to feel suffocating and large enough to have most everything I could ever need. If not everything I wanted. It wasn't Vancouver, but I'd been here long enough to appreciate the friendly West Texas city. I wouldn't have opened a business here otherwise.

I didn't think my father felt the same way about the city he'd left behind more than three decades ago. His nose wrinkled at the sight around him, and he brushed the orange dust off of his suit jacket.

"We're here. Talk," I told him.

"I know you're still mad."

"Yes."

"But Jordan invited me here."

I took a step back. "What?"

"He didn't tell you?"

"No."

I didn't care that I sounded hurt. Why the hell would Jordan have hidden it from me? He knew how I felt.

"Well, he probably knew you'd react like this."

I narrowed my eyes. "Get to your point."

"I want us to have a fresh start."

I laughed and then realized he was serious. "You believe that's possible?"

"I do. I've changed, Julian."

"A *changed* man," I said slowly. "Wow. You're really going that route?"

"It's the truth."

"And what do you know about the truth?"

My dad sighed. "Please, I don't expect you to forgive me for all my vices in one meeting. I'm asking for us to try."

"The inimitable Owen Wright, asking for us to *try*," I jeered. "Unbelievable."

He ran a hand back through his hair. He looked so much like me and Jordan. Just an older version. I could see what he must have thought looked like remorse on his face. I didn't believe it.

"I know that I did wrong by you and your brother and your mother. I regret many things, but driving you away is what I hate the most. I really would like us to start over."

I almost believed him. Almost saw the illusion he was creating. A glamour determined to blind me to reality. But the magic spell had burst a long time ago. It wouldn't cover my eyes to his deception any longer. I saw the truth. Saw who he really was.

"I don't want anything to do with you."

"Julian," my dad said carefully.

My cool vanished. "You left Mom when she had cancer!

I'll never forgive you. I don't care what you want to say. It will never get over it."

My father pinched the bridge of his nose. "I didn't know about her diagnosis."

"You think that makes it better?" I snapped.

"It's not an excuse. I was wrong. Your mother and I had deteriorated years before the divorce papers. It should have happened long ago."

"You are not helping your case." I checked my phone. "Your five minutes are up."

I stepped around him to head back inside. He grasped my elbow. I looked down at it as if it were nothing but vermin.

"Let me go."

He didn't. "I'm sorry."

I shook my head. "We both know that you're only here because you want something. That's the only reason you ever do anything. So, what do you want? A job? Money? The company? Whatever it is, you're not getting it. You dug your grave; you can go lie in it."

Then I shook his hand off of me and strode back inside without him.

My mind was a haze of anger. It so infrequently took me that I didn't know how to get rid it. Jordan had the anger issues. He was the one who had been working on not being like our father for so long. I'd always been the easygoing, charismatic, younger brother. But if there was anything that riled me up, it was my father. I wasn't going to be fooled by him.

I found Jordan with Annie. She was seated in his lap, and they were laughing and kissing. I'd never seen Jordan this happy. Too bad I was about to wreck it.

"We need to talk," I said.

Jordan frowned as his eyes settled on me. "Sure. What's up?"

"Alone."

Jordan protested, but Annie was already getting to her feet. "I'll go watch the show. Find me later." She planted another kiss on Jordan's lips before disappearing.

Jordan watched her go like a man dying of thirst. Then he looked back to me and stood. "You saw Dad?"

I pointed toward the back suite. It was being used by the band, but they were playing, so we'd have some time.

Jordan nodded and then entered the room. The band sure was hard on their space. Drinks and clothes and instruments were scattered everywhere. It didn't matter right now. I shut the door.

"You invited Dad here without telling me?" I snapped.

Jordan ran a hand back through his hair. "I did. I should have told you, but I wasn't sure if he was going to come."

"Well, he's here, and he ambushed me. Said he wanted a fresh start."

"Is it impossible to believe he wants that?"

"Yes!" I cried. "Don't you remember what it was like in Vancouver?"

"I do. I remember more than you do," Jordan said. "But I also know that I'm like him. I'm just like Dad in so many ways, and Annie gave me a second chance that I didn't deserve. I can't help but think we should give him one even if he doesn't deserve it."

"What you did was *nothing* compared to Dad. And anyway, he's had second and third and fourth chances."

"He's still our father."

My eyes widened. "So?"

"Our cousins lost both of their parents young," Jordan reminded me. "We're fortunate enough to have both of our parents still alive. Hasn't there been enough loss all around? Shouldn't we get to know the man he is rather than what we idolized him as?"

"Do you think he's changed?"

Jordan sank onto the arm of one of the chairs and shrugged. "I honestly don't know. It's not like I'm going into this blind, Julian. I want him to be a better man, but I'm willing to believe he's the same. And if he is, then that's that."

I sighed and turned in a circle. My anger never lasted that long. Everything had already drained away from me. Jordan hadn't done anything malicious, and as per usual Jordan, he was already working with a contingency plan.

"I still don't like that I was ambushed."

"That was my fault. Forgive me about Dad?"

I waved him away. "Whatever. I don't trust him."

"I get that. He hasn't earned our trust yet."

A knock came on the door, and then Hollin burst into the room. "There you fuckers are."

I chuckled. Hollin Abbey was our cousin on the other side of the family. My dad's brother had five kids—Jensen, Austin, Landon, Morgan, and Sutton Wright. But my mom had two siblings, and we had been lucky to find the Abbeys —Hollin, Campbell, and Nora. Hollin and I had hit it off right away even though we were complete opposites. He was a burly, tattooed, motorcycle-riding cowboy to my city-slick, fashion-obsessed, sports car–driving businessman. But we just clicked.

"Anything wrong?" Jordan asked, standing.

"Nah, a reporter showed up. Probably don't want me to do that interview," Hollin said with a laugh.

Jordan and I shared a look. Yeah, probably not.

"You take it," Jordan said.

"What? Me?" I asked in surprise.

"It's all you!" Hollin agreed.

I was still getting used to taking charge of the winery. Jordan had done so much of the prep to get us the place, and Hollin ran much of the day-to-day operations. But I was the real business owner, taking on more and more of the responsibilities. It was a whole new experience.

"All right," I said with a nod, dropping the problems with Dad for another day. "I got this."

4

JENNIFER

"What's going on?" Sutton asked with a concerned look as I scurried over with my camera.

"Uh...I think Julian's dad is here."

Her eyes widened. "Owen?"

I shrugged. "Yeah."

"What does he want?" she snarled.

Sutton had every right to hate her uncle. When Jensen had left as CEO of Wright Construction and Morgan had taken over before she was even thirty, Owen had shown up like a knight in shining armor. But instead of helping her, he tried to undermine her at every turn. He'd even tried to get the board of directors to throw her out and put him in her place. Owen might be their uncle, but he wasn't welcome in Lubbock.

"I have no idea. I left him with Julian."

Sutton sighed and rubbed her temples. "Should I tell Mor?"

"I think Julian can handle it. It's his place anyway."

"Right. I have to remember that my cousins are perfectly

capable. I'm just used to going to Jensen and Morgan when things start going south."

"I wouldn't say a text to them would be out of line."

She nodded and pulled out her phone.

"Aww," she gushed.

She turned the phone to face me. On the screen was a picture of her husband, David Calloway, the CFO of Wright Construction, and their two kids—six-year-old Jason and one-year-old Madison. Only Jason was smiling at the camera. Madison was trying to eat Jason's fingers, and David was attempting to stop her. It was too cute.

"Too much."

She laughed and went back to texting.

I stepped around her and pulled my camera back up to my face. Campbell Abbey was onstage, singing his heart out to an adoring audience. The rest of the band was rocking out like they were in Madison Square Garden and not a backwoods barn in West Texas. I'd been a fan of Cosmere for years. Even before they'd broken out. Their hit song "I See the Real You" really got me in the feels. I was always the girl who wanted the guy to see the real me, but it never happened that way.

I snapped picture after picture of the show as they moved from one song to the next. I was completely in the zone that I didn't even notice that others had gathered nearby until someone tapped my shoulder.

I whipped around. "Hey." Then my friends Piper Medina and Blaire Barker materialized in front of me. "Oh, hey!"

I threw my arms around Blaire, and Piper fended off a hug.

"Hey, girl," Blaire said, tugging on her signature baseball cap. This one was for her wellness blog, *Blaire Blush*, which had started with her discussing things that made her blush.

A makeup company had asked her to create her own blush on their line, but she wanted an organic, environmentally friendly company.

"This seems to be a success," Piper said diplomatically. She brushed her dark brown hair back from her sun-kissed brown skin and eyed the backstage area.

Piper ran Sinclair Cellars, a rival winery in town that had originally been started by the Sinclairs but had been passed down to Piper's father. He worked his way up in the job after immigrating from Mexico.

"I think so," I said.

"Me too," Sutton said. "Mor and Jensen are going to come back here after the show to see what's up."

"What is up?" Piper asked.

"Something wrong?" Blaire's eyes were locked on the band.

I didn't think she was a Cosmere fan, but if I didn't know better, I'd think she had a thing for Campbell. Not that I'd blame her.

"Owen Wright is here," Annie said as she walked up to the rest of us.

"Oh?" Piper asked. She clearly already knew the history.

"Yeah, Julian came to talk to Jordan about it. He looked pretty pissed."

"With good reason," I said.

Sutton nodded. "Agreed."

"Anyway," Annie said with a wave of her hand, "what I really want to talk about is you disappearing with Julian!"

All the girls faced me.

My face turned as red as a tomato. "Uh, what?"

"You disappeared with him. You were talking and laughing and then poof!"

"Are you and Julian..." Sutton asked, arching an eyebrow.

"No, no, no, no, no," I said quickly.

"I thought you were into him," Piper said.

Blaire nodded. "You always come to our soccer games."

The Tacos was a recreational soccer team that a bunch of my friends played on. Annie's brother, Isaac, had started it. Annie, Julian, Hollin, and Blaire all played along with Annie's friend Cézanne and her boyfriend, Gerome. I *did* attend all the games, but it was for my friends, not Julian. Or at least...not expressly Julian.

"You and Annie play," I grumbled.

"And Julian!" Annie crooned.

"I feel attacked."

Sutton laughed. "Let up, y'all."

"Oh, come on. Dish!" Annie said.

"He wanted me to take some pictures."

I thought about telling them about the kiss, but what was the point? It hadn't been real even if he said it was great. That was just Julian.

"All right, fine," Annie said, slipping an arm around my shoulders. "You're still doing that whole *no guys for ninety days* anyway, right?"

"I...yes, I am."

"Boys are overrated," Blaire said.

"True story," Piper agreed.

Blaire rolled her eyes. "Aren't you on-again with Bradley?"

Piper shrugged. "I need new shutters."

Annie cackled, and Sutton just shook her head.

"It couldn't also be the sex that you're missing?" Blaire asked.

"Could be," Piper said with a wink.

I laughed with the rest of the girls at Piper's not-quite love life. It hadn't been long ago that Annie and Jordan had similar relationship woes. Sutton and David had had their level of complications while she was dealing with the death of her husband. I'd had my string of bad dates. It was only Blaire who didn't seem to date much. With her level of success, I didn't understand that at all.

My friends changed the subject back to Cosmere's show. Annie danced around in a circle to their next song, singing all of the words perfectly. I could have joined in. I knew the lyrics forward and backward.

But at that moment, I felt my phone vibrate in my pocket. I fished it out and saw my mom's number on the screen. I groaned. Maybe I could skip the call, but knowing my mom, she'd call back until I answered and then blame me for wasting her time.

I held my phone up. "Going to take this."

The girls waved me off, and I headed away from the concert, answering the phone, "Hey, Mom."

"Jennifer Sue, it took you long enough."

"Sorry."

"Where are you?" my mom asked. "It sounds like a rock concert."

"Um...I'm at work. Remember I mentioned that I was photographing the Cosmere show at the new Wright Vineyard?"

"You never told me that."

I bit my lip. I definitely had. Not that she cared about anything to do with my photography.

"What can I help you with?"

"What, a mom can't want to talk to her daughter?"

Not my mom.

"Of course, Mom. But again...I'm at work."

My mom scoffed, "Taking pictures isn't work."

I swallowed back a retort. Here was the company line: photography wasn't a real job. I'd been hearing that for years from my mom. Four years ago, I'd been nannying Sutton's oldest, Jason, and applying to pharmacy school. They hadn't approved of the nanny job, but at least I was on the right track. Then I hadn't gotten into pharmacy school. Now, I was a failure.

I could have retaken the PCAT until my score was where it needed to be and reapplied until I got in. Plenty of people did it. My mom had expected that of me. I kept thinking I'd go back. It wasn't like it was a forever decision.

But then I'd lucked into an amazing second-shooter position for a wedding and never looked back. My business had taken off, and now, I was here. Not that my parents acknowledged this as anything but a passion project. Not a reality. Nothing I said that would change that.

They'd both struggled and come from nothing to give me and my brother, Chester, the comfortable lives we enjoyed. My mom just couldn't understand me giving it up to go backward. At least as far as she saw it.

"Okay, Mom," I said quickly. I needed to end this call before she went off on one of her rants.

"Well, I don't mean to interrupt your little concert," she said, "but I wanted to confirm that you were coming to Austin next weekend for Chester's graduation. He and Margaret have been planning this party for months. He even got a two-bedroom Airbnb near campus. You know how Dad hates hotels."

"I do," I said, my throat tightening.

My brother was...a genius. There was no other way to put it. He'd started winning chess tournaments at seven. He won the National Spelling Bee at twelve. He graduated from high school two years early and had three bachelor's in four years from Baylor. They'd offered him the most amount of money, which was how he'd chosen them from the two dozen universities that had recruited him. He was only two years older than me and graduating from University of Texas-Austin with his PhD in biochemistry.

I'd never measured up, and going to Austin to celebrate his latest achievement felt like another knife in the chest. But how could I deny them?

"I'll send over the details to your email. It'll be good to see Chester and Margaret. I'm so happy he's in such a stable relationship."

Unlike me. Though she hadn't said it, I clenched my teeth together.

"Anyway, we can all drive together on Wednesday."

"Wednesday?" I asked.

"Yes. Is that a problem?"

"I have to check my work schedule. I think I'm shooting a senior portrait on Wednesday. I can probably come down Thursday though."

My mom huffed, "Fine, Thursday then."

"Okay, Mom. I have to go. Looking forward to it," I lied.

She tried to keep me on the phone for a few more minutes, and after saying good-bye twice more, I finally got off.

I hung my head. What the hell was I going to do?

5

JULIAN

"I think that's all. Thank you so much for your time," the reporter said.

"It's my pleasure," I said.

Jessie lowered her microphone, and the camera stopped rolling. Her smile was bright as she brushed her hair back off her neck. The Texas summer heat was definitely uncomfortable.

"That was great," she said. "You're a natural on camera."

I laughed. "Nah, I'm sure I looked nervous."

"Were you nervous? You didn't look it."

"Thanks. Is there anything else that you need?"

She shook her head. "We're good. I'll take this back and edit. Should air tomorrow. We'll send you a link and the write-up."

"Perfect."

"Good to see you, Julian," she said and then sauntered off with her cameraman.

I blew out a breath as soon as she was gone. I actually hated being on camera. Jordan was the one who did well with public speaking. He was better in front of a camera.

Even though I had the charm one-on-one, it was a different matter in front of a crowd. But I was the face of Wright Vineyard. Jordan was counting on me. He'd handed over all the responsibilities, and I had to take up the mantle. That included getting over my nerves with public speaking.

I shook out my hands. A problem for another day.

I headed back inside and watched the end of the show. Our new manager, Alejandra, had tours set up for after the show along with coupons for customers to come back another day for a tasting. She was handling the rest of her team beautifully as Cosmere's show ended and people streamed out of the venue.

"Congrats, cuz," Morgan said as she strode backstage with Jensen on her heels.

My Wright cousins were a blessing. They were the part of my family that I'd never known I was missing. It was like having five more siblings. Always up in our business and meaning well and joking and laughing and ready for a good time. Jensen was the oldest and ran Wright Architecture, a passion project that he paired with Fortune 500 Wright Construction, which Morgan ran. Austin also worked there as a senior vice president with Jordan. Landon was the quin-tessential middle child and a professional golfer. He'd even started a PGA course here in town. Then, there was Sutton, who had rebelled against it all and ran a local bakery in town, Death by Chocolate.

"I didn't know you were here," I said, hugging Morgan. Then I shook Jensen's hand.

"Wouldn't have missed it," he said with a smile.

"We're excited to build on the Wright brand," Morgan said.

Jensen nudged. "No work talk."

She arched an eyebrow at him. "Don't tell me what to do."

Jensen crossed his arms in the typical big-brother move. "I'm older than you."

She held her hand up. "Don't care." She winked at me. "Heard your dad showed up."

I sighed. Of course that was why they were here. "He did. Yeah."

"Everything all right?" Jensen asked.

"I don't know. Jordan invited him."

Morgan balked at that. "What? Why?"

"Crisis of conscience," I volunteered.

Morgan laughed. "That's something. So, is he here to stay?"

"I don't know. He said that he's a changed man." I rolled my eyes. "I didn't believe him, and I told him to leave. I'd guess he wants something, and he's trying to get in with me and Jordan to get it."

"Sounds like his MO," Morgan said.

"I agree. He's trouble. But maybe he's being sincere," Jensen said.

Morgan shot him a look of disbelief.

"I don't support him. just mean...if I could have our parents back," he said, his eyes meeting Morgan's, "I'd do anything."

"He's not," I insisted.

Jensen nodded, backing off.

Their mom had died from cancer when they were young, and their dad had died when Jensen was just out of college. He'd had to take over the mantle at a young age. I appreciated what they meant, but their dad wasn't like my dad. Just because they were brothers didn't mean anything.

"Well, congrats on the opening," Jensen said. "Can't wait

to come back and do some wine tastings when I can get away again."

"How are Emery and Robin?" I asked.

Emery had delivered a healthy baby girl last month by emergency C-section. Both were fine, but Emery had taken longer to recover.

"They're both great. Her mom has temporarily moved into our guest bedroom. She's been a big help with Robin," Jensen said. "I know Emery's ready to get up and get moving again."

"I bet."

"Well, we'll get out of your hair," Jensen said, shaking my hand again and then disappearing with Morgan.

I waved them good-bye and went to find Nora to help her close down the event. Nora was Hollin's younger sister and the in-house event planner. She'd graduated from Texas Tech earlier this month, but she'd been interning with an event planner in town for a few years. She was a pro, and I was lucky to have her working with us.

"We're all good here," Nora said, patting down the bar top over an hour later when almost everyone had gone home. "I'm heading out for the night. I'm exhausted."

She'd been working on the event night and day since she'd graduated. She'd gotten to the venue this morning at five a.m. and not stopped since then. She was a champ for only being all of five feet tall.

"All right. Have a good night. Take tomorrow off."

She saluted me with a yawn and headed out. Jordan and Annie followed her, leaving just me and Hollin behind.

I took a seat on a barstool as Hollin hopped behind the bar.

"What'll you have?" he asked.

I shook my head. "Too tired to drink."

"That's not the energy I'm looking for here, Wright," he said, cracking a smile. "You don't want me to choose for you."

True. I really did not. "All right. Just a beer then."

"Boring," he said as he popped the top on a Blue Moon, poured it into a glass with an orange slice, and passed it to me. "Enjoy."

I tipped the drink to him and took a good, long sip. Maybe I needed this more than I'd thought. Between Ashleigh, my dad, and the interview, I was wrung out.

"Good news, boys," Alejandra said, striding forward in her mile-high heels. She'd worked all day in them, paired with a tight-fitting top and jeans. Her headset dangled from one hand.

"Yeah?" I asked.

Hollin's eyes tracked her. There was no way that was happening. He'd said so when he hired her. Even if she wasn't off the market, she'd bust his balls for even trying. "I like good news. Lay it on us, Villareal."

"We're booked out for tours the next two weeks."

"Shit!" Hollin said.

"I know. We sold off a few cases of wine already, too. Not to mention, the admission costs more than covered the event, even with Cosmere's fee."

When it had just been Campbell, he'd done it for free, but we hadn't expected the rest of the band to comply with that. Also, I was sure their manager, agent, and record label wouldn't have liked it either.

"That is good news." I lifted my glass to her. "Want to stay for a drink?"

"Unfortunately, no," she said. "I'll leave you to celebrate. I'm going to go home to Adrian. I don't think I've seen him all week."

I finished off my beer, and Hollin passed me another.

When I started to protest, he held up his hand. "Cuz, we've earned it."

"Fine." I pulled it toward me.

Just then the door to the backstage opened, and out walked Jennifer, talking to Campbell with wide, adoring eyes. I'd never seen her look at anyone like that, and something twisted in the pit of my stomach. I didn't care if Campbell Abbey was a famous rockstar and Jen loved his music; I didn't like it.

I stood. "Hey, Jen. Celebratory drink?"

Her eyes snapped up to mine, and her smile brightened. "Uh, sure. I need to get home to Avocado and Bacon, but maybe one."

"Avocado and Bacon?" Campbell asked.

He nodded his head at Hollin as Jen slid into the seat next to me, and Campbell walked around to make his own drink.

"They're her cats," I explained.

Jennifer wrinkled her nose. "I don't like cats. They're just cats that live on my street."

"That you feed."

"Well, yeah. I don't want them to starve."

"They have names."

"I can't just call them Cat One and Cat Two!"

Campbell laughed. "I think I get it. You take care of stray cats?"

"I...well, yes."

"Cute," Campbell said with a wink.

Jennifer flushed and took the drink that Hollin had passed to her. I glowered at him. Hollin tried not to laugh as he leaned his elbows against the bar.

"So, next weekend." Campbell arched his eyebrow.

"What about next weekend?" I asked.

Hollin buried his face in his drink at my tone.

"I liked Jennifer's images, and she asked if I'd be interested in sitting for a portrait series she's working on. She said she could get us studio space."

Oh. Not a date. What the fuck was wrong with me? Why had I immediately jumped there?

"That's cool," I added lamely.

"I'd really love to shoot the portrait session, but I'm not free next weekend. Sorry," Jennifer said with a wince. "It's my brother's graduation in Austin, and my parents would skin me alive if I missed it." She rolled her eyes. "It's going to be terrible."

"Why?" Hollin asked. "Don't get along with your brother?"

"No. I mean, we get along okay, but my mom's...tough. She doesn't approve of my job, especially because Chester is kind of a genius. And then I'll get the third degree about not having a date. My mom even made some comment about how my brother's girlfriend will be there and I won't have a date."

"Oof," Campbell said. "Tough."

"Fuck that shit," Hollin responded eloquently.

She shrugged her shoulders and took a sip of the drink Hollin had poured her. "It's fine."

There was that word again.

Fine.

It *wasn't* fine.

"Well, no problem. We can reschedule," Campbell agreed. "I miss being home. Hoping to spend more time in Lubbock this summer. Maybe another show in a month?"

"Definitely," Hollin agreed.

"Fuck," I whispered as I checked that date on my phone.

"Just not that last weekend in June. I have a gala I'm supposed to attend."

Jennifer slid her eyes to mine. "The one Ashleigh mentioned?"

"Ashleigh was here?" Hollin demanded.

"Uh, yeah...meant to tell you," I muttered. "I took care of it. She wanted to cause trouble."

"That's all she does," he snarled.

Hollin had never forgiven her for trying to sabotage the winery. None of us had, but Hollin had taken it personally.

"Yeah. Well, we planned this gala to help promote the winery when we were still dating. Now, I have to go stag. Kill me." I downed the rest of my beer.

Hollin shook his head. "That fucking sucks."

"Maybe there's a solution here," Campbell said, his gaze shifting between me and Jennifer. "Maybe y'all should go together?"

"What?" I barked.

"I mean, you're friends, right? It'd be easy enough for you to go to Jennifer's brother's graduation party and woo her parents, and she could go to your gala and make Ashleigh jealous."

Jennifer's eyes went wide, and she shook her head. "I don't think—"

Hollin nodded his head. "It'd be great. Julian, you can woo anyone. And having Jen there would make Ashleigh go crazy. It'd be beautiful."

"The perfect fake dates," Campbell said with a knowing smile.

Jennifer stood, shoving her drink farther away from her. "I think we've all had a long night. I'm going to go check on the cats. Thanks for the drink, Hollin. Night, y'all."

I watched her walk out with something heavy settling on

my chest. I'd pushed her too far. That kiss had ruined any chance I'd had. Just the idea of *fake* dating me and she'd literally run out of the room.

"What the fuck are you doing?" Hollin asked.

"What?"

Campbell arched his eyebrow and tossed back his drink. "This is your cue to go after her."

"Fuck," I muttered and dashed from my seat and into the cooling summer evening.

6

JENNIFER

*O*h my God, what was wrong with me?

Seriously, why couldn't I act like any other normal person? Just laugh off Hollin's and Campbell's joking and change the subject. Instead, I'd freaked out at the very idea of what they had suggested.

I couldn't force Julian to do something that asinine. He didn't want that. I knew that without a second thought. I wouldn't put him in a situation where the guys had bullied him into going on some fake date with me. I couldn't hide how I felt about him in a quick interaction with him. There was no way I'd be able to do it at my brother's graduation. Let alone some fancy gala. What would I even *wear* to a fancy gala?

And then there was the fact that the thought of actually taking anyone to my brother's graduation made me feel sick. I didn't like having anyone around my mom. Not even Sutton or Annie. Julian would never look at me the same. It'd be so humiliating.

I fumbled with the keys as I hurried to my car, trying to

fight back tears. I was such an idiot. I wished that my anxiety hadn't fucking spiked like this.

I dropped my keys and cussed, grabbing them off the freshly paved parking lot. I took a deep breath and tried to calm my racing heart the way my therapist had been teaching me.

Then I dug through my purse for my pills. I took an everyday anxiety medicine to regulate the day-to-day anxiety, but for spikes like this, I had emergency medicine that I always kept with me. I popped a half of a Xanax into my mouth and downed it dry.

"Jen!"

I whipped around, hastily stashing my pills again. My eyes widened in shock at the sight of Julian Wright heading in my direction.

"Hey, wait," he called.

I froze in place. Why was following me? Hadn't I embarrassed him?

"Hey." He smiled that charming Wright smile when he caught up to me. "You move fast."

"Uh, yeah. What's up?" I clutched the keys tighter to keep my hands from shaking.

"I didn't mean for Hollin and Campbell to run you out of there."

I could barely manage a smile. "No, it's fine. I really do need to feed the cats."

"Of course." He took another step forward. "But...maybe what they were saying wasn't actually that crazy."

I winced at the second use of that word tonight. *Crazy* was a word that had been used *about* me enough that hearing it in other contexts still hit me a little too hard.

"Unless you really don't want to do it?"

"The...fake dates?" I asked in confusion.

"Yeah. I mean, I think it sounds like a great idea."

My eyes widened. "You're serious?"

"Yeah."

"But...why?"

"Think about how well we worked together tonight. I saved you from Evan, and you saved me from Ashleigh. We played it all off fine then. We could do it again for bigger stakes. You really don't want to go to that graduation, and I can think of nothing less I'd like to do than attend that gala."

"Yeah. I mean, I don't want to go to the graduation, but I couldn't subject you to that."

"To what?" he asked with a laugh. "It's a graduation. We'll tell them I'm your boyfriend. Parents *love* me."

"But I haven't told them we're dating."

"So? Make it a surprise. You didn't know how to tell them on the phone or something."

"I guess I could do that," I said.

The possibility materialized before me. Bringing Julian Wright to graduation would make everything better for me. He could keep my mom from vocalizing her biggest disappointments in me. She was usually better around strangers than when it was just me. Usually. Not to mention, I'd have someone to talk to and laugh with about all the rest of it. And no one was immune to the Wright name. It would make me look good either way...even if it was fake. It would get me through graduation.

"But what about you? I don't make Ashleigh Sinclair jealous," I said with a self-deprecating laugh.

"You did today."

I scoffed, "Did you hear her?"

"Don't let her poison infect you," he said immediately, reaching out to touch my arm. "There is no hierarchy like her bullshit. She shouldn't have even said it."

But it was true. Ashleigh Sinclair might have a shit personality, but she had everything else. Even Julian for two years. If she had been satisfied with where he worked, she'd still have him. They hadn't broken up because he'd stopped caring about her.

"Okay. I just...don't know that I'm the kind of person she'd take as a threat."

Julian waved his hand. "It'll be fine. You don't have to do anything about Ashleigh. I'd actually prefer if you weren't anywhere near her. As long as you're there, it'll be good. Just like me being there for you."

My face flushed at the comment. I'd been so adamantly against this at the mere mention from Campbell and Hollin. But that was when they were pushing it on Julian. It'd felt like they were forcing him into something that he didn't want. Now, he was trying to convince *me* to fake date him.

Julian Wright.

The man I'd been pining after for years.

Why wouldn't I say yes?

It might be a disaster to have him around my parents. I was sure that I wasn't going to make Ashleigh jealous in the slightest. If we could even keep her thinking we were dating for a whole month. But still...that meant I would have a whole *month* of his time.

Didn't I want that?

Yes, it'd be fake. It wouldn't mean anything. If I was going to have ninety days of no dating, it'd be better to fill that time with fake dates with a friend than nothing.

"All right," I said tentatively.

"Is that a yes?"

"Are you sure that you really want to do this? It'd probably be a whole month, right? The gala isn't until the end of June."

"Yes, I'm sure."

And he looked so damn sincere. Those dark eyes considering me so carefully, looking deep into the windows of my soul. For a second, it was as if he knew how much I wanted this in reality and not just as a fake date.

Then he smiled and held his hand out.

I blinked down at it.

"Partners?"

I laughed softly. Of course he didn't see the real me underneath. It was an arrangement. A fake relationship that meant nothing else. And I wanted it regardless.

I put my hand in his and shook. "Deal."

PART II

A FAKE RELATIONSHIP

7

JENNIFER

Buzz. Buzz. Buzz.

I half-opened one eye and reached for my phone. I swiped at it to silence the alarm, only managing to throw it onto the floor. I groaned loudly, but it did nothing to turn off the alarm.

"Shut up."

It didn't listen.

I pushed the covers off of my chest and reached for the phone. I finally hit the button to cancel the alarm.

"Finally," I said as I flopped back into bed.

I yawned and checked the time—seven a.m. Ugh. Normally, I was up at six thirty without an alarm. I'd forgotten that I even *had* an alarm set. It must have been from my last sunrise graduation shoot. I was and always had been a morning person. Anything past seven felt like I was wasting the day. But today, I wouldn't have minded a few extra hours of sleep.

I'd been at Wright Vineyard until past midnight. It might be lame, but I was usually in bed by ten and sometimes even earlier. Today was definitely going to be rough since I was also a terrible napper *and* I didn't drink coffee. Which Annie thought was sacrilege.

My yawn was as wide as the Grand Canyon as I fumbled out of bed and into a super-hot shower. I blew out my brown bob—which almost reached my shoulders by now—and got into lounge clothes. I grabbed my camera and computer and headed for the dining room table, where I would likely live the rest of the day. Editing was the bulk of the job. If I was lucky, I wouldn't get carpal tunnel for at least a decade from all the micro-clicks as I worked.

I deposited my work on the table and grabbed a banana and the cat food. Another yawn hit me as I went outside.

"Avocado! Bacon!" I called into the early morning.

I nudged their two bowls before pouring cat food into each of them. Everyone made fun of me for feeding the stray cats, but I didn't want them to go hungry. Yes, they could probably fend for themselves. It made me uncomfortable to think that they might be hunting and not find food. I couldn't do it.

I didn't even *like* cats. Yet here I was. The cat lady feeding cats that didn't even belong to me.

"Cado! Bakey!" I called again. I peered into the bushes, and two sets of eyes looked back at me. "There you two are. Come eat."

As if they understood me, Avocado, an orange-and-white cat, and Bacon, a black cat, slunk out of the bushes and began to eat their breakfast. I stroked Cado and then Bacon before heading back inside and sitting at the dining room table to get to work.

Time moved at an unreasonable rate when I sat down to edit. Hours flew by without interruption. By the time the door opened, my eyes were bleary, and the sun was sinking.

"Annie?" I croaked.

"Hey!" she said. "How's it going? Have you moved at all today?"

I looked around the room and shook my head to clear it. "I think I need some lunch."

"It's dinnertime."

"Sure." I rubbed my tired eyes. "I forgot to stop and eat."

Annie rolled her eyes. "Emergency pizza it is." She pulled out her phone and started to order. "By the way, we need to talk."

"Are you breaking up with me?" I asked as I stood up. My body creaked from lack of use, and I stretched to try to release the tension.

Annie laughed. "You can't get rid of me that easily."

"Well, thank God."

"Like, what would you even do without me?"

I shook my head. I remembered the first twenty years of my life without Annie Donoghue in it. We hadn't become friends until I'd started taking care of Jason for Sutton. Annie and Sutton had been popular cheerleaders in high school. Annie was the captain, who always wore name-brand clothes and had more confidence than the rest of the school. I'd learned later that so much of it was a facade, but from the outside, looking in, I hadn't known that.

I'd been a loser in high school. Annie and Sutton barely knew my name. I had been on yearbook and in the marching band. I didn't play the flute anymore. The flute jokes in high school had been enough to make my anxiety peak at a young age. If my home life hadn't done it. My parents were *pull yourself up by your bootstraps* people. They'd done it and expected it from their children. It had not gone well for me, especially with my undiagnosed dyslexia and anxiety.

Things were better now. Well, as long as I wasn't dealing

with my mom. Dad had lightened up some over the years. Annie, Sutton, and I had put our differences long behind us. I didn't know what I would do without them now.

Once the pizza was here, Annie and I curled up on the couch and started a rewatch of *Bridgerton*. We watched it for the plot. Seriously. Not for the many shirtless Regency men.

"Okay, I have been left in suspense," I told Annie. "Spill. What's going on?"

She spun to face me. "Jordan asked me to move in with him."

I screamed. "Oh my God! That's so awesome! You said yes, right?"

"Well, I said that I had to check with you."

"What? Of course you're going to do it. You already practically live there."

"Yeah, I know, but you're my roommate. I wouldn't want to abandon you without first figuring out our situation."

"I appreciate it. Situation figured out."

Annie laughed. "Well, I'm so excited. But what are you going to do? I don't know anyone who is looking for a place. I'm sure you don't want to pay rent all by yourself."

Reality washed back over me. I'd been so happy for Annie that I hadn't thought about what I was going to do. What *was* I going to do? I couldn't afford this house alone. That was for sure. I made good money but not that good, especially after cutting back on the weddings.

Annie held her hands up. "Don't stress!"

"Like that helps."

"I don't want you to have a panic attack. This is why I wanted to talk to you. We can figure it out together. I'm sure there is an easy solution. Even if it means I'm not moving."

I laughed. "That's not an option."

"It is."

I rolled my eyes at her. "Okay. Maybe we could find another roommate. I don't know anyone either. Maybe Piper and Blaire do?"

Annie snapped her fingers. "Good idea. You know Piper has that unused third bedroom."

My eyes widened. "You think she'd want another roommate?"

"Wouldn't hurt to ask, right?"

"Yeah, for sure. It's an option." I smiled at her. "Though I'll miss these nights."

"I'm going to crash with y'all all the time."

"No, you're not. Not with that hot piece of Wright in your bed."

Annie burst into laughter. "Did you just say *hot piece of Wright*?"

I snort-laughed. "I did."

"Speaking of the other hot piece of Wright ass."

I buried my face into my hands. "Stop."

"You and Julian? Tell me the truth. You were being all weird about it yesterday before you disappeared."

"That was really nothing."

"And?"

I sighed and lifted my gaze. "He's coming with me to my brother's graduation."

Annie's eyes whipped wide, and she gasped. "Oh my God, like a date?"

"No," I said quickly. "It's not like that. We kind of... agreed to fake date."

Annie looked skeptical. "Explain."

"So, I have to go to my brother's graduation, which my parents are being dumb about. You know how they are."

She nodded. "Sure."

She wasn't around them much, but she'd heard the

arguments.

"Anyway, he has a charity function that he planned with Ashleigh for the vineyard. And, well, Ashleigh was at the winery yesterday."

"What?" Annie gasped.

"Uh, yeah...and Julian and I hid in his office to escape her. But she found us anyway, and he kissed me."

"He kissed you?!"

"It was fake," I said, waving her away.

"No. Way! He's into you."

"Shush! Let me finish. It made Ashleigh angry, and he thinks having a date there will do the same thing again. But he's not ready to date, and I'm not dating either. So, we're going to go as each other's dates to help one about out."

Annie crossed her arms and looked at me with a sly smile. "Remember how Jordan and I were all *we're not into each other and we just like sex*? Friends with benefits? Blah, blah. That was a lie to get together."

"This is *not* like you and Jordan. The two of you couldn't keep your clothes on the *first day* you met each other."

"Whatever." Annie dismissed the idea so easily. "I will put money on it."

"We're not betting on my love life."

"So, it is a love life?" Annie's eyes twinkled.

"Sometimes I hate you."

She cackled. "I know. I'm rooting for y'all."

"Thanks. But seriously, we're just friends."

"You owe me a Coke if you turn out to be more."

I shook my head. "I'll give you a whole twelve-pack. He's not into me."

Annie's smile went full Cheshire. "Oh, I'm in."

Part of me hoped that she was right, but the rest of me knew that hope only made the disappointment hurt worse.

8

JENNIFER

*B*ertha's trunk snapped shut with a *thunk*.

"That'll do it," I said with a smile as Julian looked on in dismay. "What?"

"Nothing," he said quickly.

Bertha was my hooptie white Honda Civic. She had intermittent AC issues, no automatic locks or windows, and lacked cruise control. I'd had her since high school. We'd had our ups and downs, but I couldn't give her up. We were a pair.

I opened my driver's side door and reached across the console to pop the lock her Julian. He slipped into the passenger side as I revved the engine.

By revved, it was really more of praying and clicking the engine over until it caught.

"Phew, okay," I said with a smile. "Bertha has her moments."

"You want to drive this to Austin?"

I glanced over at him. "Why not?"

"No reason," he said with a smirk.

It was uncomfortable how attractive he was. His dark

55

hair was styled artfully, short on the sides and a little longer on the top. His toned body was hidden underneath a cerulean-blue polo and khakis that ended a few good inches above his knee, revealing his muscular quads. I realized I was staring and returned my attention to Bertha.

I flipped the air-conditioning on and prayed to a higher being that it would turn on. It had been going out for years. It probably needed to be repaired, but I could get a whole new car for the cost to replace the AC unit.

Unfortunately, it didn't come on.

"Fuck," I ground out. I banged on the top of the console. "Turn on, you piece of shit. What the fuck is wrong with you?"

This time, Julian couldn't keep it together. "I don't know that I've ever heard you cuss."

I blushed. "I use it to color conversation, not to make conversation."

He chuckled. "Does yelling at Bertha usually make her work?"

"Yes," I said, hitting the car again. When the AC didn't kick on, I sank back into the driver's seat with a huff. "She usually works...eventually."

"You know, I could drive us."

I glared at him. "Do you have a problem with Bertha?"

He held his hands up. "Absolutely not. I have a problem with driving six hours through Texas without AC...in May."

"It builds character," I quipped.

He quirked a smile at me. "You did say you wanted to make an impression."

I glanced over at the fancy new sports car he'd parked in my driveway. It was a silver Jaguar convertible that had to have come straight off a conveyor belt. I'd never owned anything that new or shiny in my entire life. Neither had my parents. It probably *would* be more comfortable, plus the bonus of working air-conditioning.

I sighed. "Fine."

Julian chuckled and nudged me. "Don't act like I held you at gunpoint to make this decision."

"There's nothing wrong with Bertha."

"Of course not. She's perfectly wonderful."

I narrowed my eyes at him. "Don't condescend to me, Wright."

He put his hand to his heart. "Never."

I rolled my eyes and then hopped out of the car. "Don't forget to lock the door."

He pushed the lock down. "No problem."

His car *beep-beeped* next to me, and I jumped. I hadn't expected it. I covered my embarrassed flush by popping Bertha's trunk open again. I removed my duffel, and Julian extracted his sleek rolling suitcase.

"May I?" he asked, reaching for my duffel.

I let him have it, and he opened the Jag's trunk.

"Is it even going to fit?" I asked, staring dubiously at the tiny trunk space.

He smirked. "That's what she said."

I covered my face. "Oh my God, you did not just say that."

"You set me up," he countered, sliding the suitcase and my duffel into the trunk.

"Well, now, I'm mortified. I didn't mean..."

He laughed and opened the passenger door. "Just get in the car, Jen."

"Are you sure you still want to go with me this weekend?" I asked when I stood before him.

"I'm sure."

"It might be...awkward."

Julian leaned forward against the door and smiled a smile that nearly knocked me off my feet. "I think it's going to be fun."

"Okay," I whispered.

It was now or never. Once we were on the road, I was committed. I'd agonized over whether or not to go through with this enough the last week. I hadn't even told my parents about bringing a boyfriend, just in case. But now, we were here, and he was smiling at me, and fuck it, I wanted him with me.

I dropped into the passenger seat. "So, what have you named her?"

"Who?"

"The car."

He laughed. "She doesn't have a name."

He jogged around and got into the driver's seat. The engine purred when he barely touched it. As if it really were a jaguar responding to his touch.

"She's not real until you name her."

"You name her," he said automatically.

I shrugged. "Okay. You might regret that. I did name my car Bertha."

"I'm already regretting the decision."

"Cornelia," I told him.

His eyes bulged as he veered us away from my house. "How does my new Jaguar look like a Cornelia?"

"It was that or Millicent."

"Hey, I like Millicent. We can call her Milli."

I snort-laughed and covered my face. "Milli!"

"All right, Milli. I'll let you take it from here."

He gunned it, and then we were out of the city and into the countryside beyond.

* * *

As we pulled into Austin city limits, Julian forced us to stop at a local coffee shop, so he could survive the impending traffic. He was more used to it than me, having grown up in Vancouver, but it had been almost four years for him. Both of us were irritable as we merged into the mess.

"I really don't miss this," he said with a yawn. He took a sip of his coffee. "Still not as bad as Vancouver, but fuck."

"Yeah. I'm kind of glad that you're driving now. I'd be a wreck."

He shot me a grin. "See, we took Milli for a reason."

After an hour of bad traffic conditions and a few close calls, we made it through the city and to the Airbnb that Chester had reserved for us near the UT campus. It didn't look like much, but that wasn't surprising. My parents wouldn't have wanted to spend much money on...anything.

Julian parked Milli in the driveway. A brand-new Jag had never looked more out of place. But he didn't say anything, just went to grab our luggage.

"Ready?" he asked.

I nodded. "I think so."

I wasn't sure though. It hadn't occurred to me until now that we'd really be *lying* to everyone. I was a terrible liar. Even if it was a small deception that would make it easier to endure this weekend, I was starting to feel weird about it.

"Hey, what's wrong?"

"It's just...I don't know how I feel about lying to my parents. Now that I'm here."

"You never lied to them when you were growing up?"

I shrugged. "Not really. They always found out."

He dropped my bag and reached for my hand, pulling

me a little closer. My eyes widened. "We don't have to do this if you don't want to. We can tell them the truth—that I'm your friend and you didn't want to drive alone. That would be fine, too, Jen."

My pulse jumped at how sincere he was—and how much I wanted him to lean down and kiss me. "No, it'll be fine, right? We don't have to go into details. Just that it's new."

"Yes, and I didn't want you to drive down alone."

"Right. Yes."

"We'll do whatever makes you comfortable," he assured me. "It's not like we're planning to make out in front of your parents."

I laughed as if the very idea was ridiculous and stepped back. "You're right. It's just nerves. It'll be fine."

He frowned and opened his mouth to say something else, but whatever he was about to say was lost to the front door opening. My mom stood on the porch in mom jeans that she'd probably had since the '80s and an Atlanta zoo T-shirt she had gotten on a trip for one of Chester's chess tournaments. I didn't think my mom had purchased much clothing since then either.

"Hey, kiddos," she said with a wide smile. "What do we have here?"

"Hey, Mom." I strode across the yard, and she pulled me into a hug. "This is Julian."

"Ma'am," Julian said, holding his hand out.

"Oh, we're huggers here, dear." She squeezed Julian tightly. "I'm Connie."

"Pleasure to meet you. I'm Julian Wright."

"Wright," my mom said with an eyebrow raise in my direction. No one was immune to the name.

"Yes, ma'am."

"Well, all of these ma'ams. Aren't you precious? Come on inside. Jennifer, you didn't tell me you were bringing a boy."

I laughed awkwardly and followed her inside. "Last-minute decision."

Julian hefted the luggage into the living room. "I didn't want her to drive all the way to Austin alone."

"That's sweet of you."

Julian's eyes swept to me. Something passed between us, like a light flickering on. There wasn't just friendship in that glance. He'd turned something on, and now, I had the full weight of Julian Wright's gaze. A tenderness in those deep, dark eyes.

"I care about Jen's well-being," he said softly.

I cleared my throat and quickly looked away. I wanted that look to be real. How had he faked it so easily?

"Well, I wish you'd told me you were bringing a...date," she said the word cautiously.

"Boyfriend," Julian said with ease, slipping his arm around my shoulders.

"A boyfriend." My mom's eyes widened. She was going to have this out with me later. I could feel it. "It's certainly been long enough since I've heard that word associated with my daughter."

I tensed. *Seriously?* She had gone there.

My smile fractured, and Julian squeezed my shoulder.

"I'm so glad to finally meet you," Julian said smoothly.

"Finally? How long have you been dating?"

Julian looked down at me. "Gah, how long has it been?"

I squirmed. "Feels like it started yesterday."

He laughed. "Doesn't it?"

"Ah, young love," my mom said with an almost-mocking tone.

"Which room is mine?" I asked, shuffling out of Julian's grip. God, he was a little too good at this.

"Of course. You two will be right back here."

You two.

My head spun at that notion. Right. We were dating. We'd be sharing a room. My parents were annoying in a whole host of other topics, but they weren't prudish. I hadn't considered that when we agreed for Julian to accompany me. It was only a two-bedroom house. My parents would be in one room. Julian and I would share the other one. But maybe it'd have two queens or bunks or something. BNBs sometimes did that to try to accommodate more people.

But then Julian pushed open the door that led to our room, and I froze.

There was only one bed.

And not just that...it was one *double* bed.

What were we going to do?

9

JULIAN

"We have dinner plans in an hour. I'll leave you two to unpack and get dressed. Let me know if you need anything," Connie said. Her eyebrows rose as she looked at her daughter. "Jennifer, we should talk later."

"Okay," she said softly.

Connie pulled the door closed behind her, leaving me and Jen all alone in a room with only one small bed. A double bed. I hadn't slept on a double bed since I was a kid. Definitely not with another person in it. I hadn't considered this option about our subterfuge. I actually hadn't known we were even staying in a house until we pulled up. I'd figured a hotel with multiple beds. That was what I got for assuming.

As much as I wanted to get in that bed with Jennifer, that wasn't what she wanted.

"I'll take the couch," I told her immediately.

"Oh," she whispered. "No. I don't know. I wouldn't know how to explain that."

"I'll say that I wasn't comfortable."

She eyed me skeptically. "You're a Wright."

"What does that mean?"

"Your family reputation precedes you." Jennifer shrugged when I moved to object. "Sutton had a shotgun wedding. My parents have never forgotten that. I put money on my mom asking if I'm being careful." Her cheeks brightened as the words left her mouth.

"Ah," I said. "Then I'll take the floor."

"Yeah...we could alternate if you want."

"No way. You take the bed. I'll make a pillow fort."

"I'm sorry, Julian. I didn't think about it."

"Don't even worry. I want you to be comfortable."

She smiled shyly. "Then, uh...I'll just...change in the bathroom."

My eyes roamed her body. Fuck. Right. She'd change in the bathroom. Where she wouldn't be naked in front of me. My cock swelled at the thought. This weekend was going to be...hard. In more ways than one.

Jennifer grabbed clothes out of her duffel and shuffled into the connected bathroom. I adjusted myself in her absence. When I'd suggested that we do this, I'd thought it would be a good way for us to be around each other a lot. I couldn't deny that I would be interested in trying with Jennifer.

When I'd first moved here, I'd been in the wrong place for us to have a relationship. With my mom's cancer, it felt like too much to concentrate on anything else. Then I lifted my head from the clouds, and Ashleigh was there. She had been *so* into me. Look where that had gotten me.

I wasn't going to push Jennifer for something she didn't want, but I wasn't going to resist my flirtations. If she was my girlfriend this weekend, maybe, just maybe, I could find out if my affections were reciprocated.

* * *

I changed into fitted khakis with a thick brown belt, a bright blue button-up, rolled to my elbows, and a fresh pair of white tennis shoes. Jennifer's eyes rounded slightly as they trailed down my body. I smiled confidently. At least she wasn't completely immune to me.

"I like your dress."

She flushed and rubbed her hands down the front of the yellow floral number. She'd paired it with a dusty-blue cardigan and brown sandals. I decided that I liked her blush.

"Oh, uh...thanks. I like your outfit too. You're dressed up."

I arched an eyebrow. "Too dressed up?"

"No. It's very you."

True. I'd always been into fashion. When I was growing up, other guys wore baggy cargo pants and oversize T-shirts. I never felt like myself in that kind of outfit. I wanted sharp lines, tailored cuts, and bright colors. I'd been made fun of for it in middle school. Jordan had stopped that with his fists. He used to take all of his anger issues out by fighting. I was so glad that he had Annie now to quell that response.

"What?" Jennifer asked.

That was when I realized that I had been staring at her. At the shine in her light brown bob, the strands brushing against her collarbone. It was the longest I'd ever seen it. She had on almost no discernible makeup, except some pink gloss on her lips that made me consider licking it off, and kohl lining her eyes. The eyeliner made her eyes almost impossibly large. The hazel turned a soft green in the slanted light coming in from the shutters, revealing the gold flecks that surrounded her pupils. Her pale skin was lightly freckled across the bridge of her nose. I couldn't stop staring. Not when I had an uninterrupted view.

"You look beautiful," I admitted.

She drew her bottom lip into her mouth. "There's no one here for you to impress right now."

"Yes, there is."

Her cheeks heated. "You're such a flirt."

A deflection if I'd ever heard one. I *was* a flirt, but it hadn't even crossed my mind. I couldn't stop looking at her. But I had to.

I laughed and held my arm out. "You're right. Shall we?"

She took a deep breath. "Yes. Let's do it."

We exited the bedroom to find that her mom had changed into some rust-colored dress. Her light-brown hair matched her daughter's but appeared to have recently been permed. And then her dad walked into the room. A slight man with glasses and a flannel tucked into denim.

"Ah, you must be the boyfriend," he said, pushing his glasses up his nose. He held his hand out. "Dan."

"Julian." We shook. "It's a pleasure, sir."

"This is the part where I say you have to take care of my daughter," he said with a laugh.

"Dad," Jennifer said.

He winked at her. "I know that you can take care of yourself, sweetie."

"Barely," her mom said under her breath.

"Connie," he said softly. "Let's have a good night."

"Of course, dear. Are you all ready to go see Chester?" She nearly bounced at the name of her son.

Jennifer practically deflated.

What was I missing? Jennifer had said that graduation was going to suck and that she didn't want to subject me to it. She'd said that her mom was tough on her. But it was one thing to be tough because of her job or boyfriend status and another thing to have a clear preference for Chester over Jennifer. I'd met Connie less than an hour ago, and I could already see that. No wonder Jennifer hadn't wanted to come if she was always being compared to her brother by a parent with an obvious preference.

"Yes. Let's go ahead." Dan put his arm around Jennifer and kissed her cheek. "We're really glad to have you here, honey."

"Thanks, Dad," she said softly.

"Tell me all about your latest project. You mentioned a portrait session?"

Jennifer brightened at the question. "Yes. I started a series of close-up artistic shots and just got a musician to sign on for the project, too. I think it'll be the centerpiece. We're going to do the shoot when I get home."

"What does that pay?" her mom asked as we walked to their car.

Jennifer shrunk in on herself at the question. Some things weren't all about money. Some things were art.

Then her dad looked up and whistled. "What is *that*?"

"You like cars, sir?" I asked as he ogled my brand-new Jag.

"Like cars? Sure. *That* car is altogether different. This your ride, son?"

"It is. Would you like to give it a whirl?" I produced the keys.

"Maybe later. It's a two-seater."

"You and Jen can take it. I'll follow with Connie," I said immediately.

Jen's head whipped to me at the comment. I'd put money on it that she'd been dreading the idea of riding in the car with her mom, especially alone, and I'd found an easy solution.

"Dan, really," Connie complained.

"Why not?" He took the keys from me. "Get the top down, kiddo."

Jennifer laughed and dashed off after her dad.

"I can drive if you'd prefer, Connie." I shot her a sweet smile.

She touched her chest and laughed. "No, that won't be necessary."

I covered a laugh. I'd done that on purpose to save Jennifer's sanity, but she didn't need to know that. I'd also won over her dad in one fell swoop. One down. One to go.

10

JULIAN

*W*ell, this was more like it.

Connie pulled up in front of a mansion with a circular driveway. She'd filled me in on the fact that we were going to Chester's girlfriend, Margaret's, parents' house. Apparently, her parents were rich. This house in Austin had to cost a fortune, almost like it would in Vancouver.

"Margaret's father works for the state," she explained. "Her mother is a surgeon."

"Interesting," I said as I got out of the car.

Jennifer's hair was wild from the convertible top down being down during the drive with the with her dad. Her smile was just as wide and wild. I wanted to see that look on her face all the time. It was so infrequent that she let loose.

"We might have to drive all the way back like that," she said on a laugh.

Dan tossed the keys back to me. "I approve. Smooth ride."

I slipped them back into my pocket. "Glad you think so."

"Let's not keep them waiting," Connie said.

Jennifer sidled up to me and slid her hand onto my arm. I jolted slightly at the surprised contact. Jen rarely initiated anything.

"Thank you."

"For what?"

"You know what," she said with that same genuine smile.

"Of course. You look so happy."

"My dad *loves* cars."

"Well, aren't you glad we brought Milli then?" I asked as I guided her to the front door, trailing behind her parents.

She grinned. "I admit that it was the correct choice."

The door opened, and a slender woman with a light-brown complexion answered. She wore a white eyelet sundress and wedges. Her black hair was in natural coils, framing the contours of her face. Her eyes were nearly as black as night with gold dusted on her lids, and her lips were painted a soft pink.

She smiled wide and welcoming. "Hey, y'all. Come on in."

"Margaret, it's so good to see you," Connie said, pulling her into a hug.

"You too." Then she turned to Jennifer. "Jen! It's been too long."

Jennifer hugged her back. "Hi, Mags."

"And who is this?" Margaret asked.

"Margaret, this is Julian Wright." She paused before adding, "My boyfriend."

Margaret arched an eyebrow. "Well, hello there. I see Jen's picked a good one." She held her hand out, and I shook it. "I'm Margaret."

"It's a pleasure."

"Have you met Chester yet?"

"Not yet. This is all new for me," I told her.

"Well, come on in. My parents are finishing dinner, and we can eat soon."

I followed her into the mansion with an assessing eye. They'd had an interior designer. I could tell by the careful placement around the house. My dad had hired a designer for our place in Vancouver. As much as I'd loved the house, it had never felt like home. As if someone else had inhabited it for years and we were just its current occupants. I felt more at home at my place in Lubbock or my mom's cozy '70s-era home than I ever had in that cold house. This house had the same cold feel.

"Mom, Dad, you made it," Chester said, appearing in the living room and hugging his parents.

He...wasn't what I'd expected. I didn't know what stereotype had let me picture him as a frumpy nerd, but he wasn't. He wore a light-gray suit that had been taken in to accommodate his narrow waist and broad shoulders. His dark brown hair was brushed backward and long, coming down just under his ears. He wore black-framed glasses that were more style than I would have guessed.

"Jen," Chester said when he caught sight of his sister.

"Hey, Chess."

His brow furrowed. "You know I don't like that nickname."

Her lips quirked up as if she had in fact known he didn't like the nickname. Which was all the more reason for her to use it.

She stepped back and gestured to me. "This is my boyfriend, Julian Wright."

Chester held his hand out as he looked me over. "You're the Wright cousin, yeah? From Vancouver?"

I blinked in surprise after our handshake. "I am. Wasn't aware that news had traveled."

"Jennifer said she was working at Wright Vineyard, so I looked it up. You're a co-owner and technically her boss."

Everyone looked between us awkwardly, as if Chester had just dropped a bomb. Jennifer shifted uncomfortably, opening and closing her mouth in response. But she also didn't seem surprised that Chester had gone to all of this trouble.

"Technically," I said with a shrug. "She works for the winery, but it's a contractor situation, and she reports to my cousin Hollin."

"Hmm..."

"Chess," Jennifer grumbled, "let it go."

"Just trying to figure out how this happened."

"Are you interrogating them?" Margaret asked with narrowed eyes.

The look that passed between them was not the love and devotion of people who had been dating for a few years, like Jennifer had told me. Margaret had daggers in her eyes, and Chester's face was full of disdain. What was happening between them? Whatever it was, no one else seemed to notice.

"Of course not," Chester said. "I like to get the feel of people."

"Well, cut it out."

Chester laughed and took a step toward Margaret. He reached for her hand, but she jerked hers back.

"Chester," his mom said, "why don't you tell us about the new job that you have?"

It was clear that she already knew all about it, but she wanted to show off her firstborn and favorite.

Chester watched Margaret walk into the kitchen toward her parents for a second longer and then turned back to us.

"I'll be moving back to Lubbock next week to work as the head researcher in a biochemistry lab."

"Our boy is going to change medicine," Connie said with a wide smile.

"I still can't believe you went to all the trouble of getting a PhD and aren't staying to be a professor," Jennifer said.

Chester's head snapped to her, and she shrank back. It had seemed an innocuous enough statement. I really didn't understand the family dynamics. My own family was a hot mess, but Jennifer hadn't mentioned that Chester was a loose cannon. Or at the very least, not used to being challenged.

"I was recruited for several academic positions, but they all felt too...mundane for me. I want to work hands-on and see my research implemented in my lifetime," he said loftily.

Margaret's parents appeared then. Her father was even taller than I was with a deep brown skin tone and the look of a retired professor—thick-rimmed glasses, tweed jacket, bow tie, and all. Her mother was also tall. Apparently, the entire family was. Her peachy skin was mostly hidden by a long black dress with gauzy sleeves.

"Dinner is served," she said.

We all moved to the long dining room table and served up the delicacies that they'd concocted for us. The exchange was as tense as it had been in the living room. Something was going on with Chester and Margaret, but at least it took the focus off of me and Jennifer.

Except Jen was quiet...too quiet all through dinner. It was as if she were invisible and could blend right into the background. With Chester's booming personality, Margaret spitting back at everything he said, and both sets of parents talking up their kids, I could see how alone Jennifer must feel. No wonder she hadn't wanted to come.

By the time we finished dinner and Margaret's parents were offering drinks, I barely stifled a yawn.

"Thank you, but I have to decline," I said. "I think Jen and I need to get back. We drove into Austin today, and I'm wiped."

"Oh, of course," Connie said sympathetically.

Jennifer's head jumped at my suggestion. Her eyes assessed me in confusion. Like she couldn't figure out why I was bowing out of the rest of the evening.

I shook hands with the rest of the family and hugged Connie one more time. Then I ushered Jennifer out of that house as fast as humanly possible.

"What are you doing?" she asked.

"Getting you out of there."

"What? But...what?"

We stopped in front of Milli.

"Did you want to stay for drinks? Sit around and hear about how amazing Chester is? Watch Margaret and Chester barely keep from boiling over at each other?"

"No," she whispered. "But...how did you know that?"

"I have eyes. Anyone with eyes could see that you were disappearing in that room."

Her eyes widened, and then she flushed. "Yeah. Okay. Disappearing."

I grasped her hand before she could push away. "Hey."

She drew back and headed toward the passenger side. "Let's just go."

But I followed her. "Did I say something wrong?"

She shook her head. "No."

"Jen..."

She looked up at me, and I saw for the first time that she was hurt. Hurt by what I'd said?

"You didn't disappear to me," I said softly.

She took a step backward in surprise. "What?"

"You were fading into the background but not to me. You needed a breath of fresh air. That's why I suggested it. Not because I think that you're walking in your brother's shadow."

Her eyes were round and lined with gold from the light of the moon. "It's all that obvious, isn't it?"

"I've had a lot of experience observing people."

"I was afraid of this," she whispered and looked away.

"Of what?"

"That you'd see me differently once you met everyone."

I barked a laugh. "Differently? If anything, I see everyone else differently. How can they not appreciate what's right in front of them?"

My words held a double meaning. How had I not appreciated her there all this time? Our constant friendship. Her easy demeanor. The friendship that had blossomed so effortlessly over the last few years. That now, we were standing here, and all I wanted to do was kiss her.

She bit her bottom lip and looked down. "We should... we should just go back."

Right. This was Jennifer. She was all of those things to me, but we weren't in a place where I could kiss her. I didn't want her to push me away.

I straightened, swallowing down the urge to kiss her, and headed to the other side of the car. We drove back to the house in silence. Just the gentle purr of Milli guiding the way. The house was dark when we arrived, and Jen flipped on the lights as she headed back for the bedroom. By the time she got there, she was yawning for real.

"Maybe I'm more tired than I thought," she said.

"Traveling is draining."

So was pretending to be something that she wasn't and hiding her entire personality because of her parents' expectations and suffocating under her brother's supposed brilliance. Things I couldn't say. She'd been uncomfortable enough when I mentioned that she was invisible. Obviously, she'd been dealing with all of this a lot longer than the handful of hours I'd been present. This wasn't new to her. But that didn't mean I had to like it.

Jennifer grabbed her clothes and headed into the bathroom. She returned, wearing adorable glasses, a short-sleeved, mint-green, silk, button-up sleeping outfit. Her hair was piled into a messy bun on the top of her head with the shortest strands loose at the nape of her neck.

I snatched up my own sleeping clothes before my dick could respond to seeing her long, curvy legs and the shape of her in silk...with no bra.

Normally, I slept naked. Or at the most, in a pair of boxers. But I couldn't do that here, of course. So, I'd packed some sleep shorts and an old traveling soccer team shirt. Jennifer was already in bed when I got back. The lamp on the side table light was on, and she had a historical romance set next to it.

"Any idea where I should look for the extra pillows and blankets?" I asked her.

She cleared her throat, as if she were about to prepare a speech. "I actually thought...there is room." She gestured next to her. "I mean, I don't move around a lot in my sleep. I'll stay on my side."

"You want me to sleep with you?"

Her cheeks turned a hint of pink that made me want to keep saying things to get that expression. She was usually so embarrassed when I flirted with her, but she never took me seriously. But now, we were about to sleep in the same bed. There was no way to *not* take this seriously.

"Sleep...next to me," she chirped.

"All right."

I closed the door behind me, flicking the lights off, and carefully slid into the bed next to her. The only illumination in the room came from her side table. The bed was not big. My feet hung a little over the edge, but it was infinitely better than sleeping on the floor. The worst part was how *close* together we were. Or maybe it was the best part? The most torturous part?

Her body wasn't touching mine, but she was close enough that I could *feel* the heat coming off of her.

My brain short-circuited when she shifted and her hip touched mine. She jumped backward, as if she, too, had been hit by an electrical surge at the contact.

"I'm going to get some sleep," she said hastily, turning off the side lamp and casting us into darkness.

"Night," I whispered.

She turned on her side to face away from me. While I sat there and envisioned her naked and underneath me.

I squeezed my eyes shut and told my dick to get itself together.

Fuck. I was already hard.

"I actually think I'm going to take a shower," I told her.

"Okay," she murmured softly.

There was something I needed to take care of if I was going to sleep next to her all night.

11

JENNIFER

Graduation was bright and early the next morning.

I'd barely slept. My brain wouldn't shut off, no matter how hard I'd tried. Not when I could hear the shower running from the bathroom and picture the water running over his naked body. Not when he lay inches away from me. Not when we were in *bed* together.

I'd eventually gotten up at three in the morning to pop a sleeping pill that I reserved for emergencies. But I'd taken it too late and woken up groggy. My brain was cocooned in a cloud, and every movement felt like I was dragging.

"We could get you a coffee," Julian offered with a smile.

He hadn't seemed to have any trouble sleeping and was his same chipper self the next morning.

I made a face. "I don't like it."

"But you *need* it. There's a difference."

"It tastes like bitter bean juice."

He gasped. "You offend me."

"Feel free to enjoy it. I will stick to my water."

"Tea? Coke? Chocolate? Something with a stimulant in it."

I bit my lip and nodded. "Maybe a Coke. But there's a hierarchy of Coke."

He arched an eyebrow. "A hierarchy?"

"Definitely. Not all Coke is created equal."

He snorted. "Pray tell." He leaned his elbow on the island as he waited for his pot of coffee to brew.

"Mexican Coke in a glass bottle is the absolute number one."

"Fair."

"Then Freestyle machine Coke. You know, the one that has the touch screens."

He smirked. "Yes."

"Fountain Coke. Preferably McDonald's, followed by Coke in a can. Then comes the problem children."

He couldn't keep the full-blown smile from reaching all the way to his eyes. "Problem children?"

"Two liter, then twenty-ounce bottle, and then the dreaded bar Coke." I shuddered. "Bar Coke is the lowest of lows. Only to be had when all else fails."

"You are adorable." He reached forward and booped my nose.

I flushed and looked away with a laugh. "Ask any Coke drinker. They'll tell you! I didn't invent the hierarchy. I just enforce it."

My mom appeared then, decked out in her nicest dress for graduation. I'd carefully avoided being alone with her since we'd gotten here. I'd even waited much longer than normal before leaving the bedroom so that I wouldn't have to endure her lecture. I wanted to have a good weekend. Julian was definitely making it better, but I couldn't escape her forever.

"Ready to go, kiddos?" she asked with my dad trailing behind her.

79

"We are," I said.

"Just waiting for my coffee."

"Pour me a cup, too, would you, Julian?" my dad said. He sidled up to Julian and started a conversation about his car.

"Don't think that I don't know you're avoiding me, young lady," my mom said quietly.

"I've been with you the entire time I've been here."

"We're going to need to talk."

"Yes, ma'am," I whispered. I'd known it was coming. I didn't have to look forward to it.

Once the coffee was done and in travel mugs, we headed out of the house. The BNB was walking distance to campus, which was lucky so we didn't have to hope to find parking. We stopped in front of Bass Concert Hall, where we found Chester and Margaret waiting.

They appeared to be in a heated debate that quickly trailed off when they saw us. She couldn't even manage a smile for us. In fact, she looked close to tears. I wanted to hug her for putting up with my brother. What was his problem?

"Chester dear," my mom said, dragging my brother into a hug. "I'm so proud of you."

"Thanks, Mom." He pulled back. "Here are the tickets for the hall. I'll see you all after."

"Good luck, Chess," I said with a wide smile.

His eyes caught mine, and for a second, I saw that same antagonized irritation that always passed between siblings. But then it vanished, and he just smiled.

"Thanks, sis."

He disappeared with the rest of the graduates and left us alone with a distraught Margaret.

"You want to show us the way?" I asked before my parents could ask what was wrong. They were so tactless.

"Sure," she whispered. Then she gave me a half-smile. "Thanks, Jen."

"Anytime."

We all packed into the gorgeous Bass Concert Hall, the largest performance venue in Austin.

I sat between Margaret and Julian, followed by my dad and then my mom. We waited in awkward silence for the commencement ceremony to begin. I wanted to ask Margaret what had happened, but it didn't feel like the moment to broach the subject.

Then my focus was dragged elsewhere as Julian slid his arm across the back of my seat. He wasn't quite touching my shoulders or holding me, but I still felt wrapped in him. Hyperaware of his body, as I had been last night.

Thank God I'd taken my anxiety medicine this morning. Maybe I should have popped half of a Xanax as well to deal with all of this. But it was too late now, and Julian was almost touching me, claiming me.

I wanted to say it was all fake. That was what we'd agreed to after all. But he didn't have to do that, and he didn't have to take care of me, like he had been this whole trip either. I glanced over at him and found him staring down at me. Our eyes met as the lights dimmed. Shadows moving through his dark irises. I couldn't read him, and I so wanted to know what he was thinking.

"What?" he whispered as the first speaker walked out to a round of applause.

"Nothing."

Then I faced forward, like a coward.

* * *

Commencement ended with fanfare, and we spent the rest of the day taking pictures and doing all the things Chester insisted needed to be done for him to leave Austin. Margaret abandoned us by lunch with the promise to come out for the graduation party tonight.

"What's going on with them?" Julian asked.

"I don't know."

"Doesn't look good."

"No. Chester has always been...volatile."

"I was going to say narcissistic."

I laughed softly. "Yeah. Being told you're a genius at a young age really hits you in the ego."

"I bet."

"But I've never seen him act this way with Margaret."

"Well, I hope everything works out."

"Me too," I said, watching her leave.

"So, about this party," he said thoughtfully. "What should I wear?"

I chuckled. "Whatever you have is good. We're just going to an event at a bar downtown."

"Well, how about this?" he asked, leaning against the table next to me while my parents ordered lunch.

"Hmm?" I was distracted by his nearness, the soft touch of his arm against mine.

"You tell me what you're wearing."

"I brought, uh...a sundress. It's green," I said helplessly.

"Green." He nodded. "I can work with that."

I didn't think anything more of the conversation as my parents brought subs back for us. Not until much later when I came out of the bathroom in my green sundress and found Julian standing in an outfit that perfectly complemented mine. Soft gray slacks, a purple V-neck with a little green logo, and loafers. He looked sharp as hell. I would have liked nothing more than to stay in and take all of those clothes off of him.

"How's this?" he asked with a smirk. He must have already seen my assessment.

"I like it."

He nodded, pleased. "Good."

My mouth was dry as I stared at him. I took a step backward, trying to keep my brain from short-circuiting. Because, holy hell, Julian Wright was so fucking hot. It was practically sinful.

I snatched my purse off of the table, and it rattled with pills. I winced at the sound, hastening out of the room, nearly running right into my dad.

"Hey, where are you going in such a hurry?" he asked with a laugh.

"Sorry."

"It's fine, pumpkin. Are you ready for the graduation party?"

I nodded. "Yep."

But I wasn't sure I was ready. Chester and Margaret were fighting. Julian Wright matched me, as if we'd planned our outfits. My parents were accepting of all of it. Everything felt strangely uncertain. Still, I swallowed down my unease and followed everyone out to my parents' car.

We drove in circles until we finally snagged a spot in a parking garage not too far from the banquet hall downtown. A group of STEM students passed us into the graduation event. Chester was one of three PhDs graduating along with a dozen master's students. The entire chemistry department came out to celebrate their achievements.

We loaded up on appetizers and grabbed drinks from the bar before staking out a space away from everyone else.

It was a long hour before the party had begun to dwindle. My parents had been speaking to the dean for at least twenty minutes. Chester had disappeared.

"This is lame," I said. I stood from where we'd turned into wallflowers and brushed off my dress. "Want to head to another bar? I think I've been to one or two down the street."

Julian shrugged. "Sure. Should we say something to your parents?"

My gaze slipped over to them, and I sighed. "Probably."

Just as I headed over there, Chester reappeared. His cheeks were flushed. "Leaving already?"

"We were going to go get a drink."

Chester nodded. "I know just the place."

"You want us to go with you?" I asked dubiously.

"Why not, little sis?" he asked.

Because he'd been avoiding us since we'd gotten here. Something was up with my brother, but I had no idea what it was. I wanted to ask if Margaret was going to meet us since she'd never arrived at the party, as promised, but I had a feeling I already knew the answer.

It'd be easy to just tell Chester no and walk away. But I couldn't say no to anyone, let alone a brother who seemed to actually want my attention.

"All right," I said. I glanced up at Julian.

He shrugged. "Fine by me."

We said good-bye to our parents and then headed out onto the balmy Austin street. Chester chatted amicably the entire time. I barely heard what he'd said, but thankfully, Julian kept up the conversation easily. This was why I'd brought him anyway, right?

Chester finally stopped in front of a large metal door.

"What's this?" I asked curiously.

"Our stop," he said with a wink.

Julian and I exchanged a glance and then both shrugged.

"House party?" I said.

Chester smirked and knocked on the door. A slot opened, and he slipped a small card into it. We waited outside for a few minutes in silence. Then the door creaked open.

"Welcome to the Lounge," a gravelly voice said.

"Where have you taken us?" I whispered reverently as I looked inside.

Chester grinned. "A secret bar. It used to be a brothel."

I squeaked.

He just laughed. "Can't handle it, sis?"

His eyes were a challenge. This wasn't my scene. Not at all. But I couldn't back down from that look either. I reached for Julian's hand for strength and then pulled him across the threshold with me.

12

JENNIFER

The former brothel was a cascade of shadows. Reds and grays and blacks decorated the room, shading the black leather booths in darkness and revealing the brown lacquered bar. We passed the booths, only getting eclipsed views of the people within. They could have been as devious or innocuous as possible, but everything felt charged with energy and awareness.

"This is your room," the attendant said, stopping before a frosted sliding glass door.

He tapped twice, and the door slid open. Inside, there was a floor-level sunken tub and a dozen people that I'd never met. Half of them had dropped down to their unmentionables and were submerged in the bath. The rest were drinking fancy concoctions.

Chester entered first, and everyone cheered at his presence. "I brought my sister and her boyfriend."

"The more, the merrier," a guy said, tugging on Chester's collar and dragging him toward the bar to choose a drink.

"What am I seeing?" I whispered to Julian.

He laughed. "A bar."

I narrowed my eyes at him.

"A fancy bar, but that's all," he added.

"Do you think they clean this place?"

He snorted and covered his mouth as he walked us around the room to look at the drink menu. "I'm sure it's been scrubbed clean."

"I'm glad there aren't black lights."

He stopped and turned to face me. "What? Prudish?"

"In public? Yes!"

"This is mostly private," he offered.

I shook my head and then checked out the drink list. There were amazingly bubbly and elaborate concoctions that I'd never heard of before. Most of the ingredients didn't even look familiar.

I shrugged. "Just pick one out for me."

Julian nodded and wrote down our orders, stuffing the slip of paper into a slot that must have taken it back to the bar. Only a matter of minutes later, our drinks were rolled in on a gold trolley by a man in the shortest shorts I'd ever seen and nothing else.

I blinked and tried not to stare. Everything about him was exposed. Though not much more than Chester's friends lounging in the sunken tub with soaked boxers or thin lace panties and bras, revealing practically everything underneath.

I thankfully took my drink and downed most of it in one long gulp. I needed to be drunker for this.

"Whoa there," Julian said with a laugh.

"It's delicious. I'll take another."

He shrugged. "Okay, but do you normally drink this much?"

"She doesn't normally drink. Isn't that right, sis?" Chester asked, appearing at our sides. His shirt had been removed, and he was surprisingly built with long, lean muscles. The last time I'd seen him, he'd still been the scrawny chess player I had known.

"I drink," I countered. "Just...not a lot."

"What do you think of the Lounge?"

"It's...different."

Chester snorted. "In the best way."

"Do you come here a lot?"

He shrugged. "Sometimes. We're celebrating."

"Where's Margaret?"

His face soured at the mention of his girlfriend. "Not here."

"Are you all right?"

"Peachy," Chester said with a sigh.

I opened my mouth to ask more, but Julian touched my elbow. I was pushing Chester's buttons the way he pushed mine. But I should let it go for now. It clearly wasn't helping anything.

"Is that a number seven?" Chester asked, looking at the yellow drink in my hand.

"Yes," Julian said. He held his drink up. "And a number five."

"Good choices. Try a number twelve," he said, his smile returning. "It'll loosen you right up."

"Chester, get in here!" the same guy who had pulled him into the room called. He was sitting in the tub in nothing at all.

My cheeks heated, and I quickly averted my gaze. I guzzled the rest of my drink. Yep. More alcohol.

I dropped the drink down. "I'll take a twelve."

Julian looked at the menu and frowned. "There's eight shots in that. You'll die."

"Oh, wow. Eight?"

"Why don't we go somewhere else?"

"What? Why?" I asked, suddenly self-conscious.

"You're not comfortable here. I'm starting to think Chess brought you here, knowing you'd be uncomfortable."

I met his dark gaze. "You don't seem uncomfortable."

Julian smiled, the look he gave me was licentious and inviting. "I can't say that I mind being here with you, Jen."

"Oh?" I whispered as the drink I'd finished buzzed around in my brain, slowing my response time.

"Can you honestly say you don't feel it?"

"Feel what?"

He sighed. "Anything."

I blinked at him. What was he asking? Whether or not I felt something for him? Wasn't it the most obvious thing in the world? Could I be any more obvious about my feelings for Julian Wright? I didn't think anyone in all of Lubbock was unaware that I'd been into him since the day I'd met him. That couldn't be what he was asking.

"What do you mean?"

He shook his head, disappointment clouding his handsome features. "Nothing. Do you still want the twelve?"

"Share it with me?"

"All right."

He wrote it down on another slip of paper, and our drinks appeared again. He'd gotten me the twelve, as promised. Another number five sat on the tray for him as well.

That last drink must have been stronger than I'd thought because, suddenly, everything felt very warm. Very heady. My legs wobbled, and I could feel every one of my fingers, like little pins were pricking them. I blinked slowly and picked up the twelve.

When was the last time I'd been this drunk? I had no

idea. I wasn't really supposed to drink on my anxiety medication. They interacted in some way, so I avoided it. But it was a celebration, and then there were the naked people in a brothel bathtub. I'd needed the drink. Now, I was floating. And the eight-shot drink in front of me only helped along the feeling.

"How does this taste like a Dreamsicle?" I asked Julian, leaning into his broad chest.

His arm snaked around my waist. "You should go easy on it."

"Mmhmm," I purred, taking another sip.

Julian reached out and took the drink from my hand. He took a sip. "It does taste like a Dreamsicle. What even?"

I giggled and nodded. "Right?"

"Fuck, it's good."

My head tilted up toward him. His gaze swept to mine and held, intent and lustful. The space between us disappeared. Something passed between us. And I was drunk enough not to question it.

"Let me taste," I whispered.

"You want a taste?"

I nodded. He slowly took another drink. His Adam's apple bobbed as he swallowed. I listed into him as I traced the movement.

Then his head dipped down, finishing the descent. A pause, and everything stalled and went dark and heated. Those beautiful lips pressed against mine, soft and hard, all at the same time. His tongue flicked out, brushing against mine. The taste of Dreamsicle exploded in my mouth just from the barest touch of him.

I moaned, a deep, throaty thing that, any other time, I would be embarrassed by, but right now, I had no other thoughts than this: Julian Wright was kissing me. Really kissing me.

No stolen moments in his office to make his ex jealous. There was no one here for him to impress. No one, except me.

My fingers fisted into the front of his shirt as I came onto my tiptoes to try to get closer to that perfect mouth. He set the number twelve down before dragging me tight against him. His hands splayed wide against my back before sliding to my hips. My pelvis pushed forward an inch until I was tight against him, could feel exactly how he felt about me.

Our lips moved like a synchronized dance, as if we'd been doing this all our lives. He kept one hand on my hip while his other moved along my side and up to my stomach. My skin heated at every brush of him against my body. Then he was running fingers under my breast, along the underwire.

I gasped at the contact, and he broke free of my lips, trailing kisses down my neck and across my collarbone. My core was on fire, and I was set to combust at the slightest touch.

"Jennifer," he groaned and tugged me closer.

"Oh my God," I whispered.

A hand slid to the hem of my dress, caressing the soft skin of my thigh. I moaned again unabashedly. It was hard to think straight with him here, touching me like that.

His mouth moved to my ear. His tongue darted out to flick against the lobe. "We should get you home."

"N-now?" I stammered out.

"I can't do what I want with you here."

I shivered at the words. "What-what do you want to do with me?"

His laughter was rough and gravelly. "*Everything.*"

13

JENNIFER

"Oh," I gasped.

Everything. It took my brain a minute to catch up. He meant...he meant, everything.

His hand moved up to the lace of my panties, and his words crystallized. He meant, he wanted *me*.

"*Oh!*"

Julian wanted me. Right now. He'd actually been asking me earlier if I felt something. Now that I knew the question, the answer was yes. So much yes.

He removed his roaming hands and stared down into my shocked face. He pressed another kiss to my swollen lips. "Ready to leave?"

The drink made me bolder than I ever would be otherwise. "God, yes."

He smiled vibrantly and pulled me out of the bar. I didn't even bother to say good-bye to Chester. We took an Uber back, tiptoeing through the darkened house. My parents were clearly asleep down the hall, but we didn't want to risk waking them.

I dropped my purse on the counter as we stumbled into

the bedroom. Then Julian was there again. His hot body pressing into me. It was so much that I could barely breathe as his hand tilted my chin up to look at him, and then when he saw what he was looking for, he pressed his lips to mine again. I sighed like a drowning girl getting her first taste of air.

"Julian," I whispered, a plea.

He'd had more to drink than me. He'd even finished the number twelve, and somehow, he wasn't slurring or stumbling. He cupped my face in his hands as if I were as precious as diamonds and as fragile as glass. My eyes fluttered when he pulled back to stare down at me.

"Do you want this?"

"You?"

He nodded, his thumbs drawing circles along my jaw. "Tell me you want me."

I swallowed and bit my lip. "I want you."

His gaze remained on mine. A flush suffused my skin at the direct contact. "Say it again."

I laughed, managed to be embarrassed, even while drunk. "Isn't it obvious?"

"With you? Never."

"And what do you want?" I asked with a huff.

His smile was practically feline. "Shall I show you?"

He didn't wait for my reply, just dropped his mouth onto mine. Slow and languid, nipping at the bottom lip and sending shivers down my spine. I clung to him. My fingers moving up into the dark strands of his hair. I'd wondered how the silky strands felt, and here I was, discovering it for myself.

Julian stepped backward, and I tripped, nearly landing in a pile on the floor.

He laughed softly. "You're drunk."

"So are you," I muttered as he helped me back up.

"Tipsy," he corrected.

He swept an arm under my knees and effortlessly lifted me into the air. I threw my arms around him. He chuckled as he carried me the short distance to our small double bed and laid me out across it. I let my sandals slip off the side of the bed. Brazenly, I left the skirt of my dress hitched up high on my thighs.

His gaze traveled across the milky skin. I could see a spot of indecision on his face, and then I steeled myself and reached for him. I took his hand in mine and drew him down onto the bed next to me. That was apparently all the invitation he needed before his mouth covered mine again. And God willing, he still tasted like a Dreamsicle. I'd never taste one again and not think about him.

Alcohol battered against my anxiety, releasing its hold on me. It was only me and Julian in the room. I'd wanted this with him from day one. I didn't plan to refuse whatever he was offering. Whatever the outcome.

His hands were more hesitant than they'd been at the bar, staying firmly planted on my sides as he kissed me. But I wanted more. My core was pulsing in tempo with our kisses.

"I thought you said everything," I whispered.

His eyes flared wide at my words. "And I meant it. Show me what you want."

The alcohol silenced my inner panic. In a bold gesture, I pushed his hand lower, lower, lower, over my hip and across the top of my thighs until he was precisely where I wanted him.

Shock mingled with desire in his irises as his hand settled between my legs. "Is that so?"

His fingers skimmed the hem of my dress, slipping

under the material and reaching the cotton panties. He dragged one finger down the center of the fabric. I jolted in shock as the contact sent sparks through me.

"There," I whispered.

His head dipped to my ear. "You want me to touch your pussy?"

I groaned at the filthy words as he leisurely rolled a finger around my clit. I was already wet from just this, soaking through the material. Surely, he could feel it. I was too heated to care.

"Please."

He made a noise in the back of his throat that shot straight between my legs. He slid a finger under the fabric, finally—*finally*—touching me. He slicked a finger through my wetness and dragged it up to my clit.

"Oh fuck, Jen," he growled.

His pelvis ground against my hip, and I could feel the length of him through his pants.

My head fell back onto the pillow as he continued to bring me to new heights. Then the pressure on my hip disappeared, and suddenly, his body was positioned between my legs. He released my clit, slipping the panties over my curvy hips and tossing them to the floor.

Before I could think what would happen next, he buried his face between my legs. I stifled a cry as his tongue flicked against my clit. I jerked and squirmed under the contact, but he forced my hips back down on the bed with his forearm. My hands flew over my head in shock as my orgasm hit me full blast. Still, he licked me until he drew out every ounce of my climax.

He released me when I was left panting on the bed. My eyes remained firmly closed, and I tried to process what had happened. But processing wasn't exactly possible.

His weight shifted off the bed, and I turned in his direction. Julian stood next to me. He peeled off his shirt first, revealing the glorious six-pack beneath. He was lean and ripped from hours of soccer, running, and weight lifting with Hollin. Then went his belt buckle.

My mouth watered at the sight, and I came up to my knees on the bed. His eyes flashed to mine as he drew the buckle back and let it hang open. I scooted forward, pushing his hands away.

"You're doing my job," I told him.

His eyes widened again. "All yours, Dreamsicle."

I giggled at the nickname. "You're the one who tasted like it."

His hands grasped my jaw, and he pressed a firm kiss to my lips. "Get to work."

I heated under that tone. Confident, demanding, and oh-so predatory. I hadn't known Julian had that tone. But my body tightened all over at the sound of it.

He released me, and I popped the button on his slacks. My fingers fumbled with the zipper, but then I got it. I pushed his pants over his narrow hips, leaving him in nothing but baby-blue boxers. My nails skimmed the waistband, dipping an inch inside before retreating. It was his turn to hiss and try to get more. I grinned and did it again.

"Who the fuck knew that you were this much of a tease?" he growled.

My eyes met his, and I pushed my hand all the way in, taking his dick in my hand. "I'm not a tease."

"Fuck."

His eyes rolled into the back of his head at my contact. I didn't consider any other options, just withdrew him from his boxers and dropped my mouth onto the head. Pre-cum tasted salty on the tip, but I swallowed it down.

"Oh God," he breathed. His hands delved into my hair, tightening his grip but not directing. "You feel fucking spectacular."

"Mmm," I groaned as I took him in my mouth.

As nervous and anxious as I was under normal circumstances, blow jobs had always been easier to think about than sex. I'd gotten really, *really* good at them, thanks to a lot of douche bags in high school and college. It was the only thing I could thank them for. But it was also something I'd learned to really enjoy. Not because I could deep-throat without gagging or my jaw didn't hurt or anything. It was the sounds of pleasure Julian was making. Knowing *I* was responsible for that, it was a power that I didn't have anywhere else in my life.

"Jen," he said. "Please."

He stilled me, and I frowned.

I stroked him up and down. "I'm going to finish." I licked my lips. "Don't you want me to?"

"Fuck. Yes."

"Then...what are you doing?"

"I need to be inside of you." He said it so naturally. As if it wasn't a revelation to my senses.

He fished a condom out of his pocket and held it in the air. "Just to be safe."

I took it out of his hand, tore the wrapper, and unrolled it over his dick. Then I sat back on the too-small bed and tugged my dress up and over my head. I flicked the clasp on my bra and let my breasts fall out.

"Fuck, Jen," he groaned as his body covered mine. "You're so fucking beautiful."

Music to my ears. *Beautiful* wasn't the word most men used to describe me. I'd firmly been *cute* most of my life, but when he'd said it, the way he'd said it, I believed him.

The first touch of him between my legs made my eyes roll backward. He squeezed my hip reassuringly before sliding the rest of the way in. It was a tight fit, even as wet as I was. He filled me to the brim in a way that I'd never been filled before. It wasn't just that I hadn't had sex in a while. This was Julian. Everything felt so much bigger and better and more momentous.

He leaned forward over me, dragging our lips together as he started thrusting inside of me. I brought my legs up around his hips, meeting his thrusts with my own. I could barely breathe, barely think. Everything was hot and needy and building, building, building.

"Fuck, your pussy is so tight," he ground out into my ear.

I cried out at the filthy words, and he covered my yells with his mouth, fucking me harder. I didn't want him to stop. Not ever. My second orgasm was knocking on the door of the first. I could feel it coming on so close. I'd never come twice in one night, except by my own hand.

"Close," he said.

"So close," I repeated.

Then he lifted one of my legs onto his shoulder, and I swallowed back a shout as he managed to get even deeper.

"Oh fuck!" I moaned. And then I was coming, and there was no way to stop the cascade as it burst free like a broken dam. I tightened around him to the point of pain.

Julian came hard inside of me as my climax triggered his. He was stiff for a few seconds before finally collapsing forward on top of me.

"Fuck, fuck, fuck," he mumbled incoherently.

I stroked his dark hair out of his face and pressed a kiss to his forehead. "Mmhmm."

He trailed his fingers over my stomach and to my hips,

kissing across my chest and to my breasts. "You're incredible."

I was so relaxed that I nearly fell asleep right there with him still buried inside of me. *Me*. The girl who took an hour to get her brain to calm down enough to sleep every night. I'd never been this relaxed in my entire life.

Finally, Julian retreated and went to the bathroom to clean up. I followed after he was done. When I came back into the bed, still naked, I crashed into his awaiting arms.

Then without preamble, I let sleep take me over as if I had never had a concern a day in my entire life. As if I were a different girl entirely.

14

JENNIFER

I was still naked when the first ray of morning hit me. Julian had one arm wrapped loosely around my waist. He didn't even stir as I shifted to look at him. He snuggled in closer under the comforter and sighed happily when I ran my fingers across his back.

Julian Wright was in bed...with me.

Part of me couldn't process that. I was still waking up. Dawn had broken, but my brain hadn't caught up. It was likely because I was hungover as shit. My head pounded. My stomach roiled. The light was too bright. But still, I wanted to preserve this memory forever.

Last night had been a dream. It didn't even feel real despite all the obvious reality around me. I didn't normally get drunk. Definitely not drunk enough to sleep with Julian Wright. Definitely not drunk enough for *everything* that had happened last night. Yet here I was.

I wanted to lie in this dream forever, but I couldn't.

With a sigh, I scooted out of the bed. Julian's arm dropped into the empty space. I flicked the covers up around him and then tiptoed to the dresser. I threw on my sleeping clothes and tugged my wild hair up into a half-ponytail. I needed something to drink, Tylenol, and my anxiety meds. None of which were in this room with Julian.

I snuck one more glance at his sleeping form before stepping out of the bedroom. My foot hit a creaky board, and I winced.

"Jennifer?" my mom's voice called from the kitchen.

I cursed under my breath, deeply regretting leaving the sanctuary of Julian's arms, and then stepped into the kitchen. "Hey, Mom."

"Breakfast?" she asked, cracking eggs into a bowl.

"Sure." I poured myself a glass of water and fished out my pills from my purse. I downed one with two Tylenol, hoping it would do its trick fast enough to let me deal with my mom.

"How was your night?"

"Good." I took a seat at the island.

"You came in late."

"We went out with Chester."

My mom smiled brightly at my brother's name. "I'm glad to see you two are getting along." Then she frowned. "Did he tell you?"

"Tell me what?"

"He and Margaret broke up."

"Oh," I whispered.

Well, that explained his behavior last night. My brother was a chameleon. He took on the shape of the people around him. Around my parents, he was the perfect son. Around Margaret, the perfect boyfriend. Around me, the antagonistic, older brother, smarter and wiser and better in every way. But last night, he hadn't been any of those things. He'd existed with people I didn't know, in a world I didn't understand. But I'd seen a weight lifted off of his shoulders.

K.A. LINDE

"He didn't say."

"Well, you know your brother. He's very private."

"I could see that they were fighting. What happened?"

My mom shook her head. "He said that she wanted to move home with him and find a job in Lubbock, but that the spark wasn't there anymore."

"That's sad. I liked Margaret."

My mom slid a plate of eggs in front of me. "Speaking of relationships."

Oh boy.

"You and Julian?"

"Yeah?" I asked, reaching for the fork.

"He seems like a nice boy, Jennifer, but are you sure this is what you want?"

"What?"

"He's a Wright. You know what they're like."

"I don't know what you mean, Mom. One of my best friends is a Wright."

"And look how she treated you before she became your best friend," my mom said adamantly. "She was cruel to you in high school, and she didn't even know your name before she hired you to nanny her child. The child she had a shotgun wedding to cover up."

I winced. That was all true and looked bad, but I didn't judge Sutton for her past. We were friends now. That was what mattered.

"I don't see what Sutton has to do with this."

My mom sighed and leaned against the island. "I'm looking out for you, dear. You show up here with a man we've never met and say he's your boyfriend. He's driving a Jaguar and wearing fancy designer clothing. He's your *boss*."

"It's not like that."

"Maybe *you* think so, but what about everyone else at your work? Don't you see what it looks like?"

My face bloomed red. "Mom..."

"It looks like he's screwing his secretary." She held her hands up and stepped back. "Excuse my crude language, but I don't want him to use my baby. What is that man doing with a photographer at his work?"

"Are you saying that he's *slumming* it?"

"No, honey, I would never say that." She shrugged. "I mean, if you were a pharmacist, I might understand it better."

"Mom!" I gasped.

"But that isn't what I'm saying," she said quickly. "I don't want you to get in over your head. I see the way you look at him, Jennifer, like the sun rises when he's in the room. What happens when he's had his fun and leaves? What happens to my bright girl?"

I looked away from her, a deep hurt burrowing in my chest. What would happen? Julian and I were fake dating. Just a fake relationship for the month. We had a plan, a goal. Make the next month bearable. Deal with graduation so that I wouldn't be alone and make Ashleigh jealous. Then everything had gotten complicated.

Of course, I'd always had feelings for him, but they weren't reciprocated. We were lying to my parents. Lying to Chester and Margaret and everyone we had come in contact with this weekend. Julian wasn't madly in love with me. He wasn't my boyfriend.

I almost confessed it all to my mom. But what would that do but prove her right? The deep, yawning chasm in my chest deepened at the thought of how bad he could hurt me. He held my heart in his hands, and he didn't even know it. We'd had sex. It had been...unbelievable. But I couldn't *just* have sex with Julian Wright. I wasn't Annie. One-night stands and friends with benefits would never, ever work for me. I fell fast and hard. And crashed just as devastatingly when it all inevitably went south.

My mom stepped around the island and dropped an arm around my shoulders. "I know you like him. I like him, too. He's charming and funny. I want to make sure that you don't get hurt."

"Is there a way to ensure that?" I asked her desperately.

She laughed softly. "No. Unfortunately. But the one thing I do know is that it has to be equal. Does he feel the same for you as you do for him? If the answer is yes, then ignore me, dear. If he doesn't though...well..."

I swallowed and nodded. If he didn't, then he'd hurt me. And Julian didn't feel that way about me. That was why we had started faking it to begin with. Sex only made it more difficult. As much as I wanted to do it again, I couldn't. Not if I wanted to have a heart after this month was over.

My mom kissed my cheek. "I love you."

"I love you, too, Mom."

She went back to the stove as a rumpled Julian stepped out of the back. He found me with bedroom eyes, a quirk of his lips letting me in on our secret from last night.

"Morning," he drawled.

"Good morning," I whispered.

"Eggs?" my mom asked him.

"No, thank you, ma'am. I was thinking of ducking out and getting us Voodoo Doughnuts. Jen, you want to walk with me?"

I shook my head. "I need to shower. Still feel the bar on me from last night."

He frowned at my words. "All right. Doughnut preference?"

"Whatever you get will be fine."

"Okay," he said, drawing out the word. He looked up at my mom. "Anything for you, Mrs. Gibson?"

"Oh, I can't stomach the calories," she said, touching her waistline. "Jen probably shouldn't either."

My blush moved to the tips of my ears. Yes, I'd gained some weight in the last couple years. My body had changed, too. My hips widening and thighs going with it. Plus, I truly *hated* working out. Nothing about it was fun. I wanted to be like Annie, who cared about running and soccer and shit, but I just didn't care. I'd never been coordinated either. The best I'd managed was two years of marching band in high school.

Julian's gaze narrowed at my mother. I'd never seen him look at anyone but Ashleigh and his father like that. "Jennifer can eat whatever she likes."

"Oh, of course," my mom said. She seemed oblivious to his disdain.

"You can jump in the shower. I'll wait for you to get doughnuts," he offered.

I bit my lip. Might as well get this over with. Ripping the Band-Aid off wasn't going to be fun here or in the Jaguar, driving six hours back home.

"Sure," I said tightly.

I took the quickest shower of my life and didn't even blow my hair out. Just dropped it into a messy bun on the top of my head, the short strands still wet and slightly curling against the nape of my neck. I pulled on a gray T-shirt, tucked into a flowy floral skirt, and sandals I'd worn last night.

Julian was waiting outside. "That was fast."

"I thought you'd still be inside."

He averted his gaze to the door. "It's a nice day. Want to

walk?"

"Yeah, sure."

The day was about as beautiful as Texas summers ever reached. As if the universe knew how incredible our previous night had been and wanted a sunny spotlight on it.

My mind was still reeling from the conversation with my mom. Like...fuck. She meant well. I knew that much. She really did. But the things that she'd said, whether or not true, were the reason I hadn't wanted to have that conversation to begin with.

"You're quiet," Julian said.

"Just talked to my mom. I guess Chester and Margaret broke up."

"Thought that was clear when he got into the tub at the bar last night," he said with a laugh.

"I mean, I knew they had been fighting." I glanced up at him, and his eyes were on mine. Same Julian. Perfect smile, perfect look, perfect everything. He didn't seem to be a totally different guy. He was the same guy I'd known for years. "I didn't realize it had gotten that far."

"Eh. It was probably for the better. She seemed upset."

"True."

"It sucks when relationships end, but not every person you meet is forever."

That was the damn truth. I'd dated enough duds to know that. I had thought that Margaret was the one for Chester. Showed how much I knew about relationships. And anyway, I was using this distraction so that I didn't have to discuss what was happening with me and Julian.

"Here we are." He yanked the door open on the bubblegum-pink building with a Voodoo Doughnuts sign hanging from the top.

We entered a room that smelled like straight sugar and

looked like a kaleidoscope had exploded. We moved against the brick wall to get into the line behind a spattering of bedraggled college students.

"What do you like?" he asked.

"There are so many choices," I whispered as I stared at the plethora of doughnut options before me.

"I'm partial to the Mexican Hot Chocolate and The Blunt."

I coughed, and then my eyes tracked to what was actually a doughnut rolled into a blunt. "Well, they have everything here, don't they?"

"Pretty much." Julian leaned against the wall as we waited our turn. "So, about last night."

I bit my lip. I didn't want to talk about it. I didn't want to ruin it. "What about last night?"

"It happened."

I laughed. "I know it happened."

He smirked. "Good. I was worried when you weren't there in the morning."

"Well, actually..." I ran a hand across the back of my neck.

"What'll ya have?"

I jumped at the woman standing before us. I hadn't realized we'd gotten to the front of the line. The woman was all of five feet tall with bright blue hair up in giant Leia buns on the sides of her head. Her eyes were heavily winged, and she was clearly high as fuck.

Julian didn't even glance back as he said, "She'll have The Dick." My jaw dropped open. "With Bavarian cream."

The woman glanced over to my look of shock and then snorted. "Absolutely."

He grinned at me devilishly. "What?"

"Nothing," I said with an embarrassed laugh.

He ordered a dozen other doughnuts, paid, and took the bright pink box to carry back with us. We stepped outside, and he opened the box and held out my doughnut on a napkin.

"I cannot believe you ordered that for me."

"Go on. Eat it," he teased.

And I couldn't keep myself from cracking up as I took a giant bite of the chocolate-covered dick doughnut. White cream exploded out of the end, spraying onto the sidewalk in front of us. I was sputtering with laughter at the display.

"Oh my God," I gasped.

Julian stepped forward with a napkin and wiped the cream from my chin. "It's polite to help clean up."

"You're ridiculous." I couldn't stop laughing.

"Ah, but you're laughing now, and that's better." He tossed the napkin into the nearby trash. "I thought you might be freaking out."

"I..." I paused.

He was right. I had been freaking out.

He smiled intuitively. "And there's no reason to, Jen. This was supposed to be a fake date, and now, it looks complicated. It doesn't have to be. Let's just keep it casual."

"Casual." Could that even work? I took another bite of my doughnut, so I didn't have to ask the hard questions.

"I'm having fun. You're having fun, judging by how you're *devouring* that dick doughnut."

I sputtered again. Fuck this fucking doughnut.

"It's delicious." I challenged him by taking another bite.

He chuckled. "So, let's just, you know, have fun. Okay?"

My mom's words echoed in my head. That I liked him more than he liked me and I was going to get hurt. She was probably right.

But I wanted this anyway.

PART III

CASUAL

15

JULIAN

*H*ollin spewed drink all over the barn floor. "You made a dick joke?"

"I know." I pushed my computer back across the bar. "You're cleaning that up."

"Yeah, yeah," Hollin said. He was still laughing hysterically as he grabbed a rag and started to mop up the floor. "I just...can you run me through it one more time?"

"Ass."

"I'm serious. I don't know how you got here."

"We hooked up, and the next morning, I could tell she was all squirrelly. Like she was going to give me some big speech about how we couldn't date."

"Seems fair."

"So, I ordered her a dick doughnut and made her eat it."

Hollin tried to keep a straight face, but he lost it again. "Holy shit, man! The great Julian Wright. *The* charming, charismatic, flirtatious jackass that gets every girl in the place falling all over themselves. And you went with a dick doughnut?"

"I panicked, all right? She throws me off my game."

"*Throws you off* is a fucking understatement. You resorted to base humor. That's some shit that I'd pull. Next thing you're going to say is that you're going to dress like me, too. Need some new cowboy boots, bro?"

"I hate you," I grumbled. "Why did I tell you anyway?"

"I don't know, but, man, you're never living this down."

That seemed to be apparent.

No matter how stupid I felt about the whole thing, it had worked. Jennifer had calmed down. She didn't open her mouth again about breaking up our arrangement. Her mom had seemed surprised when we walked back into the house, laughing and cutting up. That woman was a new breed. I'd seen plenty of moms like her in Vancouver, trying to get their perfect princess to marry a prince. But this was different. She actually enjoyed cutting Jennifer down. I was glad I'd been there for her during that.

And a hell of a lot more than saving her from a controlling mother. The sex had been out of this world. She'd enjoyed it, even if she wouldn't talk about it. I'd count it as a win and figure out where to go with her from there. I still had a few weeks until the gala.

"When are you seeing her again?" Hollin asked.

"I don't know. I drove her home yesterday. Maybe at the soccer game next week. But I said casual, so I can't exactly look eager."

"You're Julian Wright. Why the fuck not?"

I glared at him. "Did you miss the entire conversation? If I push, she'll spook."

"You're so difficult," Hollin said. He dropped onto the stool next to me and pulled his own laptop across to him.

Despite both having offices in the cellars, we gravitated toward the quiet of the barn. The tours were closed on Sunday, but the staff was still in the building. I'd spent too many years locked away in an office. It was nice to be out in the open with Hollin, not worrying if my boss was going to come down on me...or my brother.

"What would you know?" I asked him. "You haven't dated anyone longer than three dates the whole time I've known you."

"No one interesting enough."

I snorted. "Sure."

"Three dates tell you all you need to know."

"And what would it tell me about Jen?"

"Don't know, man. I'm counting the entire weekend as date one. Get back to me on date three."

I shook my head. "And you say *I'm* complicated when you have a fucking three-date rule."

"It's not a fucking rule, douche," Hollin grumbled. "You just *know* by then."

I arched an eyebrow skeptically. "If you say so."

"Like, I knew after your first three dates that Ashleigh Sinclair was a fucking psychopath."

I winced. "Low blow."

"Not that you heard a word of it."

"I don't want to talk about her."

"I know you don't, but you need to move on. Jennifer is way cooler than Ashleigh ever was."

I returned my attention to my computer. He wasn't wrong. Jennifer was unlike anyone else I'd ever met. Whereas Ashleigh was exactly like every girl I'd ever dated back in Vancouver. Maybe that was why I'd stumbled into her open arms the second after my mom's cancer cleared up. She was comfortable and convenient. And no matter how many times I said she was different with me than anyone else, it didn't excuse her behavior. She was terrible to everyone in her warpath, and I let it pass until it couldn't be ignored. Until she did something so incomprehensible that I had to walk away. It hadn't made it easy.

"I have this video conference," I reminded him.

"Fine. Change the subject."

I tipped my head at him as I pulled up the conference software.

"Remind me, who are you talking to again?"

"The Dallas-based distribution company. They were here a few weeks ago doing that tasting of our wine. We're in talks about getting us into stores and letting us sell wine off premises. Everything that we need to make actual money."

"Right. Right. I'll leave you to charm them. I'm going to go check on Alejandra."

He clapped me on the back as he left the barn.

I shook out the nerves for the meeting. This was why Jordan had transferred all of the responsibilities to me while he worked on building the new Division II soccer complex on the north side of town for Wright Construction. He couldn't handle both and still have time for Annie. It was all on my shoulders now.

I squared them and entered the meeting. *Here it goes.*

* * *

"Hey, bro. Heard the meeting with the distributor went well," Jordan said, striding up to my Audi SUV in the soccer complex parking lot five days later.

Annie stood next to him in the red uniform for The Tacos—our recreational team started by her brother, Isaac. "Congrats! Is it a done deal?"

"Oh, not yet. They liked the wine. So, that's good at least. We're in negotiations now," I told her. "There are a lot of hoops to jump through."

Despite my apprehension, the meeting had gone as well as planned. They were eager to meet me at the gala event. Part of me was glad that Ashleigh had set it up so that I could meet these wine distributors in person without having to fly into Dallas for a face-to-face. The other part of me resented the fact that she had made this happen. One more obstacle to overcome without her.

I jerked my soccer bag out of the trunk and slammed it shut.

"Well, I think it's only a matter of time," another voice joined the conversation.

I stopped in surprise to find my mom stepping out of Jordan's Tesla. I dropped my bag and rushed over to help her.

"Oh, stop that. I'm fine," she said, shooing me away.

"How are you feeling?"

My mom crossed her arms. "I'd be doing better if you made more time to visit."

I laughed, admonished. "You're right. What are you doing after this?"

"Something with you," she said with a wink.

I exchanged a glance with Jordan. He hadn't told me that he was bringing Mom to the game. It was a blistering day, and there was no shade out on the pitch. I didn't like this at all.

My mom had confided in us that despite all the treatments last go-round, her cancer had returned. She was starting chemo again next week to beat this thing once and for all. We'd moved to the States for her to get excellent treatment here. I'd given up a year of my life to take her to and from her appointments and make sure she was cared for. Now, I was running a vineyard full-time. Jordan was an executive director at Wright Construction. Neither of us had the time, and I *hated* it. She told us not to worry. That she had her brother and Hollin's dad, Gregg, her sister, Lori, and Lori's wife, Vail. But it didn't make it any easier to deal with.

My mom fell into step with me, Jordan, and Annie as we headed for the soccer pitch. I located our field and found my mom a place to sit on the bleachers.

"Stop treating me like an invalid," she said with a smile. "I can still kick your ass."

I laughed. "I believe it. I can't help but worry."

"Lord, don't I know it?" She had that twinkle in her eye when she said it. "It's a little heat. I brought an umbrella. I'm not going to melt."

"Old habits."

"Speaking of," Jordan said, "can I talk to you?"

I frowned. "About what?"

"Just hear him out, Jules," my mom said.

She was the only one who ever got away with using that nickname. My dad hated it. I never used it or let anyone else call me that. But my mom did what she wanted. She also used it when she needed to get her way.

"What?" I demanded.

"Dad is coming back into town."

"So?"

Jordan sighed. He ran a hand back through his dark hair, the mirror image of mine. And yet he was in a button-up with the sleeves rolled up and khakis while I was in a red soccer uniform. So similar and so different. "He wants to have dinner."

"So?" I repeated.

"With you and me."

"No thanks."

"Julian, please. He's trying. He's flying all the way here to see us."

"Not interested."

"Could you please stop being petulant for one second?" Jordan asked.

"Petulant?" I seethed. "He's a bastard, and I have no interest in seeing his face again. Especially after the ambush at the opening."

"That was...the wrong way to do it."

"Oh, my big brother admits fault?" I gasped.

He sighed. "Come on, man. Just one dinner. He's invited Annie, too. It's going to be casual. If it doesn't go well, then I'll leave it alone."

I could see the desperation in my brother's face. I wanted to tell him to go fuck himself. But this was Jordan. This was my best friend and protector. The best brother I could have ever asked for. He hadn't always made the right choices, but he'd always been there for me. He'd even moved here for me when he really didn't want to. Would it kill me to suffer through one dinner with our dad to please Jordan?

"If it's as bad as I suspect, then that's it, Jor."

He nodded and held his hand out. "Deal."

I ground my teeth together but shook his hand. "Fine."

It felt like a death sentence.

Then I found a spot of sunlight in a sea of faces, and another thought occurred to me. If Jordan was bringing Annie, maybe I could bring someone, too, and this wouldn't be a total loss.

16

JENNIFER

"*A*re you sure?" I asked Piper and Blaire before I could stop myself.

It was an old habit, believing that no one else would want my presence near them.

"Yes!" Blaire cried. "I think it'll be awesome."

"It's your house, Piper," I said.

"Jennifer," Piper said, putting her hand on my shoulder, "we want you to move in with us."

"Bradley just finished a remodel on the guest bathroom," Blaire explained. "Before, it was really a half-bath that connected to the living room, but now, it's the full-blown deal. So, there are three full baths. We won't even have to share."

"It does still connect to the living room," Piper said, as if that would talk me out of it. "Guests would still use your bathroom."

"Would that be a problem?" Blaire asked with her wide blue eyes. She recently died her dark-brown hair black as night and it made her eyes pop even more under the shag of her bangs.

They both looked at me with worry. As if I might suddenly change my mind about moving in with them. Tears came to my eyes, and I had to force down the swell of emotions. I'd never really had girlfriends. When I'd gotten Annie and Sutton, I'd felt like I'd won some lottery. Weren't girls catty and terrible? But, no, that was some bullshit that I'd been force-fed. Girls ruled the world, and they made mine so much better.

Now, I had Piper and Blaire in my circle, too. High school Jennifer would have never believed it. Especially because Piper had been a year older than me in high school. She'd always seemed so much more *with it*. I hadn't known Blaire. She was two years younger, still only twenty-five, but she'd grown up with Piper, and now, I couldn't imagine life without them all.

"It would be amazing," I told them truthfully.

"I'm so excited!" Blaire threw her arms around me, jumping up and down in her Tacos uniform. Her long pony-tail swinging around wildly from the back of her characteristic *Blaire Blush* baseball cap.

I laughed and hugged her back. "Me too."

"I'll get together a lease," Piper said, all efficient. "When do you want to move in?"

"Annie is moving Wednesday," I said with a sigh. I was still sad to see her go. "I'll need to track down boxes, but then I don't know...Saturday?"

"Oh my God, Saturday!" Blaire cried.

Annie jogged over then with Sutton and her toddler, Madison, in tow. "What's happening Saturday?"

"Jen is moving in with us," Blaire said, her arm still around my shoulders.

"Yes!" Annie said.

"Wow, Jen," Sutton said.

Madison, in response, burst into tears and started screaming. Sutton's eyes widened in horror and tried to shush her one-year-old. Madison squirmed and flailed until Sutton was forced to put her down into the grass. There, she flopped over and began to wail.

"I have no idea what's gotten into her lately," Sutton said in despair. There were black thumbprints under her eyes from lack of sleep, and she seemed to be on her last leg. "Jason was such a good toddler."

I laughed and leaned down to Madison's level. Jason had been an exceptionally well-behaved toddler. He still was a really good kid. It had been the easiest nannying job I could have asked for. But I'd babysat toddler monsters for years before taking on Jason full-time. I could generally wrangle even the hardest-to-navigate toddler.

After a few minutes, Madison was in my arms, laughing, and Sutton was staring at me with wide eyes.

"How?" she gasped.

I shrugged. "I'm not exhausted or with her twenty-four/seven. Plus, she knows that she can be herself with you. I'm new and different."

Sutton just stared, perplexed.

"If y'all need a night to yourself, I don't mind taking them," I reminded her.

She laughed. "Yeah. I'm going to have to take you up on that."

"Godsend," Annie said. She tapped Blaire's arm. "We have to go warm up."

"See you after, roomie," Blaire said.

They jogged off toward the field, and my eyes snagged on the person they were dragging away—Julian. His eyes were already on me when I found his, and we snapped together like a magnet. He smiled with that look that made my stomach flip and waved before following the girls onto the field.

"What's up with that?" Piper asked.

"They went away together last weekend," Sutton filled her in as we headed to the blanket Sutton had laid out for the kids.

Jason was running a small soccer ball up and down the sidelines with David.

Piper's head whipped to me. "What?"

"We didn't go away! He came with me to my brother's graduation."

"Holy shit! Are you dating?"

I bit my lip and then shook my head. "No. It's not like that. Just helping out a friend."

"Yeah, right," Piper drawled.

"That's what I said," Sutton said. "Like, sure, if you hadn't hooked up, then maybe."

"Sutton!"

"You hooked up?!" Piper said.

"Shh," I said, putting a finger over Piper's mouth. "Way to tell everyone."

"Oh, sorry. Didn't realize it was a secret."

"It's not a secret. It's..." Was it a secret? Had Julian told anyone? What did that make us?

Casual. Just having fun. That was what he'd said over that ridiculous doughnut. I'd laughed and felt all good about it then. Now, it felt more complicated, and I didn't want it to be.

I set Madison down next to the blocks that Sutton had brought and played with her.

"It's not a secret," I repeated. "It's just not...a relationship."

"Hey, I've been on-again, off-again with Bradley for

years," Piper said. "Who am I to judge?"

"Seriously, what is up with y'all?" Sutton asked.

Piper shrugged. "He wants more. He always wants more."

"And you?" I asked.

Piper frowned. "I feel like it's missing something, but I haven't found anything better either."

"How exactly do you find someone better when you're still sleeping with the last guy?" Sutton arched an eyebrow.

"Point taken," Piper said with a laugh. "But how do I find a guy in this small town?"

That was a good question. Annie and Sutton had gotten lucky. David and Jordan had moved here from out of town. Julian was new here, too. But guys from Lubbock? I'd known them all my entire life. The only new guys were usually college students here for Tech. There was some medical and oil money in town, but it wasn't a huge draw. Which left the guys we'd always known. It was probably why Piper kept going back to Bradley.

With Madison temporarily occupied, we turned our attention to The Tacos game. I went to their games every weekend that I was in town and much preferred the outdoor games to the indoor ones, where we all froze our asses off. There were more players for the outdoor games, too. They'd tried to get me to play, but I had no skill with a ball, just with my dutiful camera that I pulled out of my bag.

Blaire was their star forward. Julian and Isaac played mid along with Hollin's sister, Nora. She was a tiny pixie of a thing, but she was *fast*. Her boyfriend, August, played forward with Blaire, but he was mostly there for assists since girl goals counted for two. Hollin and Annie played defense with Annie's med school friend Cézanne. And Cézanne's boyfriend, Gerome, was their goalie. Nora and August were the latest recruits for outdoor, and as far as I could tell, they were a big help on the larger field.

I put the camera to my eye and trailed the players, focusing in on my friends and snapping shots. Blaire scoring a goal, Annie passing to Hollin, Isaac getting fancy and pulling a nutmeg—passing the ball between the opponent's legs—and then finally landing on Julian.

My heart stuttered at the sight of him. His shorts were shorter than average, revealing inches of his tan, muscular legs. His hair flopped side to side as he ran with the ball. His footwork was impeccable. There was something about him. About having been under him.

I'd never thought that I'd be the kind of girl who would get drunk and have a one-night stand with a guy. That was Annie. Not me. But I couldn't regret that it had happened, no matter what my mom had said. And part of me hoped it wasn't actually a one-time thing.

The game ended with The Tacos winning at an embarrassing twelve to two. The teams shook hands, and then the guys stripped out of their shirts, mopping up their sweat with them. My eyes hungrily roved over Julian's body.

"You're drooling," Piper joked, nudging me.

I coughed and looked away. "I can appreciate a nice body."

"So can I. Hollin looks hot as fuck."

My eyes rounded.

Sutton looked at Madison and was glad to see that she was still napping.

"Sorry," Piper said, "but look at his body. He's built like a tank."

We both looked. He certainly was, and he was tatted to high heaven. I'd never really noticed how many tattoos covered Hollin Abbey's body. I'd been too busy admiring Julian.

"But I thought you and Hollin were like oil and water," I said.

"We are," she agreed. "Being around him makes me want to stab something."

"But he's still hot," I volunteered.

Piper's gaze was stuck on Hollin with a glare in her brown eyes. "He's still hot."

I laughed and came to my feet, shaking the grass off of my legs. "I'm going to go congratulate them."

"Say hi to Julian for me," Piper said with a smirk.

"Hollin for you."

"You wouldn't." Her cool demeanor slipped.

One day, I wanted to know what had started this huge feud between Piper and Hollin. But for now, it was fun to tease her.

"Love you," I said, waving at her.

I veered for Annie and Blaire, but as I got there, Julian stepped into my path. He was still shirtless, sweat dripping down his chest. His shirt was slung over his shoulder, and his bag was at his feet. He'd changed out of his cleats and into his indoor Pumas.

"Hey, I heard that you're moving in with Blaire and Piper," he said with a panty-melting smile.

"Good news travels fast."

"I knew you were worried about what you were going to do now that Annie is moving in with Jordan."

I was. I'd told him that last weekend on the drive to Austin.

"Looks like I was worried for nothing. It all worked out in the end."

"Definitely. Need help with the move? I'm sure I can borrow Jordan's truck and coax Hollin into helping."

I flushed at the thought of him and Hollin, shirtless, moving my belongings. I cleared the thought from my head. "That would be amazing actually."

"Not a problem." He grinned. "Might even be able to convince my cousins to help. You know, Jensen also has a giant pickup. Good ole boys."

"Wright Construction would now be Wright Movers."

"Hey, we do business where it's necessary."

"I'd really appreciate it."

"I just have one question," he said, crossing his arms over his amazing pectorals.

"Uh-huh." I tried not to be distracted by the gesture. The last time I'd seen him in this little clothing, we'd been having sex.

"What are you going to do about the cats?"

"Oh fuck," I whispered.

What *was* I going to do about Avocado and Bacon?

17

JENNIFER

I never thought I'd be a cat person.

I was definitely *not* a cat person.

And yet the thought of leaving the two babies behind that I'd named and been feeding for over a year was heart-wrenching. It was impossible. There was no way I was doing that. Just because they weren't indoor cats didn't mean they weren't *my* cats.

So, I'd stayed up all week after I finished packing and editing to research what the hell I was supposed to do in this situation. Cats didn't like to be introduced to new environments, even when they belonged to you. Stray cats that I'd been feeding and such were definitely not going to be happy.

Poor Avocado and Bacon. This was not going to be fun.

At least Julian had agreed to come and help.

Which was why he was now setting up a spring-loaded cat trap. I hadn't wanted to use them at all. They seemed so scary, and I didn't want to traumatize the cats that I'd *just* decided belonged to me.

So, I'd gone out and gotten pet carriers along with fancy,

smelly cat food to entice them to get inside. I'd rather get them into a regular carrier than trap them and have them freak out. With my luck, they'd never forgive me.

"Okay, all set," Julian said, coming back to my side.

I bit my lip and nodded. "Me too. Hopefully, they don't hate me."

"You're going to keep feeding them. They'll get over it."

"You've never had cats, have you?"

He laughed. "Admittedly, no. You?"

"My mom had one, growing up. Total bitch. Thing hated everyone. Even my mom."

"Eesh. Well, I think Avocado and Bacon will be different."

I crossed both of my fingers and held them up. "Let's hope."

With the enticing smell of fish too potent to resist, Avocado stuck her head out of the bushes. Her orange tail swished back and forth as she scented the air. She walked over to me first, running her body against my legs.

"Wish I could pick her up here," I said. "Would be a lot easier."

"I could," he said, bending at the waist and touching Cado's back.

"Wait..."

But it was too late.

Avocado was the more finicky of the two cats. Bacon didn't mind being pet by strangers as long as they were near me, but Cado was still getting used to it all. Especially men. She really hated men. I never wanted to know the trauma she had gone through at the hands of some asshole. I never wanted to see her full rage either.

She whipped around so fast that Julian never saw it coming. Avocado raked her claws along his arm.

Julian yelped and reared back. "Fuck!"

Three long red welts rose on his forearm. He clapped his hand over the scratch, and blood welled underneath.

"Oh God, are you okay?"

"Fine," he said through gritted teeth.

"She really got you. God, let me get you something for that."

"No, look," he said, pointing toward the crate I'd set up.

Avocado had her tail in the air as she followed the bread crumb trail toward the opening.

"She's so close," I whispered. "But someone is going to need to close the door."

"Hence the spring-loaded box," he reminded me.

"I know, but it's so mean."

He shrugged. "So are the cats."

I laughed. "You poor, poor thing."

He flashed me a grin. "I didn't know she was going to scratch the shit out of me."

"She's a stray!" I gestured to the cat who was almost inside the carrier. "What did you expect?"

"Well, you pet her just fine."

"I'm her owner," I argued.

He put a finger to his mouth. "She's going inside."

"Did you guys figure it out?" Annie asked, bounding out of the house.

"Shh!" we both said at the same time.

Annie's eyes widened, and she put her hands up. "Sorry," she whispered. Her eyes landed on Julian. "Oh my God, are you bleeding?"

"Shh," he hissed.

Then Avocado walked into the pet carrier.

"Jennifer, go!" he said, all but shoving me off the front steps.

This was the one problem with the pet carrier over the other ones that Julian had wanted to use: someone had to close it. Which meant, I should have been waiting nearby. So that as soon as the cat walked inside, I could snap the door closed. Instead, I was running like an idiot the short distance across the lawn to try to get there before Cado ate all the fish and realized she wasn't in her natural environment.

I dashed across the yard and smashed the grate closed as Avocado tried to stick her little head out. She snarled and yowled, slashing at the metal. I secured the grate in place and carefully pulled my hand back. If I hadn't been quick, she could have gotten me.

When I turned back around, Julian and Annie were both laughing hysterically.

"What?" I demanded.

"You should have seen yourself," Annie said. "You, like, slid into home to get that gate closed."

"She would have gotten out!"

Julian tried to cover his laugh, but it didn't work. "It was amazing. And good news: Bacon made it into the other one."

I found the spring-loaded carrier had worked, and Bacon was inside, contentedly eating the fish. Cado never would have gone willingly. Should have seen that one coming.

I flopped back onto the grass. "Thank God that's over."

Julian dropped down next to me. "Remind me to never offer to help you catch cats again."

The adrenaline of the moment was gone. "I can't believe it worked!"

Tears rolled down my cheeks as laughter hit me right in the pit of my stomach. Julian was right there with me.

Until Annie came to stand over us and shook her head.

"I want whatever y'all had."

I wiped the tears from my eyes. "I trapped cats that a few days ago, I wouldn't have even claimed as mine. And I'm taking them with me across town."

"I knew you loved those cats."

"At least one of us did."

Avocado was still crowing. I was going to have to figure out what to do with her. She was probably going to be pretty pissy for a while once we got her out at the other house. But at least Bacon seemed fine, and Cado loved Bacon.

A giant pickup pulled up into the driveway, and Hollin hopped down out of the driver's seat. "What the fuck are you doing in the grass, Wright?"

Julian propped himself up onto his elbows. "Getting a tan."

Hollin snorted. "Are we moving today or what?"

"Thanks for offering to help," I said, brushing grass off of me as I stood. "Piper, Blaire, and Chester should be here soon."

"Chester?" Julian asked.

"Yeah, I'm as surprised as you are."

"Your brother is going to help?" Annie asked.

"He moved in earlier this week, and I helped him. He offered to return the favor." I shrugged.

"What's up with your brother?" Hollin asked. "Why is everyone shocked?"

"He's just..."

"Self-centered," Annie finished.

"Narcissistic," Julian added.

"An asshole."

I swatted at them both. "He's trying, y'all."

"Hell, I'm a self-centered, narcissistic asshole," Hollin said, crossing his beefy arms over his muscled chest.

Julian and Annie shared a look and then shrugged and nodded.

"Pretty much," Annie said.

"What do you say about me when I'm not here?" Hollin joked.

"Nothing we wouldn't say to your face, cuz." Julian got to his feet and clapped Hollin on the arm.

"Dude, are you bleeding?"

And the rest of us broke down into laughter again.

* * *

By the time Piper, Blaire, and Chester showed up to help me move, Julian and Hollin had already gotten the furniture onto Hollin's truck. Annie had brought Jordan's truck over for the day, and Piper had shown up in Bradley's pickup. I was thankful because that meant I didn't have to rent anything.

Jordan had paid for someone to come and box up all of Annie's stuff and move it into his mansion on the south side of town. But I didn't have a billionaire boyfriend, so I was on my own.

"What do you have in here?" Chester grunted as he lifted a box from my bedroom.

"Books."

"More like bricks."

"A book a day keeps reality away."

He snorted and hauled it out of my bedroom. I grabbed one from the bathroom and followed him outside.

The whole thing was going remarkably fast with six people moving instead of just me, like the last time I'd moved. My arms had hurt for a week straight afterward.

"Last box," Hollin said, hauling the box onto his

shoulder as if it weighed nothing. He was easily the biggest guy I'd ever seen in my life.

"Phew! That was quick," I gasped.

My eyes traveled across my friends. Hollin deposited the box in the back of his truck. He dapped knuckles with Julian. Piper was chugging from a bottle of water. She passed it to Blaire, who took a sip. Chester leaned against the truck next to Blaire. Annie grinned at me, as if understanding the look of awe on my face.

They'd all come here for me. Just for me. I'd always been a loner. More interested in my camera and books. Too much social anxiety to reach out and find my own niche. Sometimes, I was pulled into a vortex by proximity, but I hadn't found anything until Sutton and Annie. And now, I had my own little world. Even with my brother unexpectedly in it.

"Thanks for helping me today," I said, unable to keep from choking on the words.

They smiled and said it was no problem. Only Annie knew what it all meant to me. Or so I thought.

Then everyone piled into the trucks to head over to Piper's house.

Julian grabbed my arm. "What got you all emotional?"

I laughed softly and glanced away. "Just nice to have a friend group like this."

"You have Annie and Sutton."

"Yeah. It's just...new."

"The whole family thing is new for me, too. I only ever had Jordan."

I nodded. "I get that. I'm the opposite. I'm more surprised that Chester even bothered today."

"He seems totally chill now. Not at all how he was at graduation."

"I know. I don't understand his moods."

"Well, I'm just glad."

"Same."

"You can ride with me," he offered.

Annie had driven Jordan's truck over, and we'd gotten the cats into the backseat of Julian's Audi SUV. I still had to come back to clean and do a final walk-through. I could get Bertha then.

"Sounds good."

I slipped into the passenger seat, and we followed behind the three trucks. It took us half the time to unload the boxes than it had to stack them into the trucks. I ordered pizza and gave Annie money to grab some beer for the entire party. It was my thanks. While she was gone, I dealt with the cats.

I put food and water out before letting Avocado and Bacon out in the backyard. Bacon went straight for the food, seemingly unperturbed by the new location. But Cado disappeared as soon as I opened the crate. I bit my lip as I watched her dart off. She'd come back when she was hungry, but I still worried. She had left a few times in the past and always came back. I'd never considered her *mine* before. So, now, I had anxiety about my cats. Great.

The pizza came in record time, and we all crowded around the living room, eating off of paper plates and drinking the cheap beer. I was seated next to Julian, who kept accidentally touching my hip with his.

I glanced over at Julian, and he smiled, taking another sip of his beer. Maybe not accidental?

"So, yeah, it's been a *week*," Piper said with a sigh.

"What did I miss?" I asked. Julian had completely broken my concentration.

"Peter and Jeremy broke up," Piper said.

I frowned. "Oh no! What happened?"

Peter was Piper's twin brother. He and Jeremy had been dating for a long time. I didn't even know how long. They'd been inseparable.

She shook her head. "I have no idea. He won't talk about it."

"But he's distraught," Blaire added. "He was here last night and cried the whole time. We don't know what to do for him anymore."

"Fuck," Hollin said eloquently.

"I know that feeling," Chester agreed. "I just went through a rough breakup. Two years, and then it ended."

"Maybe you could talk to him!" Blaire suggested. "I mean...if you're okay to talk about it."

"Yeah. It was the right time for my relationship, but it still hurts."

I stared at my brother. He hadn't spoken one word about Margaret since the breakup. He hadn't even told me himself. I was surprised he was volunteering this information.

"Well, why don't we go out tonight?" Julian suggested. "We could get Peter out of the house. Might help."

"Yes!" Annie cried. "I'll drag Jordan out, too."

"I'm down," Blaire agreed.

"I'll try anything," Piper said.

Chester and Hollin both agreed to go out. All eyes swung to me. I was still distracted by Julian. Now, his hip wasn't the only thing pressed against mine. Half of his leg was also touching. And fire was running down my entire body at the contact.

I looked up at him again. The last time we'd gone out together, I'd gotten wasted, and we'd hooked up. Was going out a good idea if we were keeping this...casual?

He smirked. "Well, Dreamsicle?"

I flushed at the nickname. "I'm in."

18

JULIAN

*D*esire had simmered in Jennifer's eyes when I suggested we all go out tonight. It had been pointed. The whole damn day had been. Helping her with the cats and moving and feeling her pressed against me while eating. It was all because I couldn't keep myself from being close to her, and I wanted her to feel that, too. I wasn't sure that she had until I called her Dreamsicle. Then our entire night at graduation flashed in her eyes. And she'd agreed to come out.

Saying we were casual and just having fun was one thing when I was trying to get her not to destroy what we'd built that weekend. But when she was around me, it didn't feel casual at all. I didn't want to scare her. Sometimes, she was as skittish as Avocado.

"How did I get forced into this?" Jordan asked as he came to stand before me and Hollin inside Walkers, a coffee shop by day and pub by night.

I leaned back against the bar and took a sip of my Jack and Coke. "You're whipped."

Jordan snorted. "Sure, that's it. Not that I want to please the love of my life."

"I'm sure you could do that a thousand other ways," Hollin said with a suggestive shift of his belt.

"Subtle," Jordan drawled.

"Why are you here without Annie anyway?" I asked.

"She wanted to help Jennifer get ready." His eyes slid to mine. As if he already knew exactly what had transpired between me and Jen. "Were you going to tell me that you were dating our photographer?" He flagged down the bartender and ordered a drink.

Hollin crowed, "Good luck nailing him down on that."

"We're not dating."

"Fake dating," Jordan said. "Whatever."

"Don't big-brother me," I said, bumping his shoulder. "You friends-with-benefitted Annie."

"She was *leaving*," he growled. "It was different."

I didn't want to get a lecture from my overprotective, older brother. I loved Jor. I just didn't need it today.

"And what about Hollin? He managed to carry on an entire conversation with Piper without either of them biting each other's heads off."

Hollin scoffed, "We didn't make it that long. You missed the cutdown every time I passed her while we were moving."

"What is *with* you two?" Jordan asked.

Hollin shrugged. "Fuck if I know. She hates everything that comes out of my mouth."

"And you love baiting her," I added.

"How could you *not* enjoy baiting someone who reacts like she does?" he asked with a chuckle.

"So, are you going to three-date-rule her?"

Hollin punched me in the shoulder. "That is not what I said."

"What the fuck is a three-date rule?" Jordan asked, grabbing his drink off the bar.

"It's nothing. Julian is making shit up," Hollin grumbled at me. "And I'm not dating Piper. I'm not dating anyone. I'm too busy, living up the bachelor life."

"Enjoy it while it lasts," Jordan said with a laugh.

Said the happiest motherfucker I knew. He and Annie had had a bumpy start, but it was worth it to see that stupid smile on his face when he thought about her. At least that made one of us.

All thoughts fled my mind as the girls arrived en masse. Though I only had eyes for one. Jennifer's new roommates had clearly decided to give her a full makeover. Not surprising, considering the resources at Blaire's disposal and Piper's flair for the dramatic. Jennifer wore an orange dress that I'd never seen before. It didn't seem like something out of her closet, not with that neckline. I tried not to let my eyes wander to the way her breasts popped out of the top. Or imagine having my hands on them graduation weekend.

I straightened when our eyes met. Those hazel eyes were lined and bright as could be, almost gold in the lighting. She gave me a tentative smile, and something tightened in my chest. Just that one smile, and I was done for.

Annie tugged Jen forward, Blaire and Piper following in their wake. Piper practically dragged Peter along after them. Annie launched herself into Jordan's arms. His eyes lit up, even as he laughed at her enthusiasm.

"Hey," Jen said when she reached me.

"You look great."

She flushed. "Thanks. Blaire got ahold of me."

"And didn't I do a fabulous job?" Blaire asked with a flip of her black hair.

I rarely saw her out of a baseball cap and workout clothes. It was a jolt to see her hair down and her in a dress. That just wasn't *Blaire*.

"You did," I assured her.

"Could have gone for better company though," Piper said. She brushed past Hollin and leaned forward across the bar.

Hollin smirked. "You know you want a piece of this, sweetheart."

Piper's glare was fierce. "Hasn't *everyone* already had a piece?"

"And that precludes you how?"

"I'm not a fan of sloppy seconds."

"Guys," Blaire groaned. "One night. Just please, *one night.*"

Piper rolled her eyes and ordered drinks. Peter looked between them and sighed, taking a barstool without a word. He looked like he'd been run over.

"Hey, man," I said, holding my hand out.

Peter shook it and nodded. He accepted a drink from Piper and began to down it as if it were water. I winced.

Jennifer frowned and then drew my attention back to her. "How's your arm?"

I showed her the three perfect cuts down my forearm. "Pretty mangled."

"Do they hurt?" She trailed her fingers down the raised lines.

My pulse jumped at the contact. Fuck. I was going to need to figure this out.

"Oh shit, sorry," she said, mistaking my jump as pain.

"They're not too bad."

"I'm still sorry about Avocado. She really hates men."

"That makes two of us," Piper muttered.

"No Bradley? What a shame," Hollin said with another pointed grin.

I nudged Hollin. Why did he have to antagonize her?

He just shrugged, mouthing, *What?*

Peter yawned, finished his drink, and dropped it down on the bar. "He's working."

Piper flicked her eyes to Hollin and dismissed him as easily.

Chester appeared then at the front door. He'd gotten dressed up, and his smile was wide. "Sorry I'm late. Not used to the city anymore and got lost."

Blaire laughed. "In Lubbock?"

"Where you grew up?" Annie added. She sounded like she wanted to call him on his bullshit but didn't.

"Yep," he said amicably. He held his hand out to Peter. "You must be Peter. I'm Chester. I heard we should get fucked up together."

Peter startled at Chester's overbearing personality. Then he actually smiled and shook his hand. Not the sad thing he'd done to me. "Uh...yeah, sure."

While the girls crowded together to get drinks, Hollin clapped Jordan on the back and grabbed Peter and Chester, leading them over to the darts at the back of the bar. Annie shared a look with Jen, and then when they got their drinks, the girls headed over to the darts as well, leaving us alone.

"Drink?" I asked her.

She shook her head. "I apparently make bad decisions when I'm drunk."

I arched an eyebrow. "*Bad* decisions?"

"Well, I make decisions I wouldn't normally make when sober."

I frowned. I didn't like that.

She saw my assessment and flushed, looking down. "I'd rather make them while sober, I mean."

Okay. That I could work with.

We probably shouldn't have tumbled into bed for the first time while we were drunk, but neither of us had thought it was going to happen until it did. I'd *wanted* it to happen, but I hadn't been certain she did. Then the sex had been phenomenal and...

I needed to think about other things.

Casual. Fun. Keep it light.

"Well, I have another proposition, if you're interested."

Her gaze met mine. "Another one?"

"I know we're supposed to go to the gala. Our second fake date," I told her. "But my dad is actually coming into town next weekend, and I could use a date for that."

She furrowed her brows. "You're going out to dinner with your dad? I thought things were..."

"Bad," I finished for her. "They are. I don't want to go any more than you wanted to attend graduation."

"Then why..."

"Jordan said that if I went and it went poorly—which it will—he'd leave me be. I wouldn't get cajoled or ambushed into any more of this bullshit."

"That's an incentive," she said softly. "And you want *me* to go?"

"Jordan and Annie are going. I'd really rather not go alone." I shot her my most charming smile and pinned her with the puppy-dog eyes. She looked hesitant, so I threw in, "I'll accept it as an apology for Cado."

Jennifer burst into laughter. "You would."

I reached out and touched her elbow. She didn't stiffen, but her eyes widened slightly as I drew her a step closer.

"So, what do you say?"

"I, uh...have a portrait session with Campbell on Saturday, but I'm free after that. So, I can return the favor. Fake date in front of your dad."

A fake date. Well, I'd walked right into that one. She didn't need to know it was a real one...not until she was ready to hear it.

"Perfect." I released her elbow. "Now, are you sure about that drink? I bet I can get them to make you a Dreamsicle."

She blushed again. "I can't believe you called me that in front of everyone."

"What?" My voice dipped low. "No one knows that's what you taste like."

"That's what *you* taste like," she said muttered. Then her smile dropped. "Oh no..."

I whipped around, following her gaze to the front door... where Ashleigh Sinclair stood in all of her glory.

19

JENNIFER

Oh no was an understatement.

A more accurate response to seeing Julian's ex-girlfriend right now was...*fuck*.

Because the last person I wanted to deal with, let alone compare myself to, was the bombshell that walked into the room. Piper, Blaire, and Annie had done their best with me. I was wearing this kick-ass dress that Blaire had sworn a designer had sent her from Montreal but that—quote—"looked better with my complexion." Piper had a knack with a curling wand, and after Blaire had finished with my face, I had been half-certain that it wasn't actually *me* looking back at me in the mirror. I was a *lip gloss and mascara* kind of girl. This was daunting.

Now, I was a little glad for the proverbial body armor when Ashleigh walked in. She wore a cherry-red bustier dress that matched her fire-engine lipstick. Her hair was down in these supermodel waves that was her signature. She had a sun-kissed tan that made me look pasty as hell since the sun hated me. Not to mention, the four-inch heels and the glowing self-confidence that I also lacked. It was a tough act to follow.

"Just ignore her," Julian said. He turned back around, as if her presence meant nothing to him.

Sometimes, I wished that Lubbock wasn't so small. What were the chances she'd show up at the same bar as us?

"Do you think that will work?" I asked.

She hadn't exactly walked away the *last* time we ran into her at Wright Vineyard.

"No," he said under his breath.

"I'll take that drink now."

He laughed softly and flagged down the bartender.

Before the drink ever made it into my hand, Ashleigh and her band of minions traipsed right over to us. I was desperately wishing for Annie at my side right now. Annie wouldn't take Ashleigh's shit. If only I had that level of confidence. But seeing Ashleigh tower over me only made me want to run. Instead, I shot straight past fight or flight to freeze, where I stood in front of her like an idiot, deer in headlights.

"What a coincidence," Ashleigh crooned like it wasn't a coincidence at all.

Julian took a breath next to me and then faced her. All the humor and charm he'd been laying on all evening evaporated. "Ashleigh."

"Hey, baby."

His jaw tightened. "What are you doing here?"

"Just out with the girls." She twirled her fingers at the three girls behind her—a brunette, redhead, and black-haired girl. As if she'd picked them all out so that her blonde would stand out.

"Well, have fun," he said dismissively.

He turned toward me, sliding his arm across the bar. He wasn't quite touching me, but the insinuation was clear. We were together. Even though we weren't.

Which meant that the full fury on her face was only there for me. Julian wasn't looking at her. He must have felt her anger like a brand. How could he not? But it wasn't about him anymore; it was about me.

"And who's this?" she purred.

Oh, she hated his dismissal. *Hated* it.

Julian didn't respond, but I was locked in on Ashleigh. Her eyes searing through me.

"Is this the girl you were in pictures with in Austin?" she asked.

Julian sighed. "How would you even know that? I blocked you on social."

"Tiff showed me." She gestured to the redheaded minion.

"Of course she did," he muttered. "Yes, this is Jennifer. You met her at the opening last month."

Ashleigh's eyes rounded when she put two and two together. She'd cared so little about me at the vineyard that she'd actually forgotten my existence. She was now realizing that her calculations had been misguided, and all the gears in her brain were clicking over to incorporate me into her hatred.

"Are you two...together?" she asked. Her voice careful, neutral.

"Yes," Julian said.

A lie to maintain the fake relationship, but I still warmed at the word out of his mouth.

"Does she speak?" Her words were clipped.

"Ashleigh, leave it."

Ashleigh held her hand up. "Just trying to figure out who you'd leave me for."

He blew out a sharp breath. "I left you because you tried to ruin my business, Ashleigh. Jennifer has nothing to do with this."

"Obviously." Her eyes swept to me. "I see what's happening here."

"We're done," Julian said. "Come on, Jen."

But I was rooted in place. Still frozen by her words, by the fear that whatever was going to come out of her mouth was the truth.

"You're slumming it."

"Ashleigh, enough," he snarled.

The words hit like a punch to the gut. The same words my mom had insinuated. She hadn't said that right out, but they'd held the same force. I wasn't good enough for Julian Wright.

"She doesn't even *speak*," Ashleigh said with a smirk. "We both know that *this* isn't what you want or deserve. A small, meek thing to agree with you. Where's the Julian that I know, baby? She'll never push you. She'll never give you what you really need."

"I said, enough," he spat.

Julian jumped between us, breaking whatever spell she'd cast over me. I blinked awake, as if from a deep slumber, sucking in a breath. My heart pounded in my chest, loud as firecrackers in my ears.

I didn't hear what Julian said to her. I didn't want to know what words he'd use to defend me. Ashleigh had been right. As much as it hurt to admit it, I could see the truth when it hit me in the face.

What the hell was I doing?

And then I couldn't stand there any longer.

I bolted for the back door. The back of Walkers was an open courtyard patio with benches and a small garden. I needed the fresh air. I needed something to clear all of this from my head. From the anxiety taking me over.

A part of me knew that was what this was. It was the anxiety that I usually managed so well. But I couldn't calm down. I needed to pop a half-Xanax or something, but anyone could see me. Anyone would *know*. And I couldn't let them know about the anxiety. Not when I'd been called crazy before because of it. Not with the stigma that clung to me like a second skin. Annie knowing was one thing, but Julian? Ashleigh? I shuddered.

No. I needed to get under control. I slammed my eyes shut once I was in the courtyard and regulated my breathing. Tried to do the meditations that I'd been practicing. Eventually, my heart rate came down, and the unceasing panic released me from its clutches.

By then, a hand gently touched my arm.

"Jen?" Julian said tentatively.

"Hey," I whispered.

"I am...so sorry."

"For what?" I pushed my hair back off of my face and met his concerned, wide-eyed gaze. "You didn't do anything."

"It's still my fault. And for everything."

I huffed, "It's fine."

"Stop saying that," he said with more force than I'd expected from him.

"Sorry."

He sighed. "You don't have to apologize, and you don't have to say you're fine. Why the hell would you be fine after

Ashleigh said all those horrible things to you?" He slid his hand down my arm. "All *untrue* things, mind you."

I snorted. "Sure."

"I'm serious."

"I just...froze," I muttered. My bottom lip trembled. "Why can't I tell her off and come out ahead? Why do I have to be...me?"

"Who you are is perfect, Jen," he said as if he believed those words. "And you shouldn't have even had to react. I should have gotten us away from Ashleigh before she could even start. No one deserves to be spit on."

"Thanks."

"I mean it."

"I know. It's sweet," I confessed.

He smiled down at me at that. That charming Wright smile that made my knees weak. As if I would give anything to this man. Anything at all.

His hand came up then and brushed a stray strand of hair out of my face, tucking it behind my ear. He lingered there, softly trailing his fingers down my neck. As if he were waiting for the moment when I'd jerk away. As if he could think that was what I wanted.

His eyes flicked down to my lips and back up to my hazel eyes. A question written in them. We hovered in that space, holding a breath as I drowned in his attention. I wanted to lean forward and kiss him, to take what I wanted. But I could no more do that than stand up for myself like I should have just now. Not unless I was drunk, apparently.

My heart was racing again—not from fear, but from anticipation. I wanted this. Even though everything that my mom and Ashleigh had said was true. I was sure it was all going to go down in flames. That he was going to wake up and see who I really was, that I wasn't good enough for him. Still, I wanted those lips on mine. I wanted to feel him again.

"Jen," he whispered. He leaned forward so that our breaths mingled. Then he repeated the words that had started this whole thing. And he said them with a smirk on his perfect face. "Forgive me."

His lips descended on mine. The barest brush against mine. A wave of heat flashed through my body. Everything crawled to a halt.

Then a head popped out of the back door. "Hey, y'all okay?"

We broke apart so quickly that I stumbled back against the brick wall. My face turned bright red.

Annie chuckled, holding her hands up. "Uh, sorry. Didn't mean to interrupt."

"You're fine," Julian said calmly with a laugh.

"I saw Ashleigh and wasn't sure what happened. But I'll just..."

Ashleigh. Right. Her name dropped water over my head. I'd been freaking the fuck out. How had Julian managed to soothe that sinking ship so fast?

Annie winked at me and then scurried back inside. Julian and I both started laughing as soon as she was gone.

"Caught red-handed," he said, running a hand back through his hair.

"I guess so."

"Are you ready to go back in?"

"Is Ashleigh still in there?"

He shook his head. "I made her and her minions leave."

"Minions," I said with a laugh.

"No, seriously. They follow her around like dogs."

"That's kind of sad."

He nodded. "Yeah. Well, anyway, they left. That's what I really came out to tell you."

"Oh. Well, good."

I waited for him to offer to pick up where we'd left off, but he didn't. He'd been caught up in it, too. That we'd gotten lost in the moment. Now, the moment was gone.

But it was the first time I thought that maybe it wasn't gone forever.

20

JENNIFER

*T*he doorbell rang, and I jumped, racing across my new place to answer the door. "I got it!"

Piper laughed from the couch. "All yours. Julian, I presume?"

"Uh...no."

I was jittery with nerves and excitement as I pulled the door open to find Campbell Abbey standing there. He was in ripped black jeans, a plain white tee, and a studded leather jacket. He was effortlessly gorgeous and a legitimate rockstar. My body threatened to go into shock.

"Hey," I squeaked.

He grinned that panty-melting smile. "Hey yourself."

It wasn't just that Campbell was gorgeous—because he was. It was that he was the *lead singer* of Cosmere. And I was a huge fan of their music. Their last album had gotten me through a real low point. I'd sat in my room and played it on repeat as I stared up at the ceiling, radiating with Campbell's voice in my head. After all that, he was just *here.*

"Should I wait here?" he asked with a laugh.

"Oh, no." I opened the door wider.

He must have been used to the starstruck reactions by now because he hadn't even blinked at my slack jaw or how I went nonverbal.

I shook my head to clear the fangirl. "Come on in."

Campbell entered our three-bedroom. "Nice place."

"Thanks. It's Piper's."

She waved from the couch. "Abbey."

He nodded at her. "Yo."

Then the back bedroom door opened, and Blaire stepped out of her room in a matching salmon workout set and a baseball cap slung low over her brow. She froze when she saw Campbell standing in the living room. Her entire body tensed up like she'd been electrocuted. She didn't move. I wasn't sure if she was breathing.

I didn't even know if Blaire liked Cosmere. She hadn't stuck around for the last concert in town, and she'd left early when Campbell played his solo show earlier this year. It surprised me that someone as social famous as Blaire would be a fangirl like me.

"Blaire," Campbell said her name soft, like a prayer.

My gaze shifted to him, and then I realized I had been wrong.

I had been *so* wrong.

This wasn't the same thing that I felt at all. There was something here. Blaire and Campbell had graduated the same year, but Blaire was adamant that, like me, she'd been a nobody. And even in high school, before Campbell's fame, he'd been somebody.

Blaire's jaw flexed, and then she turned on her heel and walked right back into her room. The door slammed shut.

Campbell winced at the noise. "I...didn't realize you lived with Blaire."

I wanted to ask. I had so many questions. But how the

hell would I even begin?

"Uh, yeah...just moved in last weekend."

"Are we...shooting here?" He suddenly sounded almost...anxious.

"No, I rented us studio space downtown by LHUCA."

"Great. Let's do that." He waved at Piper again, whose brow was furrowed in confusion. "Nice seeing you again."

"Let me grab my equipment," I said as he veered toward the door.

I hauled my shooting backpack over my shoulder and headed out after him. He was in a shiny rental BMW and offered to drive us across town, which I accepted. I didn't know if I could live down having Campbell Abbey in Bertha.

I was already done up more than I normally would be for a shoot. Julian was picking me up at the studio later to take me out to dinner with his dad. I had a change of clothes in my bag so that I could be comfortable in the studio, but my face was made up how Blaire had tried to teach me. She'd eventually given up and fixed my winged eyeliner and the edges of my lipstick before dotting me with blush, which I'd always insisted I didn't need, considering how often I flushed being around Julian. But this was the *Blaire Blush* we were talking about.

We parked outside of the studio, and I unlocked the space. It was a perfect day for shooting with lots of natural light. Though I'd come over yesterday to set up the lighting as well.

"So, where do you want me?" Campbell asked.

"Just sit on that chair over there while I set up. I assume you've had some experience with this."

He laughed. "*Some* feels like an understatement. I feel like I've spent the last two years in front of a camera. You'd never guess I was camera shy."

I looked up at him. "No, I'd never guess that."

Here I was, talking to Campbell like it was totally normal. Like he wasn't a famous rockstar. Like he was just a person. A person with anxieties, just like me. Unfathomable.

"Yeah, I had to get over it real fast once things started taking off. But fuck, did I need a Xanax in the beginning."

I rocked back on my heels. "Seriously?"

"Yeah, mental health is really important."

Part of me wanted so desperately to confide in him about my own problems. He was so *open* about his mental health issues. I couldn't believe he'd tell me this stuff.

"Well, thanks for sitting for me anyway."

"Hey, I asked you. Your work is great. I'd love to use it as a new headshot. My other ones are so...stuffy. Or staged."

I nodded, taking a few pictures of him to test the equipment. "That makes sense. The record label wanted that?"

"Yeah. Standard bullshit."

I snapped another picture and looked down at it. "You deal with a lot of bullshit?"

Now that I was behind the camera, everything else disappeared. I was no longer Jennifer Gibson—nerdy, anxious girl. I was just me, and I was in control. I felt *good* here. And I wanted to keep him talking. People worked the best when they were comfortable. Didn't I of all people know that?

"You have no idea," he said with a laugh.

Snap.

"Can you lean forward? Elbow on your knee."

He did what I'd said.

"Yes, good. Tell me about the bullshit."

He sighed and looked off in the distance. *Snap.* "Music is just one big bureaucracy. I love creating and making music and touring. But everything in between reminds me it's still a job."

His eyes looked straight on at me. *Snap.* "Know what I'm talking about?"

"I do. Plus, you're in the public eye. What's that like?"

He frowned. *Snap.* "Depends on the day. Right now, things are low-key. I kind of like being back in Lubbock for that. It's not like LA."

I laughed. "Understatement."

"What about you?"

"What about me?" I asked, pulling the camera from my eye.

He shifted in his seat. "How do you feel about your job?"

"I love it. Though not everyone thinks it's a real job."

He pulled his arms up over his head and leaned backward.

I jerked my camera back up. *Snap.*

"Why wouldn't it be a real job?"

I shrugged. "I'm not a doctor or lawyer or pharmacist. You know...real jobs."

He snorted. "Hell, I don't have a real job either. Seems to work out for me."

It did.

"And what about you and Julian?"

I stared at him through the viewfinder. The thoughtful expression on his face. "What about me and Julian?"

"You're into him, right? That's why he wanted to fake date you—so he could real date you."

I nearly dropped the camera. "What?"

His face froze, as if he'd realized he'd said too much. "He...told you that, right?"

"He didn't. No," I whispered. "He made all the fake dating up?"

"Uh, I didn't mean to say any of that. I thought you already knew that he liked you."

"Julian...likes me?"

Campbell stood from his seat and adjusted his jacket. My brain was frozen though. The only thing functioning was the camera. I managed to keep shooting through all of it. But I couldn't seem to process what he'd said. It didn't fit in with anything that had happened. Well, other than the sex, and we'd both just gotten drunk.

"I mean, isn't it obvious?" Campbell said.

No, it wasn't obvious.

Then I replayed every interaction over the last several weeks. Every touch and smile and flirtation.

I lowered the camera this time. My mouth falling open as I rewrote all the things we'd done together, layered with this information. I felt kind of stupid. But I'd convinced myself that there was no way Julian really wanted to date me. Why would he when he could have better? But if he'd liked me all along, then every time we had been together was him getting closer and closer to me.

"He likes me," I whispered.

"Yeah, dude, but don't tell him I told you. I don't think I was supposed to do that."

I laughed softly. A smile hit my features. Julian liked me.

And we were going out tonight. I rewound to the time when he'd asked me. *I* was the one who had suggested it be a fake date. He hadn't said anything like that. Jesus Christ, had I been self-sabotaging myself this whole time? Could I actually have Julian Wright?

"Forget I said anything. What should I do next?" Campbell asked with a sly smile. Like maybe he'd said it all on purpose. Little matchmaker.

21

JULIAN

*M*illi hummed almost noiselessly as I put her into park outside of the studio. I was a few minutes early to pick up Jennifer, but I wasn't looking forward to this dinner and couldn't help myself. I dicked around on my phone for a few minutes and then gave in to the inclination, getting out of the car and knocking on the door.

After a minute, I heard Jen yell, "Come in."

I stepped inside and froze. Campbell was lying on the ground, shirtless, while Jennifer hovered over top of him. She had one knee against his hip, practically straddling him, and grounded herself with her elbow on the other knee. She was taking picture after picture, shifting here and there to get different angles. I had no idea what was going on, but I immediately didn't like it.

"Hey," I said, clearing my throat loudly.

Jennifer pulled back from her camera. Her smile was magnetic when she swiveled to face me. "Hey. Is it time already?"

"A few minutes early actually."

She turned back to Campbell and laughed at something he'd muttered.

"We got all we need." She hoisted herself to her feet and offered him a hand, which he declined.

He reached for his discarded white T-shirt and slung it back on. "Hey, man."

He must have seen the scowl on my face because he chuckled softly. I suppressed the urge to be pissed at him. This was Jen's job. Nothing about what had happened was inappropriate...probably. And anyway, I was clearly being a jealous dick.

"How'd it go?" I asked.

"Really great," Campbell said. "Jen's a natural. I saw a few back-of-the-camera pics, and they're crazy good."

Jennifer flushed at the praise. "Thanks." She smiled back at me. That same smile she'd given me when I first walked in. Something different than I'd seen from her before. I didn't know what it meant. "I'm going to get changed, and then I'll be ready."

"Cool."

She disappeared into the bathroom, leaving me alone with Campbell. We shook hands, and then he reached for his perpetual leather jacket.

"Where are you two headed?" Campbell asked.

"Dinner."

"A date?" He arched an eyebrow.

"With my dad."

"Oh," he said with a laugh. "Why? Uncle Owen's a dickbag."

"He is. Hopefully, this is the last time I have to see him."

Campbell nodded. "Good luck with that. Parents are complicated."

That was an understatement. I'd learned that the

Abbeys' mom had died when Campbell was a senior in high school. Hit-and-run. Their dad had stepped up and tried to make up for it, but it would never be the same. Hollin didn't really talk about it. I assumed Campbell was the same way.

"Okay. All set," Jennifer said, stepping out of the bathroom.

Campbell and I both froze at the sight of her in a little black dress. But she only had eyes for me. The smile on her face was perfection. No averted gaze. No pulling back. Just me and Jen. Seriously...what had changed?

* * *

We arrived at Funky Door right on time. Punctual as ever, Jordan and Annie were already waiting at the entrance. Our father was nowhere in sight. *Shocker.*

Jennifer ran right over to Annie and enveloped her in a hug. Jordan shook my hand, his gaze drifting to Jen in surprise even though I'd told him I was bringing her. I wasn't the one who ambushed people.

"So, where is he?" I asked.

"He's on his way," Jordan said.

"And no one is surprised he's late."

"It's five minutes, Julian," Jordan said with a sigh. "His flight was delayed, or he would have been here hours ago. Can you cut him a break?"

I bit my cheek to keep from retorting. Because, no, I wasn't giving my dad *another* undeserved break. He'd done enough. I didn't believe that he was here just to see us. Not after everything.

"That's probably him," Annie said, pointing to a car that pulled into the parking lot.

Jordan put his arm around her and kissed her hair. A thank-you for backing him up.

Jennifer gently touched my arm. Just enough for me to break my attention and turn to her.

She smiled. "It's going to be okay."

I nodded and released the tension in my shoulders. She was right. I'd get through this dinner, and then I could go back to my life. It was one night.

Jennifer released me by the time my dad strode over to us. I hadn't really paid attention the last time I'd seen him at the vineyard, but he looked different. The last few years had aged him. His typical dark hair had silver at the temples. There were lines on his forehead that I'd never seen before. As if us leaving had really changed him. Or maybe it was the loss of the company that he'd tried to *steal*.

He'd clearly been talking to Jordan more frequently because they shook warmly when he appeared. Then he turned to me, that same Wright smile on his face. "Son."

"Dad." I shook his hand, withdrawing quickly.

He seemed like that was good enough for him now. He and Jordan exchanged a look. I didn't want to know what they'd talked about when it came to me.

Annie kept up a steady stream of conversation. She was good at that. Directing us so that we all went inside. Funky Door had a stunning interior with a large circular set of stairs at the heart of the building, which housed hundreds of bottles of wine. It was the best place in town for wine selection. And I was working on getting our bottles on that shelf.

The hostess sat us at a round table near the center of the room. Jordan ordered a bottle of red for the table before we were even seated. I gestured for Jennifer to sit next to Annie. That I'd bite the bullet and sit next to my dad, but she smiled that same smile at me and moved one over. I looked at her in confusion, but she was already sitting next to my dad. A buffer. Just like I'd been for her parents.

I didn't argue with her and took the seat between the girls, drawing the menu up in front of my face. Everything at Funky Door was delicious, but I barely saw the options. I was thankful when the wine Jordan had ordered was placed in front of me. I needed it to get through tonight.

"I really appreciate you boys agreeing to have dinner with me tonight," my dad said with a smile. "And your lovely girlfriends, of course."

Annie raised her glass to him. "We're all here for the free wine."

My dad guffawed. He looked at Jordan and winked. "I like this one."

Jordan's gaze landed on Annie. "Me too."

"So, your flight was delayed?" I asked.

Jennifer touched my knee under the table. Not a warning, but reassurance. She was here. We could get through this.

"Yes," my dad said, ignoring the bite in my voice. "Getting out of Sea-Tac is always an adventure."

My brow furrowed. "You flew in from Seattle?"

"Yes. I thought Jordan told you." He looked at Jordan, but Jordan's face was neutral. He clearly hadn't revealed anything to me. Dad would have to win this one on his own. Good. "I relocated a couple years ago."

"Why?" I hated to give him the satisfaction, but there it was. I hadn't even known the most basic thing about my dad.

"Well," he said, clearing his throat, "everyone and everything I loved was gone. Vancouver held old memories. I didn't want to stay there anymore and deal with it being empty."

"That sounds difficult," Jennifer said thoughtfully.

My dad smiled at her. "It was, but nothing compared to these boys moving across the country to be with their mom. That took real guts."

I almost rolled my eyes. Had he always been so transparent?

"What are you doing there?" I asked. "I can't see you moving somewhere and doing nothing."

"Julian, this isn't an interrogation," Jordan said. "It's dinner."

Our dad held his hand up though. "It's fine, Jordan. Julian is entitled to his questions. I haven't always been the best father. He has every right to be skeptical."

I almost snorted. The best father? What an under-statement.

I'd worshipped the ground he'd walked on. Then he'd shattered every ounce of that love into pieces. He was a liar. He'd always been a liar. And I didn't know how to let him build back the trust.

"I'm working in corporate America now. I'm sitting on three boards right now. Before, I was consulting with a local commercial construction company. Nothing like running my own branch of a Fortune 500 company, but I ruined that for myself." He shrugged. He almost sounded...remorseful. Like he regretted the actions that had led to him being removed from his position at Wright Construction. He'd lost everything when he bet on that.

"We all make mistakes," Jennifer said softly. "It's learning from them that's important."

Our eyes met, and she smiled again. That new smile. The one I'd never seen before. Not just when she was looking at me, but when she was looking at anyone. I'd thought I had all of her smiles memorized. This one made me want to try hard, do better, be more. And maybe that meant giving my dad an *actual* chance here.

"You're right," I agreed. I looked back at my dad, prepared to start this conversation over. "Tell me about Seattle."

22

JULIAN

*B*y the time dessert was served—a decadent chocolate fondue—everyone had loosened up. I was still hesitant about my dad. I kept waiting for the other shoe to drop. For him to step out of line and prove my point. But so far, it seemed like he'd actually flown in from Seattle to Lubbock, Texas to see us.

"So, you're saying that Julian is running the entire vineyard on his own?" my dad asked.

Jordan grinned. "Yes. I've basically handed it all off to him. I did a lot of the setup, but he's in charge."

"Hollin does a lot of the work, too," I said quickly.

"Sure," Jordan said. "Day-to-day stuff. He manages the team. That's what he's good at. He already knows the winery. He's worked in every position before this, so he's perfect for it. But you're the businessman."

"That's incredible, Julian," my dad said.

"Thanks," I said with a smile.

"Seriously, it's such a relief," Jordan said with a laugh. "Working two jobs..."

"Was terrible," Annie finished for him, dipping her piece of cake into the chocolate. "He was running himself ragged."

"Yeah," Jordan said with a shrug. "What else is new?"

"Doesn't sound healthy," Jennifer said.

Annie gestured to Jen with her cake. "Exactly!"

"Well, I'm proud that Julian can handle it all on his own. Doesn't even need me anymore," he said with a laugh.

"That's not true," I told him.

He waved me off. "I like it that way. That the winery is doing well enough on its own without me. Especially with all the distribution options."

"Distribution?" my dad asked with actual interest.

"Yeah. I'm working with the wine distribution company out of Dallas to get Wright wine in stores all over the state."

"That would be huge," my dad said with a proud light in his eyes.

"It would, but we're still negotiating. We're meeting face-to-face on Friday. It's probably the most important meeting since we bought the place."

Jen squeezed my knee again. As if she could hear the hint of fear in my voice. This distribution would make or break where Wright Vineyard was going. I couldn't fuck it up. Not when Jordan had handed everything over to me.

"I know you'll handle it the *Wright* way," my dad said with a laugh.

I sat back, waiting for him to fuck up, to offer to step in and help, to take over the vineyard in some small way. It'd be supremely stupid, but I'd never put it past him. Except it didn't happen. He genuinely seemed interested.

"And you, Jen?" my dad said, turning to her. "You're a photographer for the vineyard?"

"Yes, I'm full-time on events," she said with a smile.

"Don't be modest," Annie jumped in. "She's a genius."

Jennifer blushed and stared down at her chocolate-covered marshmallow.

"She really is," I agreed. "I'm using her work as my headshot, and she did a photoshoot with Campbell Abbey."

My dad blinked. "Your cousin?" he asked. When I nodded, he added just to clarify, "The rockstar?"

Jennifer laughed. "Yes. You all make it sound so glamorous."

"Don't undersell yourself," Annie said. "You're still doing weddings with all of the rest of this going on."

"Elopements," she corrected. Power returned to her voice as she talked about her passion. She lit up when discussing her art. I didn't know how anyone hadn't seen it before. "I actually have an elopement next weekend. I'm flying into Cabo on Saturday for a sunset wedding."

"Cabo." My dad whistled. "Are all your elopements that fancy?"

She laughed. "Sometimes. I've gone all over for them. I actually accepted the position at Wright because I was gone most weekends."

"Every weekend!" Annie corrected.

"It became taxing to always be gone."

My dad nodded. "A girl with a vision and brains. No wonder my son is smitten."

She flushed crimson at the compliment. It was my turn to squeeze her knee under the table. Her eyes met mine. I wondered if she could see that my dad had spoken the truth. I was smitten with her.

My dad flagged the waiter down then. "I'll take the check. Just one." Jordan protested, but my dad waved him off. "I can take care of my boys."

Once he paid, we all headed out of the restaurant. The girls huddled together, gossiping. Well, it appeared that

Annie was mostly rambling to Jen, and Jen was laughing at her. My dad shook Jordan's hand and then mine.

"I'm glad we could do this. I look forward to hearing how that distribution meeting goes," he told me.

I nodded, actually believing him. "Definitely. When is your flight back?"

"Sunday. I'm going to check in on your mom and see some old friends. I'd be happy to do this again if you're free."

Jordan arched an eyebrow and looked at me.

"You're seeing Mom?" I asked, my voice cracking.

"Of course. Just because we're not married anymore doesn't mean that I no longer care for her. I hate to see that she's suffering."

I stood there in shock. Of any of the conversations I'd envisioned having with my dad, this was not one of them. I knew that Mom still loved him, but I hadn't thought they were in contact. That she'd let the man who had hurt her back into her life...even as a friend. That he'd ever actually cared.

"I didn't know that," I said softly.

And just like that, something shifted. Like I could see my dad for who he really was. A broken man trying to make amends with the only family he had left.

"Well, I'd be up for a round of golf," Jordan said with a shrug. "Maybe tomorrow afternoon?"

"Absolutely. I'd love to get out on Landon's course. Heard it's a doozy."

Jordan laughed. "You have no idea." He arched an eyebrow at me. "Julian?"

Despite everything, I nodded. "Actually, yeah. Golf sounds nice."

My dad hid the look of surprise as quickly as it had come and then nodded. "I look forward to it."

It was weird to realize that I was, too.

* * *

"Well, what do you think?" Jennifer asked as we drove away in Milli.

"I don't know. It didn't go at all how I'd thought."

"Because he's as charming as every other Wright?"

I flashed her a grin. "You find me charming?"

"Oh, don't start," she said with a laugh.

"I kept waiting for him to make a mistake, to show his hand. But he never did. I don't know if that's because he doesn't have an ulterior motive or he's just gotten sneakier."

"I'd like to think the former."

"Me too," I said with a sigh. "I thought that in the past though, and then he fucked us all over."

"He's going to see your mom though. That doesn't seem like a man with an ulterior motive. It sounds like someone doing penance."

I sighed heavily. "I know. That's what gets me, too. He's going to see Mom. She never told me either. I'm going to have to talk to her about it."

"Or you could let it go. Have a little faith."

"That hasn't worked so well for me."

She nodded. "I get it. I have a difficult relationship with my parents, as you saw. But I can't imagine cutting them out of my life forever either."

"It wasn't an easy decision."

"And so, it won't be an easy one to turn around, but if tonight is any indication, he's trying to right the wrongs from his past."

"Well, I was glad to have you there."

"I didn't do much," she said.

I arched an eyebrow. "You grounded me. It was more than you know."

We pulled into her neighborhood, and I headed toward her house. She looked focused and thoughtful. I didn't dislike whatever was going on with her. But I wouldn't mind knowing why.

I hadn't planned to ask. "What are you thinking about?"

She hesitated a second before saying, "I'm not ready to go home."

My head jerked over to her. "Really?"

"Yeah. Maybe...we could go somewhere else to talk?"

I blinked. I couldn't believe she was suggesting this.

"Sure," I said without pause and turned the car around, heading toward my place. I didn't want to make it a big deal. *Casual* and *fun* were the words I'd used. I certainly wasn't going to say no.

We drove the rest of the way to my house in companionable silence while the radio played Top 40. We pulled up to the driveway of the house I'd had built my first year in town. I'd lived with my mom in her remodeled '70s-era home while she was sick and had this place built in the meantime.

I parked in the garage, and Jen followed me with wide eyes into the house. The space was a sprawling open-floor plan with vaulted ceilings and an industrial farmhouse kitchen. My mom had taught me to cook, and I enjoyed it. So, I'd put all my time and love into the kitchen design.

Jennifer's mouth hung open slightly. "Wow. This is your place?"

"Yeah. Benefits of being a Wright."

"Tell me about it. Geez," she muttered as she wandered the room. "It's beautiful."

"Thanks. Probably too big for me," I admitted.

"Probably. And you're here all alone?"

I nodded. "Yep. Just me. Hollin joked about moving in, but he likes living closer to the vineyard."

"Annie always gushed about Jordan's place. You know, she used to study there before moving in. I didn't really get it." She stopped with her hands on her hips, looking out the back windows to the pool beyond. "Now, I get it."

My eyes remained on her the entire time. I'd always thought that Jennifer was shy and maybe a little insecure but generally just really shy. My teasing had always made her blush. She didn't speak up much when in big crowds. I'd thought that was who she was. But now, I could see there was something else simmering there. Something I only saw when she had a camera in front of her face.

"You seem different," I finally said.

She turned to face me. "Do I?"

"Yeah. I can't put my finger on it."

She arched an eyebrow and crossed the room to stand before me. "I don't think I'm any different."

Then she smiled that smile. The new one. It took all my self-control not to kiss her right then.

"It's that smile. Like you have a secret."

Her eyes dipped down, and then she looked up at me from under her lashes. "Maybe I do."

"Oh?"

"I heard a rumor...that you like me." She swallowed. "That you liked me when you proposed our fake dating."

My eyebrows rose to the ceiling. "Is that so?"

She nodded. "Is the rumor true?"

"Yes," I said. "Yes, I like you. Of course I do."

Her body trembled slightly at my words. "And you wanted to fake date me...to real date me?"

"I...yes. I wanted to ask you out, but I didn't think you'd say yes."

She blinked. "Why would you think that?"

I laughed and ran a hand back through my hair. "Honestly, I didn't think you were interested in me."

Her eyes widened. "Are you serious?"

"Yeah, I mean, you hide your feelings so well. I couldn't ever tell if you were humoring me or what."

Her mouth fell open. "Oh God, you're serious. I thought everyone in Lubbock knew how I felt about you, Julian."

It was my turn to blink in confusion. "And how do you feel about me?"

She stepped forward, clearing the last bit of distance. "I've liked you since you fell into the pool on top of me at Landon's party almost four years ago."

My pulse jumped. I wanted her so fucking bad. I'd been trying to deny myself, to tell my body that whatever we were doing was fine. But I could no longer deny that I wanted her. I wanted all of her. And to hear that she'd wanted me all along...

It was so much wasted time. I refused to waste another minute.

My lips sealed to hers in a searing kiss. I should have told her how I felt from the start. I should have dived right in. Instead, I'd feared that she'd turn me down, and after my last relationship, I hadn't wanted to put myself out there.

Now, she was here, in my arms, and I didn't intend to ever let her go again.

"Oh God," she groaned against my lips as my hands trailed under the hem of her black dress.

I ran them over her thighs, reaching the lace of her panties. I didn't wait another second before ripping them down her legs. She squeaked in surprise. Her eyes were wide, but I was already standing against her, taking her lips for mine again before hoisting her up into my arms. She wrapped her legs around my waist, and I thumped her body back against the wall. She gasped again. I swallowed her cries, grinding my body against hers.

Fuck. I'd wanted this for too long. One night of her body would never be enough.

Her hands went for my belt, removing the clothes that lay between us, and pulled my dick free. She pumped it up and down in her hand, the friction hot between us.

"Need you," I grunted.

"Yes," she breathed.

Whatever I'd been feeling these past few weeks, she clearly had, too. Because as soon as I lined my dick up with her opening, I realized how wet she was and how much she fucking wanted this, too.

"Oh fuck." I pressed the tip deeper.

Her head fell back against the wall. Her hands dug into my back. "Please."

And then I thrust forward up into her, claiming her perfect body for my own. She moaned deep in the back of her throat. It went straight to my balls. I'd do anything to duplicate that sound.

So, I drove up into her again. And again. And again.

She was so fucking tight and wet. The sounds coming out of her mouth drove me to take her harder and faster. To feel every inch of her wet pussy wrapped around my cock.

I was hardly seeing clearly by the time I felt her tighten so hard around me that it was almost painful.

"Julian," she cried over and over again as she came. My name the prayer on her tongue.

"Come for me," I groaned, trying to hold off to let her come down, to maybe even get a second.

Her eyes opened then, golden irises only for me. She

was panting. Her breasts heaving out of the top of her dress. "Come with me."

It was a command out of her perfectly prim mouth that I'd never be capable of denying. I came with a fury, buried deep inside of her. I saw stars at the force of my climax, and it was a full minute before I pulled back to look at her again. She had a sated, happy smile on those lips. Another smile that I claimed as my own.

I gently dropped her back down to her feet, and after we cleaned up, we collapsed back onto the couch, nestled together under a blanket.

"I guess I should have told you how I felt earlier," I said into her hair.

She chuckled softly. "I don't know that I would have believed you."

"Why not?" I trailed figure eights into her hip.

"I don't know. It would have felt too surreal that you'd pick me."

I kissed her shoulder. "I like everything about you, Jen. The way you light up when holding a camera, your most adorable reaction to your cats, that smile when you think no one is watching, the blush on your cheeks when I tease you…" My voice dropped seductively. "That little noise you make as you come."

She flushed all over and buried her head in my chest. "Okay, I believe you."

"Mmm. I can keep reminding you of all the reasons I like you." My hands trailed lower.

"You have my attention." She peaked back up at me. "So, I have a question."

"Yes?" I asked, pressing a kiss to her neck and then her collarbone and then her breast.

"Um...I'm going to Cabo next week for an elopement. Do you...have any interest in going?"

I looked up at her from where I'd been laying kisses down her stomach. "To Mexico with you? Of fucking course, I want to go, Jen."

She grinned. "Oh well, um...good."

"My turn for a question," I said right before I reached the apex of her thighs.

"Mmhmm?" she murmured.

"Does this mean you'll go to the gala with me as my girlfriend?"

Her eyes flew open. "Not your fake girlfriend?"

I shook my head. "Real girlfriend."

"I...could probably manage that," she whispered. "And that makes you my *real* boyfriend?"

I covered her body with my own. "It sure as fuck does."

PART IV

A REAL RELATIONSHIP

23

JENNIFER

a text from Annie buzzed form my phone as I pulled up to Jordan's place three days later and parked next to Sutton's new Range Rover.

Come around back. The gate's unlocked. xoxo

I plopped a wide-brimmed hat on my head and grabbed my beach bag out of the backseat. Annie's residency started at Texas Tech in full force tomorrow. Her life was going to be a madhouse, but she had today off, and Sutton and I were taking the rare opportunity to get away for the afternoon. Jason was at summer camp all week, and they'd hired a full-time nanny for Madison. Sutton had jumped at the first opportunity to have a break.

I hefted my bag and walked around to the back. Jordan's house was on the Wright golf course that Landon had commissioned to PGA standards. But the best part of the house was the immaculate pool and spa.

Annie and Sutton had already stripped down to swimsuits. A pitcher of margaritas sat between their tables.

"Hey, y'all," I said.

"You made it!" Sutton said with a wide smile.

"I did."

I held my breath for a second and then stepped into the backyard, carrying the other thing that I'd had in my backseat with me. I walked right up to Annie and dropped a twelve-pack of Coke onto the empty table next to her.

She looked at it, then at me, and then back down. Then she shrieked at the top of her lungs, jumping out of the seat and throwing her arms around me.

"Oh my God!" she squealed. "Yesss! I knew it!"

Sutton's hands covered her ears. "Dear Lord, what is happening? I escaped the screeches of my toddler for a reason."

Annie bounced up and down. "I won a bet!"

Sutton arched an eyebrow. "What bet?"

I laughed at Annie's reaction. "Annie bet me a Coke that Julian was into me."

"And I said I was sure that he was that I'd bet her a whole twelve-pack." Annie hefted the package up to the sky. "And look what I have, bitches!"

Sutton shook her head, laughter bubbling out of her. "So, you're dating my cousin, too?"

I dropped my bag and sank into the seat next to her. "I am. As utterly surreal as that is to say out loud."

"Why?" Sutton asked. "Anyone would be lucky to have you, Jen."

I shrugged. "Well, I sort of thought that I'd make it longer than a few weeks with my *no guys for ninety days* policy."

Annie snorted. "No one thought that would last."

"Least of all if Julian showed interest," Sutton added.

"I never thought he'd show interest. You know, he was interested in someone like *Ashleigh Sinclair*."

Annie wrinkled her nose. "A two-faced, manipulative asshole who tried to ruin his life? Yes, why can't we all be as perfect as Ashleigh?"

"That's not what she means," Sutton said knowingly.

"No. I know that she tried to ruin his life and sabotage the winery. I certainly don't forgive her for it. But I'm also not a Sinclair." I gestured to Sutton. "And I'm not a Wright."

"Neither am I," Annie said quickly.

"But you're Annie," Sutton said.

"Right! You're Annie," I gushed. "You're Miss Self-Confidence. Your whole motto is, *I am woman. Hear me roar.*" Annie laughed but didn't deny it. "I'm more the David Rose type and you know, not connecting."

Sutton chuckled.

"Who cares if you're not like me? There's no reason that Julian shouldn't see how wonderful you are in your own way."

"But how could he? When I didn't see it in myself first?"

They were both silent at that question. It was true. I wasn't just shy; I actively self-sabotaged my own life. I got in my own way. I'd rather stay inside than go out. I was more comfortable in front of a camera. I preferred the company of cats that didn't even belong to me to ninety-five percent of people. And I wanted to be as bold as Annie, but that wasn't who I was.

"Part of me still feels like the nobody I've always been. And the last couple years with you two and all your amazing friends and family was just a dream." I shrugged. "I liked Julian, but I didn't feel good enough for him."

"Well, good news," Sutton said, taking my hand, "it's not a dream."

I laughed. "I'm so glad."

"And," Annie said pointedly, hands on her hips, "if anything, you're way too good for Julian."

"Yeah, right," I sputtered.

"He had his chance with you, and he ended up dating someone like Ashleigh Sinclair," she said furiously. "If he didn't see what he was missing, that was his own damn fault for having bad taste. Not your fault. Not because you're nobody. You're our friend, and *we* most certainly don't have bad taste."

"We do not," Sutton agreed easily.

I nearly choked on their words. Tears came to my eyes, unbidden, and I laughed as I swiped at them. "I love y'all."

"We love you, too," Annie said, pulling us in for a group hug.

"Now," Sutton said as we broke apart, "have a margarita and tell us everything."

I took the margarita glass out of her hand and tugged off my cover-up. "Well, first things first. I'm going with Julian to a gala on Friday, and I need a kick-ass dress."

"I thought you already had a dress," Annie said.

"I did. But...that was when I was going with him as a fake date. If I'm going as his girlfriend, then I want to show up Ashleigh."

Annie cackled. "There's my Jennifer."

Sutton smiled mischievously. "I think we can handle that."

* * *

When Friday rolled around, I still wasn't completely satisfied with my dress situation. I'd tried on the most incredible dress with Annie. Until I saw the price tag and nearly threw up. I couldn't get the gorgeous thing off of me fast enough. I'd worried that I might even sweat on the thing. No event was worth the price tag on that thing...even if it was as close to perfect as I could get. So, Blaire had called in some favors, and we had *a* dress, but it still didn't feel like *the* dress.

Piper spent a solid hour blowing out and styling my hair. By the time she was done, I hardly recognized myself.

"You should do this for a living," I told her.

She beamed. "You know, I actually considered cosmetology out of high school because I found it fun. But then I remembered it would be a job and not just something I enjoyed, so I went into business to help run Sinclair Cellars with my dad."

"Practical," I said softly. "My parents wanted me to do something practical like that. I even got the correct degree and then never went to pharmacy school. I pursued photography instead."

"Seems to have worked out," Piper said.

I smiled. "I guess it has."

Blaire hip-checked Piper. "Allow me access to the canvas."

Piper rolled her eyes and got out of Blaire's way for her to work her makeup magic. I was halfway through makeup when the doorbell rang.

"That can't be Julian yet, can it?" Blaire asked.

"No way," I said, checking the time.

"I'll get it," Piper said. She hopped up from her seat and headed out to the living room.

Blaire went back to work on my face but stopped a few minutes later when Piper still hadn't returned.

"Pipes?" Blaire called.

"Uh," she said from the living room, "y'all might want to see this."

Blaire and I exchanged a look of confusion. Then I hopped off the seat, and we headed into the living room.

What we found made my brow furrow in confusion. Piper had draped a black garment bag over the dining table, and in her hand was a shoebox.

"What's this?" I asked.

"They were just delivered." Her eyes were glued to the shoebox. "They're for you."

"Me?" I asked in confusion.

She passed me the shoebox, and I realized why she was in awe. Written in beautiful white letters across the top was one word—*Louboutin*.

"Oh my God," I whispered. "Who...who are they from?"

Piper handed me the card that had come with it. I flipped it open.

For my real girlfriend.
—Julian

Tears sprang to my eyes as emotion washed over me.

"No crying!" Blaire said, waving her hands at my eyes. "You'll ruin all my work."

I laughed at her ridiculousness. "He sent me a dress and shoes."

"Two-thousand-dollar shoes," Piper said pragmatically. "He must really like you."

"Well, open it already! We're dying here," Blaire said.

I popped the box on the shoes and felt as if I were having a full-blown Cinderella moment. The shoes appeared to be glass-encrusted with rhinestones that made them glitter in the light. And of course, the signature red-lacquered bottom brought the entire shoe together.

Blaire and Piper oohed and aahed at them.

"Damn," Blaire said. "Boy did good!"

Piper nodded. "Damn good."

I set the shoebox down, unable to process my feelings about the most beautiful shoes I'd ever seen in my life. Then I pulled the zipper on the garment bag. And inside was the designer dress that I'd tried on with Annie in Malouf's. It was *the* dress. And here it was, in all of its glory.

My throat closed up. "I can't believe he did this."

"I can," Piper said. "He adores you. Don't you see the way he looks at you?"

"Seconded," Blaire said.

"It's too much."

Blaire waved her hand. "Who cares? He wouldn't have done it if he couldn't afford it. He wants to see you in it."

"So, let's get you ready. I cannot *wait* to see his face," Piper said.

Blaire nodded. "He's going to die. Seriously."

Piper picked up the dress, and I hugged the shoebox to my chest like a prized treasure. I didn't know how the hell this was happening to me. But when a guy bought you shoes, he was a keeper.

24

JULIAN

"*L*ooking sharp, Wright," Blaire said when she answered the door.

"Thanks." I smirked at her and stepped inside in my custom-tailored tux. Fashion had always been a part of who I was, but this tuxedo blew most of my closet out of the water.

"I'll get Jennifer." She hustled around the corner and out of sight.

I stuffed my hands into my pockets and waited. I'd never thought that I'd be looking forward to this gala after what happened with Ashleigh. It had seemed like such a chore. Part of the business side that I would have to adjust to. If I wanted that distribution contract, then I'd have to play nice.

But now, I was going with Jennifer. My real date. Nothing fake about what was happening anymore. Which meant I'd gotten to be a bit extravagant. I'd worried the dress and shoes might be too much, but Annie had assured me it wasn't. I was going to do it regardless.

Then Jennifer walked out into the living room in the light-blue dress that I'd purchased for her. She was more than stunning; she was effervescent. The bodice clung to her like a second skin with an iridescent plunge neckline. The dress gathered at the waist and shimmered in a metallic silver to the ground. She lifted the hem slightly, and I caught a flash of the Louboutins, which were probably a bit over the top but I couldn't help myself.

Seeing her beam at me, looking like a goddess, made it all worth it.

"Wow," I breathed.

"Wow yourself," she said. "Look at that suit."

I ran my hands down the front of the tux and smirked. "You like?"

She arched an eyebrow. "Don't be coy. We both know you're vain."

I burst into laughter. I couldn't help it. "We do know that, yes. Now, get your ass over here."

She giggled and stepped up to me. I threaded a careful hand up into her perfectly curled hair and brought her lips up to mine. She tasted divine. Suddenly, I was having second thoughts about leaving.

"Maybe we could stay in," she said breathlessly.

I chuckled. "And miss the chance to show you off? Never."

"You two are kind of disgusting," Blaire said. I'd forgotten that she was still standing there. "Go to your gala and take lots of pictures. I want to live vicariously through you."

Jennifer laughed and held up her purse, which was much larger than the dainty little clutches most women brought to such events. "I know it isn't gala appropriate, but I brought a camera. No lens, so it fits."

"I'd expect nothing less." I held out my arm. "Shall we?"

She looped her arm through mine. "Definitely."

We got into Milli and drove downtown to Buddy Holly Hall, a new performing arts center that Wright Construction had worked on. Jordan had been the mastermind behind the construction job. I'd been on dozens of tours of the place while it was in development, but I hadn't seen it all done up.

The charity gala was in conjunction with Lubbock Volunteer, an organization dedicated to helping those in need right here at home. Ashleigh was on their board—she sat on a dozen all around town so that she would be invited to every major event—and had helped plan this one. When she'd had it in the works, she had considered how best to help the vineyard—or so she'd said. She'd invited everyone who was everyone in wine to be involved. It still amazed me that she had been doing this kind of thing while at the same time trying to tank the winery. It was like she had a contingency to every plan. I didn't know who she'd really been the whole time we were together.

I valeted the car and then helped Jennifer up the walkway and into the venue. Her breath caught at the interior of the gorgeous, new concert hall. I'd been to locations like this all over the Pacific Northwest, and even I had to admit that this was picturesque. Nothing else like it. The Wrights were bringing class to this burgeoning town.

"It's amazing," Jennifer whispered.

"Jordan really outdid himself."

"He really did. Wow. I don't even know what to say. I can't believe this exists in Lubbock."

We passed through to the main part of the hall. Three tiers of balconies overlooked the main stage. The curtains were closed, and a projector displayed the Lubbock Volunteer logo against the heavy drapery. Circular tables filled the perimeter, and an open space for dancing was already occupied by many of the guests. Twinkling lights made it look as if we were open to the cosmos.

Everything was glamorous and sophisticated. It almost felt like being back home in Vancouver. Jordan was the one who had been the face of the company with Dad and attended most of these sorts of events. I'd never had any real interest even though I'd worked there for several years right out of college. It hadn't been my passion. Not like the vineyard was. I'd gone to events with Ashleigh, but it had always been a chore. I'd forgotten how much fun it could be.

"Well, well, well, look who showed," Ashleigh said, materializing before us.

I wanted to clench my jaw, but I didn't. I stayed as calm as I could. This was why we were here to begin with. This was why I'd asked Jen for a fake date. I had to deal with Ashleigh today, and that meant putting on a happy face and not pissing her off. I didn't put it past her to sabotage this distribution agreement if she was pissy.

"Evening, Ashleigh," I said politely.

Her eyes crawled my body. She loved when I dressed up.

She stepped forward, tugging slightly on the collar of my jacket. "This is new."

Jennifer stiffened next to me.

I took a step out of her reach. "It is."

"Well, what do you think?" she asked, unperturbed. She twirled in a circle. She'd gone all out in a pink silk number that flowed over her like water. It was a great dress. Too bad it was on a such a terrible person.

"I think it's lovely," Jennifer said before I could respond.

I glanced at her, but she was just smiling.

Ashleigh's eyes narrowed. She'd been trying to pretend that Jen wasn't there. "Don't you clean up nicely?"

K.A. LINDE

Jen's smile widened. "I could say the same thing about you."

Ashleigh arched an eyebrow. "Look who got some teeth."

I was just as surprised that Jennifer was even talking to Ashleigh. Last time we'd seen her, she'd frozen up and then run out of the room. Was the difference that we were dating?

Jennifer shrugged. "No reason to be catty. We're all here to have a good time."

Ashleigh looked like she wanted to say something else with venom, but I stepped between them.

"We're going to go get drinks. Have a nice evening."

"I planned to introduce you around," she said. "But if you'd rather play with your pet, then..."

"Ashleigh, can we just have a civilized night?"

She clenched her tiny little clutch until her knuckles went white. "Can we speak in private?"

I sighed. I really didn't want to do this, but I worried if I didn't have this out with her now, then the entire night, she'd hound us with her bullshit.

My eyes swept to Jennifer. "Will you be all right?"

"I'll get in line for drinks," she said easily.

She had her hands clasped together, but I could still see them shaking a little. She didn't like this, and I hated putting her in an uncomfortable position.

"It'll just be a minute," I promised.

Then she did something that I never anticipated. She reached up onto her tiptoes and brought her lips to mine. It wasn't a long kiss. Nothing more than that one perfect press together. But she looked up at me with such intimacy that my entire being shifted toward her.

"One minute," she said with a smile.

I heard Ashleigh huff in front of us. I nodded at Jen, and then she headed for the line for the bar.

"That was unnecessary," Ashleigh spat. She whirled on her heel and stalked out of the room.

A smile tugged at my lips as I followed her. Damn bold of Jennifer to kiss me right in front of Ashleigh. I liked this side of her.

We ended up in a mostly empty area of the lobby. Nearly everyone had moved into the concert hall already. The last thing I wanted was to be alone with Ashleigh. As furious with her as I was, we'd still dated for two years. And she knew how to get to me.

I crossed my arms over my chest and waited. "What's this about?"

"So," she said, still facing away, "you managed to dress her up. Cute."

I sighed. "I'm not here to discuss my girlfriend with you."

Her shoulders stiffened. She asked very softly, "Girlfriend?"

"Yes. My girlfriend."

She whirled around. There was shock and revulsion on her face. "You're with *her*? After me, you picked someone like *her*?"

"You should get to your point. I'm not going to stick around to hear you degrade Jennifer or my choice to date her."

"You're actually serious."

"I am. I'm here like we planned, but I'm with Jennifer now. That's how it is."

Something shattered as those words hit her. Her mask faltered and fell.

Everyone had always asked me what I saw in Ashleigh.

Why I'd want to date someone who was sometimes cruel and uncaring and vicious. I'd always said that she was different with me. Up until the moment that she'd ruined it all, I'd argued that. And here, I saw the vulnerable girl who'd been hurt by a mother who didn't see her worth and a father who didn't care enough. It was the girl I'd fallen for all along. Too bad it took me dating someone else for her to find that girl again.

"Sure. Okay," she said. "That's how it is now."

She wrapped her arms around her stomach and didn't meet my eyes.

"Ash…"

"I'll grab you when the distributors arrive." She wiped a tear from the corner of her eye. "Forget about everything else."

I sighed. A part of me wanted to comfort her. I didn't like to see her hurting, but at the same time, she reaped what she sowed. I hadn't ended it because I didn't care about her, but because she'd lied and manipulated and hurt everything we had. She'd thrown us away long before I'd put an end to it.

"Have a good party," she said and then hurried away from me.

I ran a hand back through my hair and muttered, "Fuck," into the empty room.

I couldn't do anything about Ashleigh. That ship had sailed. I needed to get back to Jen and try to salvage the night.

25

JENNIFER

The drink line was outrageous.

I just wanted something to calm my nerves. I'd actually spoken to Ashleigh. That felt like a drastic improvement. Even if Julian immediately disappeared with her. He'd said a minute. It'd been more than a minute.

Of course, it was an exaggeration, but still...the nerves. I'd taken my medicine before coming here. I wasn't great in social situations to begin with. Big events like this definitely heightened my own issues. Not to mention, Ashleigh Sinclair.

Finally, I reached the front of the line. I ordered us drinks, and as I was about to pay for them, hands snaked around my waist. I jumped in surprise and whirled around to find Julian smiling down at me.

"I got it," he said, dropping cash on the bar. "Keep the change."

"You didn't have to do that."

"Yes, I did."

We picked up our drinks and found a table to regroup.

"Sorry about leaving you behind," he said as soon as we took our seats.

"It's okay."

"It's really not."

"Why did she even want to talk to you?" I couldn't help but ask.

He sighed and shrugged. "I don't know. Just to get the upper hand. It doesn't really matter because it didn't work."

I nodded. Though I was uncertain. I thought getting him alone had been a smart move on her part if her goal was to try to get between us. I had to remember that Julian was here with me. He wanted to be with me. He'd gotten me this outrageous dress and shoes. There was no reason to panic. Other than...life.

Julian downed the rest of his drink in one long gulp. Then, he rose to his feet and held his hand out to me. "Come on. Let's dance."

"Dance?" I squeaked, taking another fortifying sip of my vodka cranberry.

"Yeah. I don't think the distributors are here yet. We have some time to enjoy ourselves before I need to talk business."

I made a face. "I didn't know that included dancing."

"I'm an excellent partner, I assure you."

I laughed, finishing the drink with a wince. "I'm not worried about *you*."

But I let him pull me to my feet and out onto the dance floor. I wasn't a dancer. Never had been. Even my senior prom, which I'd only gone to because my boyfriend had wanted to go, I hadn't danced. And said boyfriend spent most of the time getting drunk with his friends in the corner by passing around a flask. They even spiked the punch. Though no one else had known who'd done it.

This was nothing like that. Julian was an excellent

dancer, and he led the entire time, so I never felt like I was out of place. Even though I had no idea what I was doing, it was fun to be swung around by him. To have him pull me close and sway side to side. To see that look in his eyes.

I even forgot for a time that other people were watching us. Which was a goddamn miracle because I was surely going to agonize about people seeing every misstep for the rest of my life. Thanks, anxiety!

"I need a break," I gasped with a laugh. "These shoes are killing me."

"But they look incredible on you."

"Incredible little spikes of death."

He snorted. "Come on. We'll have a seat for a minute. Unless my favorite song comes on."

I groaned, and he laughed as he walked me off the dance floor. We didn't make it back to our table, as we were intercepted by familiar faces.

"Fancy meeting you here," Morgan said. She winked at me. "Love the dress."

"Thanks. Hey, Mor," I said, pulling the CEO of Wright Construction in for a hug.

"Morgan. Patrick," Julian said. He shook hands with her boyfriend. "I didn't know you'd be here."

"She didn't want to come," Patrick said with a laugh.

Patrick was Morgan's brother Austin's best friend. It had been a whole to-do when they got together, especially when she'd just been promoted to CEO.

"I hate these things," Morgan said with a shrug. For someone who hated it, she fit right in with a trim black dress. Her dark hair had clearly been coiffed to perfection by a professional, and she had flawless makeup. "But it's part of the job."

"Such a hardship," Patrick teased.

"Shut up, you," she said with a smile. "What are you kids doing here?"

"I'm here to represent the vineyard," Julian said. "Jennifer is here with me."

"Well, wasn't that obvious by the cute dancing?" Morgan said, twirling her finger. "Also, Sutton told me."

I laughed. "Of course she did."

"Something about a twelve-pack of Coke?"

I flushed, and Julian arched an eyebrow.

"What am I missing?"

Morgan and I met each other's eyes and giggled.

"Nothing."

"It's good to see you," Morgan said to Julian. "I was going to ask Jordan about this, but he's a busy bee with the new soccer complex. We're having our annual Wright summer event. Usually, we do it on premises, but since it is the Wright Vineyard"—she winked at him—"might be good to try a new venue."

"Yes," Julian said enthusiastically. "Absolutely. I can have Alejandra run numbers for you. Nora is on staff for event planning. We should absolutely do it."

"Good. Well, my work here is done," Morgan said. She nudged Patrick. "See, I *can* network."

"Yes, dear," he said with a smirk on his lips.

"Sorry to interrupt, but are you Julian Wright?" a man said from behind us.

We turned around to find a man with a bald head that I'd never seen before.

Julian extended his hand. "That I am. And you are?"

"George Jeffries," he said, shaking Julian's hand. "We spoke on the phone. You met with my board earlier this month."

"George. Yes, of course. It's so great to meet you," Julian said. He gestured to me. "This is my girlfriend, Jennifer."

"Nice to meet you," I said, shaking his hand.

"Hello there. I brought the missus myself, but she's found the bar. So, I'll introduce you if we can recover her." Julian laughed with him. "Would you like to meet the rest of my team?"

"Yes, sir," Julian said.

"We'll see you later," Morgan said, pulling Patrick away.

I waved good-bye and then followed Julian across the room to the most important meeting of his career thus far. He had to be nervous, though he didn't show it. I was trying to have that same level of control. But the truth was, I had never dealt with anything like this before. And my normal level of anxiety, which had diminished while we danced, was coming back full force. And I wasn't even the one having the meeting for the vineyard.

The rest of the team was four other old white guys in suits with bulging middles and varying lengths of beards. They were exactly what I'd expected for some reason. Old Texas money was usually held by the good ole boys. Their wives were huddled together, laughing around their cocktails with their big Texas hair and shiny diamonds on their wrists, throats, and earlobes.

I felt ridiculous, standing in front of them. Julian shook hands and used his considerable Wright charm with these men. Not even the wives looked my way or acknowledged me. It was as if I had entered a different era. And sure, it wasn't like I had any business experience. I couldn't contribute to the conversation in any way. But after meeting George, I'd been relegated to the sidelines, just like the other wives.

A wallflower to the very end. And it shouldn't have made

me panic to think about being here in this life. But when had my anxiety ever been rational?

Not any time in my lifetime. It had always come at the least opportune moments. Forcing my brain to fire on extra cylinders while also completely shutting down. It shouldn't have been possible for it to happen at the same time, but it did. My brain whirred lightning fast, and as it pushed and pushed and pushed toward panic, everything else shut down. There was only blinding fear and desperation.

Thinking all of the irrational thoughts: I wasn't good enough. I didn't belong here. This meeting was too important for me to be on Julian's arm. I was going to ruin it all. And worst of all: I couldn't do this.

My hands shook, the tremors running up to my arms. I slowly took a step backward. Away from the men and their beautiful wives and this life I could never belong to.

Julian turned toward me. His face crinkled in concern. "Hey, are you all right?"

"Fine."

His brow furrowed. Fine didn't mean fine. He'd been the one to say that from the beginning. I watched him war with himself. Did he comfort me or deal with the most important meeting, one that he'd been waiting for? The answer was obvious. He had to have this meeting.

"I'm going to go find the powder room," I said with a laugh and a forced smile.

"Jen..."

"I'll be right back," I told him. "Continue your meeting."

He took a step toward me, but I turned and fled the ballroom. I didn't want to interrupt. I needed to get to a restroom and get my shit together. Fucking anxiety. Why did it have to ruin everything?

I pushed into the restroom. A half-dozen women were

inside, but no one looked my way when I went to the end of the long line of mirrors and took deep, heaving breaths, my hands braced on the cold counter. I needed to get this together. I needed to stop panicking. I needed...I needed...a Xanax.

I dumped my purse onto the counter and dug around inside. My hands were still shaking too badly that I couldn't find what I was looking for. I jerked my Canon out of the bag and set it down as carefully as I could manage on the counter. No one else was even close to me. It would be safe where it was.

Then I rummaged through the rest of the bag for the pill bottles I always kept with me. First, my everyday anxiety pill. I dropped that on the counter next to my bag. A sleeping pill that I definitely didn't need right now, but it helped calm my brain enough at night to finally crash. And —*aha*—my Xanax prescription.

I should have taken a half-pill before even coming to this thing, but I'd been on cloud nine. Everything was working well in my relationship. The sex was great. I was even sleeping because his dick apparently put me straight to sleep. I'd barely needed to take my everyday pill, but I knew better than to forget. Now, I was here, suffering for forgoing the Xanax. What had I thought—that my social anxiety would just disappear?

I popped the cap, washing the half-pill down with some water from the sink. Then I grabbed a paper towel and dabbed at my mouth and nose. I'd started sweating, thanks to the adrenaline rush from panicking. I couldn't go back out there, looking like this.

A throat cleared in the middle of the restroom, and I nearly jumped out of my skin. Then I froze in place.

Ashleigh Sinclair stood there, watching me. I didn't

know how long she'd been standing there. My anxiety pills were still on the counter, and I hastily tossed them all back into my bag. Fuck, fuck, fuck.

Ashleigh stopped in front of me. "Are you okay?"

"Fine."

"You don't look so great. Pale, dilated pupils, sweating," Ashleigh rattled off my symptoms and then looked toward my bag and back to me.

"I'm fine," I repeated more forcefully.

I turned my back on her and started the water. I got some soap and began to wash my hands, as if I'd come from the toilet. It was better than looking at her and wondering what scheme she was cooking up.

"Do you really think this is going to work?" Ashleigh asked, casually leaning her hip against the countertop.

"Is *what* going to work?"

"Hiding this from him."

I stilled completely. My heart rate had been coming down, but it skyrocketed again. The water flowed over my now-clean hands. I needed to move, needed to think, needed some comeback.

"I...I don't know what you're talking about," I said lamely.

"Well, it all makes sense, doesn't it?"

"Leave me alone."

"Don't worry. I'll keep it our little secret," she said, moving in close. Then her elbow knocked into my camera, still sitting precariously on the counter.

I gasped, reaching for it, but I was too slow. The camera fell beyond my grasp and into the sink, water soaking it on contact. I almost screamed as I yanked it out of the stream of water and grabbed a handful of paper towels to try to undo the damage.

"Oops," she said.

I whirled on her, all of my anxiety evaporating in the wake of my fury. It was one thing to be mean to *me*. It was another thing entirely to try to hurt my livelihood. I had an elopement to photograph tomorrow, and this was my only working camera, my favorite, my baby. She was easily the most expensive thing I'd ever owned. And if she was ruined, then I'd kill Ashleigh Sinclair.

"What the fuck is wrong with you?" I snapped.

"It was an accident," she said with a viperous smile.

"No, it wasn't. We both know it was no accident. Do you think *this* is going to win Julian back? Or are you past the point of that and going for flat-out sabotage? Because all it's going to do is make him *hate* you. Is that what you want?"

Ashleigh straightened to her full height. Her teeth tight together. "And you think what you're doing is going to win him?"

"News flash," I snarled, "Julian is already mine. He's mine, Ashleigh."

"For now."

"You had your chance. You had him for two years. And then you ruined everything. There is no way that he would *ever* go back to you after what you did." I took a step toward her, throwing my purse back on my shoulder and grabbing my camera, still wadded up in paper towels. "So, why don't you get the hell out of my way and get your own life?"

Ashleigh opened her mouth and then closed it, as if she had no retort to that. Miraculously, she took a step to the side. I strode past her without looking back.

I couldn't believe I'd done that. It had only taken ruining my favorite camera to get here, but I'd stood up to Ashleigh Sinclair.

26

JULIAN

I shook hands with George. I laughed at their bad jokes and smiled at their wandering-eyed wives. I did it all, and at the end, I came out with the yes. They wanted to work with me. I could look forward to hearing from them. But the entire time, I'd been worrying about Jen. She'd freaked out halfway into the meeting and disappeared. She still hadn't come back. I didn't like that I wasn't there to protect her.

At the first opportunity to get away, I took it and stormed across the concert hall to find Jennifer. I texted, asking where she was, but she didn't respond. A panic came over me when I ran into the last person I wanted—Ashleigh.

"Have you seen Jennifer?" I asked.

She smiled a dangerous smile. "She was in the bathroom."

"Is she *still* in there?"

"I think she left."

"The bathroom?"

"The party," she said.

"What did you do?" I demanded.

She gave me the biggest puppy-dog eyes she could muster. "Why would you think that I did anything?"

"History," I snarled.

Ashleigh shrugged. "I didn't do anything, but you should maybe look in her purse."

"What?" I blinked in confusion. "What are you talking about?"

"I'm just saying...if you want to know who you're really dating."

I sighed heavily. "I don't want to play games. If you don't know where she is, then we're done here."

"I'm trying to warn you," she said, reaching for my arm.

I pulled back sharply. "Don't."

"Two years," Ashleigh whispered. "We were together for two years, and you can just throw it all away? Do I disgust you that much?"

"I'm not having this conversation. You know why we broke up. Now, I'm going to go find Jen."

Ashleigh looked like she wanted to say more, but I pushed past her. I didn't know what the fuck she was talking about with Jen. It was normal Sinclair mind games. I wouldn't fall for it. And if she'd seen Jennifer in the restroom, that probably meant that she'd gotten to her. Fuck.

I dashed through the lobby until I found Jennifer seated at a table, wiping down her camera with paper towels.

"There you are," I breathed in relief. "I've been texting you."

"Sorry," she whispered. She sniffled and dabbed at her eyes. "I didn't want to ruin your meeting."

"Hey," I said, sinking into the chair next to her. "What happened? Are you okay?"

In response, she pushed the camera toward me. I looked

at it and the wad of soaked paper towels. Everything clicked together at once.

"Oh fuck, your camera. Does it work?"

She sniffled again and shook her head. "It won't turn on. I'll put it in rice when I get home, but..."

"How the hell did this happen?"

She laughed sardonically. "How do you think?"

"Ashleigh," I breathed.

She nodded. Explanation enough.

"Fuck, Jen. Fuck." I ran a hand back through my hair, not caring about how I'd meticulously gelled it to look like this. "This is my fault. I'll replace the camera."

"No. I mean, you don't have to."

"Yes, I absolutely do. This is unacceptable in every way."

"I'm sorry that I'm such a mess," she said.

I took her hand in mine, stroking my thumb along her palm. "You do not need to apologize for anything. I can't believe she'd even do this." Then I sighed. "I guess I do believe it, but I hate to think she would. That she'd try to hurt you because you're with me."

"I...kind of said as much to her," she said with a small laugh.

"Did you?" I asked.

"Yeah. I might have jumped down her throat and told her that you were going to hate her and she'd never get you back. That she had her chance and ruined it."

I blew out a harsh breath. Well, Ashleigh's reaction when I had seen her made more sense.

"Well, not inaccurate," I told her. "Though I didn't think you'd say so."

She pushed the camera toward me again. Fire was back in her eyes. "She knocked my camera into the sink while the water was running. She deserved everything I said to her."

I smiled and drew her toward me, dropping my mouth onto hers. She melted into me, as if everything that had put her on edge disappeared in that one kiss. When I pulled back, her eyes were still closed, and she looked dazed.

"Do you want to go home?" I asked her.

Her eyes fluttered open. "I don't want to give her the satisfaction."

I laughed. "You're turning into a real spitfire. Do you know that?"

She flushed. "I'm tired of being a pushover."

"You're not a pushover."

"I really am. But I stood up to her, which was a first, and I don't want her to ruin our night. Then she'd win anyway."

"All right," I said, coming to my feet. I held my hand out to her and helped her up. She put her camera back in her purse, and we headed back to the gala.

"How did the meeting go?" she asked as I pulled her into my arms on the dance floor.

"Excellent. Should be a done deal."

"Good. At least one good thing came out of all of this." She nuzzled into me as the music turned to a slow song.

"I think more than one good thing came out of this."

"Oh?"

"You in that dress." I leaned toward her ear. "In those shoes."

"You like them?"

"I picked them out."

She laughed. "Not Annie?"

I shook my head. "Just me."

"You have good taste in shoes, Wright."

I pressed a kiss to her earlobe. "Would it be bad to say that I've been thinking about you in those shoes all night?" She shivered against me. "Just those shoes."

She blushed. "Well, now, you *are* making me want to go home early."

"Who says we have to go home?"

"Scandalous," she breathed.

"My brother built this place. I know my way around well enough to find us a secluded corner."

"Oh my God." Her blush deepened.

"No?" I asked, pulling back to look into her eyes.

She bit her lip. "I've never done anything like that before."

I laughed at her look. "Just come with me. I want to show you something."

"Is that a euphemism?"

"No, I'm serious." I kissed her hand. "You'll like it."

I watched her waver, but then she nodded and followed me. I was glad that I'd gone on all those tours with Jordan. Who knew I'd use that information for my own advantage? I wended our way through the crowd and popped open a nearly invisible door that led backstage.

"Wow," Jennifer gasped.

We stepped around the corner and through the wings to see the stage in all its glory. Just on the other side of that curtain were hundreds of people enjoying the gala. None the wiser that we were here.

"It's beautiful," she murmured. Her eyes were wide as she took in the space.

"You're beautiful."

"I can't believe you got us backstage."

"Perks of being a Wright."

She laughed softly and then rolled her eyes. "Everything is a perk of being a Wright."

"And now, you get to enjoy those benefits." I pressed a kiss to her lips. "Do you want to see the best part?"

"Yes," she answered breathlessly.

I walked her across the brand-new stage and to the thick curtain. She teetered on her high heels and peered through the slit that I'd found in the curtains. The stage had the most perfect view of the entire concert hall. All the guests milling around the room for the gala, the tiered balconies, and to the stars.

"Oh my God," she whispered. "I've never been on a stage like this before."

"Magnificent, right?"

She turned back to face me, a smile on her lips. She'd been so distraught earlier, trying to suppress her tears, that I'd wanted anything to see that smile back on her face. I had every intention of replacing her camera. To make up for what Ashleigh had done. But the most I wanted now was to make up for ever seeing her that sad. I never wanted it to happen again if I could help it. If I had to give her the entire world for her to keep that smile, I'd do it.

"How did I get this lucky?" she asked me, letting the curtain drop.

"Oh no, I'm the lucky one. I've got a beautiful woman on my arm. And she's taking me to Cabo tomorrow."

Jennifer laughed and waved me away. "You paid your own way."

"We're going for your work. My work isn't that interesting."

"Oh, stop."

"I'm serious. The vineyard isn't sending me to Cabo."

I pulled her into my arms. We swayed to the music playing through the concert hall. Our own empty, private dance floor on the darkened stage.

"You just landed a huge deal for the vineyard. I think we can celebrate that in Cabo, too."

"I think we're going to be doing an awful lot of celebrating," I said, dragging her in for another kiss.

"I'm okay with that."

The music stayed slow and steady as we danced. No need for words. No need for anything else. Her heart beat against mine as I held her in my arms. I hadn't planned for any of this to happen with Jennifer, but I was damn glad that we were here. And I'd do anything to keep us this way.

27

JENNIFER

"Jennifer, I thought you might call," Evan said on the phone.

I cringed. Julian didn't know I was calling Evan, but this was important. Not only was my favorite camera broken, but my second-favorite camera had been acting up for months. No stores would be open for hours, and we had to be out of Lubbock soon. I was desperate. Which was why I'd reached out to the last person I wanted to speak to.

"Hey, Evan. How are you doing?"

"Great. You want to catch lunch?"

"Actually, this is a work emergency," I said carefully.

"Oh? You need a second shooter?"

"Well, no, my camera was submerged in water yesterday, and I have an elopement to photograph in Cabo *tonight*."

"Shit. That sucks. How did it end up in the water?"

"Bad luck," I said quickly. "Are you shooting this weekend? Could I borrow your Nikon? I'd pay you."

"I don't have anything on the schedule," he said thoughtfully. "Maybe we could meet for dinner when you bring it back."

My throat closed up. *No* was the answer. It was definitely no. And I could and *would* say it this time because I had a boyfriend. A perfectly crafted excuse that I was going to say on this line *right now*.

"I'm actually seeing someone."

He snorted softly, as if he didn't believe me. "Really? Do I know him?"

"Julian Wright."

Evan was silent on the other end of the line for what felt like a solid minute. "Well...uh, yeah. Sure. Come on over and grab it. Maybe if things don't work out with Wright—"

"Thanks, Evan," I said, interrupting him. "I'll swing by in a few minutes. You're a lifesaver."

"Anytime, Jen. Anything for you."

I hurriedly got off the phone just as Julian walked in from the bathroom in nothing but a towel. Water still ran over his shoulders, and his dark hair was wet. It wasn't the only thing in the room that was wet.

"Who was that?"

I grimaced. "Evan."

"Fuck that guy. What did he want?"

"He said I could borrow his camera."

"Is it still not working?"

I shook my head. "Backup camera isn't working either. I don't know when that happened. I'm going to have to invest in new equipment."

"As I said last night, I'm buying you a new camera. This is my fault."

I bit my lip and shrugged. It didn't feel right. It was Ashleigh's fault. But I also didn't really want to say no either.

Cameras were an investment. With fewer weddings this year, it would hurt.

"We have to swing by and pick his up on the way out of town."

Julian grinned. "I'll get it for you."

"Oh, he'll love that," I said sarcastically.

"Exactly."

* * *

I couldn't see Evan's face from the passenger seat of the Audi, but Julian's smile was so devious that I could only imagine what had happened in that conversation.

"Here you go," he said, passing me the Nikon.

"Did you scare him?"

"Just a little."

I shook my head as I fiddled with the Nikon. I needed to get used to the manual settings real quick. "You're bad."

"What? It was fun. You got to scare my ex."

"I didn't scare Ashleigh. I just...I don't know."

"Put her in her place," he suggested.

"Whatever. And Evan isn't my ex. We went on one date."

"Close enough. Do you have other exes?"

I bit my lip. "Sure. I dated a guy in high school for a year. He mostly smoked pot and wanted blow jobs. Not great for the self-esteem. And I dated a guy in college who played video games and wanted to be a gamer but was a business major." I shrugged.

"That's all?"

"Well, no. I dated a guy when I first started nannying for Sutton. He seemed with it. I thought he was the one. But we, uh...had a falling-out."

To put it nicely. He'd found out about my anxiety

medication and gone off for weeks about how people who took medicine for "mental issues" were weak. That I should be able to just fight it. He actually hid my anxiety pills for a week, and it was bad. *Bad.* He'd called me crazy. I'd sworn to never tell anyone else about it if I could help it. I definitely wasn't planning to reveal that to Julian anytime soon.

"You?" I asked.

He shrugged. "Yeah. Jordan calls me a serial monogamist."

"I don't see how that's bad."

"Right," he said, waving his hand. "Anyway, I think this is the longest I've been single since high school."

"It's only been a couple months."

"Yeah. Well, I hadn't planned to date." His smile hit me full force.

"Sorry to disappoint."

"You are anything but a disappointment." He pressed a kiss to my fingers.

"This camera is going to suck," I muttered.

"Oh?"

"Just going to have to take a million pictures before we get there." I brought it up to my eye. "Say cheese."

He laughed and I snapped the picture. "Feel free. Also I upgraded us to first class."

I nearly dropped Evan's camera. "What?"

"Yeah. Hope that's okay."

"How? How is that even possible?"

He shrugged. "I'm a Wright."

Which seemed to be enough. I was learning a whole new world while dating a Wright.

It turned out that first class to Cabo was an event. We drank a little too much champagne and snuggled up in the enormous seats while I figured out Evan's camera. By the time we landed in Mexico, I was bubbling with excitement to photograph this wedding. The Nikon was now my bitch.

* * *

"So, I should just stay out of your way?" Julian asked.

I grinned. "Well, that's not exactly what I meant. Mostly that I'm going to be busy for the next few hours. The ceremony is late."

"Can I come?"

I furrowed my brow. "I don't know why you'd want to go to a stranger's wedding."

"Because you'll be there."

"Well then, sure," I said with a shrug and a flush. "If that's what you want."

"It is," he said, dropping the bag in our swim-up suite.

I was already rummaging through my own bag so that I could change and get going. I kissed Julian on the way out and made my way to the bridal suite, which was a massive presidential suite with as much room as Piper's house. I introduced myself to everyone involved and then got to work. My mind was completely focused on taking pictures of the bridal party and then the first look with her groom— always my favorite part of any wedding—that I didn't even realize we were quickly approaching sunset.

I took my final pictures of the bride walking toward the beach before dashing forward to capture the groom. This was where a second shooter would be valuable, but most people couldn't afford to send out two people to Mexico. I had to be good enough for two of me.

But when I stepped onto the beach, my feet froze. The small contingent of friends and family who had shown up for the elopement were milling around the beachside wedding display. A towering archway wrapped in blossoming flowers stood behind the groom. The crowd was dressed in summery sundresses. The groom and his best man were in gray slacks and blue short-sleeved button-ups.

It wasn't the most beautiful wedding I'd ever attended, but it was absolutely stunning in its own right. The start of these things always took my breath away. As if I were perpetually stalled in a single perfect moment.

Then my gaze drifted to the lone person at the back of the party. The one person who didn't belong. My smile grew as Julian took me in—frazzled and excited—and liked all of it. My cheeks heated. I'd always appreciated his fashion sense, but today was above and beyond. He took my breath away in slacks and a peachy linen shirt, rolled up to his elbows. His dark hair blew gently in the beach breeze, and those eyes were solely focused on me.

For a whole minute, I forgot what I was doing. Just couldn't believe that Julian Wright was mine. This beautiful, amazing man was my boyfriend.

Then the music changed, and I needed to get back to work. No rest for the wicked.

The ceremony was short and sweet. My bride was stunning beyond measure with her new groom taking her breath away. Everyone cheered, and then we headed to their reception. It wasn't anything fancy since the couple planned to have a bigger event once they got back home. But I dutifully took pictures of their first dance and cutting the cake. All the typical additions to a traditional wedding.

By the end of the night, I was dead on my feet, and it was a miracle to have Julian there, still waiting for me.

"You're glowing," he said.

"That's the exhaustion."

He laughed. "No, it's you doing exactly what you love to do for hours on end. They were lucky to have you."

"Thank you."

"About that exhaustion," he said, wrapping an arm around my waist as we headed back to the suite for the first time in hours. "Do I need to put you straight to bed?"

"God, I don't think I could sleep even if I tried. I'm too keyed up."

"You just said you were exhausted."

"Oh, I am. And it'll all punch me in the face tomorrow. But right now, I'm living on the high of a wedding."

"Good," he said but wouldn't tell me why until we reached our room.

Candlelight suffused the room, leading out to our swim-up pool. Champagne was in a silver bucket, and chocolate-covered strawberries rested on a silver platter. Rose petals were strewn across the white comforter.

My hands flew to my mouth. "Oh my God, what did you do?"

He laughed at my question. "I thought I'd surprise you."

I whirled on him with wide eyes. "Julian…"

He took the camera from around my neck and set my bag down at our feet. "You deserve all of this and more. I wanted to do something to give you a break after working so hard."

"You didn't have to do this."

"I wanted to."

His fingers moved to the strap of my sundress that I'd been wearing all day. Gently, he released one strap and then the other. The material puddled around my hips. He stepped around me, unperturbed by the width of my body, and dragged the zipper down the back. The dress fell to the ground, leaving me in nothing but a bra and panties.

I swallowed as his fingers skimmed the clasp on my bra. He snapped it open as he pressed a kiss to my shoulder.

"God, I love to see you naked," he whispered.

I closed my eyes around his words, trying to infuse them into my body. Julian liked how I looked. He wanted to see me like this.

His hands slid down my stomach from behind, one hand slipping into the waistband of my underwear. I inhaled sharply as he moved lower. My head tipped back to rest on his shoulder. His lips found my neck as a finger touched my most sensitive area.

"Oh God," I moaned.

"Yes," he purred, rubbing me in slow circles.

His fingers slicked through my wetness. I shivered at the touch as he dragged his way back up to the bundle of nerves that had me nearly trembling in his embrace.

"You're so wet," he said into my ear.

I groaned at the words and his fingers and the surprise and all of this at once. "Please."

"I want to taste you," he said, removing his hand.

"Oh," I gasped at his absence.

I moved toward the bed, but he caught my hand. "Not there."

I arched an eyebrow. But he tugged me toward the open door. My eyes widened as I realized he was taking me outside. Yes, we had a partially secluded swim-up suite, but it was *partially* secluded. Anyone could walk by and see what was happening.

He must have seen that all cross my face. "It's after midnight. Who is going to be out?"

It was a fair point, but I still stopped right before leaving. I was in nothing but my underwear. I'd be completely exposed. I'd never done anything like that before.

He smiled at my hesitation. All warmth there. "Don't you want me to taste you?"

"I do, but—"

He pressed a finger to my lips. The same finger that had been inside of me. I could taste my want there. My own arousal only grew. My anxiety not letting up despite the sexual nature of the gesture.

Julian took another step outside and into the humid Mexican air. Then he slowly—oh-so slowly—unbuttoned each individual button on his linen shirt. Until the material fluttered open, revealing the abs beneath, leading down into a V that made me want to step right out there and remove the pants, too.

He dropped the shirt onto a nearby chair and then did exactly what I wanted him to—unclasped his pants and let them drop to the ground. My mouth watered. I could see that he was visibly affected by our contact. That he desperately wanted me. All I had to do was cross that threshold and take what was mine.

Julian Wright was mine.

Before I could move though, his boxers followed the rest of his clothes, and then he was standing completely naked before me. A small noise of want escaped me, and he smirked. He knew precisely what he was doing. Then he stepped away from me and walked right into our swim-up pool.

"Nice night for a dip," he said, waggling his eyebrows.

I wavered for approximately three seconds. We were in Mexico, away from everyone we knew, in our own private suite. Why would I say no?

"Fuck it," I said on a laugh and followed him out and into the pool.

His hands slid over my wet body as he drew me to him. "That's my girl."

I laughed. "I can't believe I'm skinny-dipping."

He arched an eyebrow before dropping his hands to my panties. Without a word, he eased them over my hips and down my legs.

"*Now*, you're skinny-dipping."

"You're a bad influence."

"Oh, absolutely, love," he said, swimming me back to the stairs. He effortlessly lifted me and dropped my naked ass onto the pool edge before gently pushing me backward, so I was laid before him.

"Julian..."

"Breathe," he whispered, his hands sliding up my inner thighs. "No one is going to see you but me."

And then I lost all coherent thought as he slid his tongue up my core. I gasped in shock. But he wasn't finished. His tongue returned to my clit, circling around the nub and causing me to buck off the edge. His hands pressed my legs open wider for him. At the first touch of his finger to my opening, I thought I was going to explode. He thrust up into me, curling his finger and making me shudder.

"Julian," I gasped.

"Mmm," he hummed against my lower half. Another finger thrust inside of me.

My hands slid into his hair. There was nowhere to go. Nowhere to escape the onslaught. And I didn't want to escape, but it was too much. Way too much all at once. Too much sensation, too much pleasure. I'd never felt so over-whelmed, as if every nerve ending in my body was responding at the same time.

I came undone all at once. A whimpering sound came from my lips as I writhed against his mouth. He pulled back to watch me, but I could barely comprehend anything because his fingers were still pumping in and out of me as I contracted. I thought I might pass out until he finally relented and withdrew from my body.

"Holy shit," I gasped, finally opening my eyes to look at him.

His cock jutted up toward me. His chest heaved, as if he could barely restrain himself from taking me.

"I could watch you come all day."

I flushed at his words, coming up onto my elbows. "That could be arranged."

His dark eyes flared molten. As if he might very well take me up on that. "Don't tempt me."

"All day, Wright."

He smirked and then covered my body. "I like this Jen."

"How so?" I whispered as he brushed the tip against my wet center.

"Unrestrained," he breathed.

Then he drove inside my body. I was so wet that I just stretched around him. He felt as if he were always meant to be there.

"Fuck," he groaned as he pushed the final inch into my body.

We were perfectly joined. His hands wrapped around my waist and drew me in even closer.

"I wanted this all day. Watching you work, watching your joy, it was so hard to contain myself. Linen was not the right choice."

I laughed softly. He eased out and drove into me again.

"I can't get enough of you, Jen." He brushed a lock of my hair out of my face and then finally claimed my mouth.

He still tasted like me, but I was beyond caring. Beyond caring that we were in public and having sex poolside.

K.A. LINDE

Julian Wright was thrusting inside of me, bringing us both to the edge.

We came undone at the same moment. My climax driving on his own. Until we were both a tangled mess of limbs against the hard concrete floor. Nothing could be more perfect. Julian Wright was mine. He'd wanted to fuck me all day. He'd even gone to great lengths to surprise me in our resort room. Now, we were here, in a perpetual state of satisfaction.

There was nothing in my life more right than this Wright.

28

JULIAN

"*H*ey. Hey," a voice whispered, pulling me from sleep.

I blinked an eye open, and Jen was draped, naked, against my chest. "Morning."

"Your phone has been going off for the last ten minutes."

"Ugh," I groaned. "Let's ignore it."

My hands slid to her waist. We'd barely slept last night. I'd been...vigorous in our activities. Always wanting more. Always taking more. She was probably too sore to even have more this morning...but I'd be gentle. Maybe.

She laughed as I slid a hand down to her lower half. "Phone first. It might be important."

I sighed and swiped a hand down my face. "I'm not awake enough for this."

She yawned. "Me neither."

I pressed a kiss to her lips and rolled out of bed. I was still naked. Right. I tugged on a pair of boxers and grabbed my phone as it started ringing again. I yawned dramatically, taking the call out on the pool, where our clothes were apparently still draped. No one walking by was going to have to guess what had happened here. I smirked. Damn straight.

Finally awake enough, I glanced down at the phone and saw Jordan's name on the screen.

"Hey, Jor," I said with a yawn. "It's early. I'm in Mexico. Is the vineyard burning down? Because I don't know why else you'd be calling me."

"Fuck, you're in Mexico. I forgot."

"Yep. So...not burning down? I can go back to bed?"

"No, I'm guessing you haven't checked your email."

"Was kind of busy."

"Right," he said. Then I heard something in my brother's voice that I rarely heard...fear. Or at the very least, unease.

I straightened and tried to wake up more fully. "What's going on? Is everything okay? Is it Mom?"

"No, no, Mom is okay. But I got an email this morning. It was sent to you, too."

"Okay?" I asked uncertainly.

"Just...just go read it and then call me back."

"Seriously?"

"Yeah. Or I can wait. Whatever."

He was serious. Jordan wanted me to read this email. I shrugged. "All right."

I put the phone on speaker and dropped into a seat in front of my laptop. I'd done some work from the resort while Jennifer had been busy. It was already up and ready for me. I clicked over to my email and scrolled through the long list of spam emails that I really should have unsubscribed from earlier.

"See it?" Jordan asked.

I didn't know what I was looking for, but there was only one email there that looked out of place. Only one that immediately drew a red flag.

"Yeah. I see it."

From: Weston Wright
Subject: Quick Question...

I clicked on it.
Then, I blinked and blinked again.
"Jor."
"Yeah," he said softly.

Hey,

My name is Weston Wright, and I think...you might be my brother.

I stopped reading there. Because...what the hell?
"This can't be true," I whispered. "Can it?"
"I have no idea. He sent it to both of us."
I finished the letter. Weston said that he lived in Seattle and worked as a musician and computer tech. He was seven years younger than me, nine years younger than Jordan. His dad was Owen. He'd had no idea that he had another family. That we could be half-brothers.
I reread the letter and read it again. Then I slumped back into my seat, wishing I hadn't woken up. "What the fuck, Jor?"
"I really have no idea what to think about it."
"Did Dad cheat on Mom?"
"I mean, time wise, it might have been when they were separated."
"Right."
I'd been young when our parents separated. They were apart for a year or maybe over a year. I didn't have many memories of it. Jordan seemed to have internalized the

whole thing way more than I ever did. I'd been six or seven and Jordan had shielded me as much as he could. As he always had.

"Are you going to respond?" I asked.

Jordan took a minute before saying anything. "I don't fucking know what to do, Julian. Like, what the fuck do we do?"

"I don't know."

"If it's true, then Dad has had a whole other family this entire time. If it's not, then what the fuck does this guy want? Why does he think that we're brothers?"

Jordan had always had a temper, and I could hear it flaring up at this news. He'd been working *so* hard to deal with his issues with Dad. And they cropped up all over again.

"I don't have the answers. But I think we should probably talk to Mom and Dad before we do anything. Mom might be able to tell us if she already knew about this. Why they would hide it from us, you know?"

Jordan huffed, "I know why they'd hide it."

"Yeah," I said. I didn't want to add the *I told you so*, but he must have heard it in my voice.

"Yeah, yeah," Jordan grumbled. "Just get your ass back to Lubbock, so we can talk to Mom. I'm not going to talk to her or Dad without you. I want to know what the fuck this bullshit is. I'll look up Weston Wright in the meantime."

"You mean, stalk him," I said with a short laugh.

"I want the truth."

"Me too," I assured him. "Jen and I are leaving tonight. We can talk to Mom when I get back. When is Dad coming back into town?"

"This weekend," Jordan said. He sounded like he was grinding his teeth. "It's Fourth of July. He wants to spend it with us, go golfing Saturday. I think we're going to have a very different conversation."

We sure as hell were.

"Enjoy the rest of your day," Jordan said.

We said our good-byes and then hung up. Have a good day. Yeah, right. All thoughts of crawling back into bed with my girlfriend had vanished. I might have another *brother*. Weston Wright in Seattle. Had Dad knocked his mom up and not known it? Had his mom given him our last name to capitalize on it one day? I didn't understand any of it. And like Jordan, I wanted to know.

"What was that all about?" Jennifer asked, padding out of the bedroom in my T-shirt.

"Jordan called." I shook my head and showed her the screen, displaying the email.

She read the screen and then gasped. "Oh my God, Julian!"

"I know."

"Is this true?"

I shrugged, running a hand back through my hair. "Fuck if I know. We're going to ask our parents when I get home."

Her eyes were round with worry. "Are you okay?"

I reached out and pulled her into my lap. She curled up easily, wrapping her arms around my neck. "I don't know. I don't know what to think."

"Is it possible?"

"With my dad...anything is possible."

"Okay. Probable?"

"I don't know. I can't imagine that even Owen Wright would hide a family from all of us for our entire lives."

"Did he do work in Seattle?"

"No," I said. "He ran the company out of Vancouver.

Sometimes, he was gone for conferences or board meetings. That sort of thing but rarely Seattle."

"Huh. Maybe it's not true?" she asked optimistically.

"I don't know, love," I said, burying my head into her shoulder.

"Do we need to go home early?"

I looked up at her in surprise. "Of course not. We're not leaving until late."

"Yeah, but—"

I silenced her response with a kiss. She laughed against my lips.

"We get at least one beach day."

She nodded. "Okay. If you're sure."

"I am."

I could put this behind me for a day. For her, I could do it.

* * *

We arrived back in Lubbock late that night. I had Jennifer stay at my place, but when I went into work, she headed home to check on the cats—Avocado was still avoiding her—and to begin work on the wedding edits.

Hollin, Alejandra, and Nora were already on-site when I arrived at the winery. Jordan's truck was also in the parking lot, which meant we were going to deal with this bright and early. If he wasn't at Wright Construction working on the soccer complex, then this was serious.

My stomach tightened. I'd been doing a good job at avoiding the topic. I'd reread Weston's email a couple times. I had become more and more skeptical, the more times I read it. What were the fucking chances that this was even true? And did I want to get to know this guy if it was? It was a lot of unanswerable questions. I just wanted to run my vineyard, be with my girlfriend, and not have to deal with more shit because of my dad.

"Julian!" Nora said as I stepped inside. "I'm so glad you're here. You look tan!"

"Thanks. I was in Cabo this weekend."

"Jealous! Sounds amazing. So, I sent you the final information for the Wright Construction party. Morgan had pinged me, and I'd worked on it all weekend. It's coming up quick. I need you to sign off on it, and then I can work with her directly about the party."

"Sure. Not a problem. Has Hollin looked at this?"

"He said to talk to you," she said with an eye roll.

I snorted. "Of course he did."

"He and Alejandra are working on the tour schedule this week. He said something about hiring some new people."

"Great," I muttered. I only had half a brain to deal with this, but I gave her a reassuring smile. "Let me know if you need anything else."

"Will do. Are you going to be back this weekend for the game? Because I have to admit that your replacement was not the best."

"Sorry about that. Who did you get?"

She laughed. "Annie brought in Chase Sinclair."

I nearly choked. "What? Seriously? And Jordan didn't blow a fuse?"

"I did not," Jordan said, appearing by us. "They're friends. Just friends."

Chase and Annie had been a heck of a lot more than friends for a long time. But if Jordan trusted them, then who was I to judge?

"But he sucked?"

Jordan grinned. "He did. That part was satisfying."

"We lost," Nora grumbled. "Even Blaire and August didn't make up for it."

She beamed when she mentioned her boyfriend. They'd been dating seriously for three years now. He was a pretty good forward, if he didn't ball hog like Hollin did as a defender.

"I'll be back this weekend."

"Thank God," she said. Then she smiled and traipsed away. Little pixie actually skipped, her long ponytail swaying as she went back to work.

"So," Jordan said, "should we go see Mom?"

"I'm really behind on work."

"You think this should wait?"

No, I didn't really think so, but I'd hoped.

"All right," I said with a nod.

I found Hollin and told him I'd be out until lunch. He didn't seem happy about it, but I couldn't tell him the real reason. Not without a conversation I didn't want to have.

Jordan and I piled into his truck, and we headed north to our mom's house.

She opened the front door with a wide smile. "To what do I owe the pleasure? Both my boys home at one time."

We followed her inside. Jordan shot me a look, and I gestured to him. He was the one who always took point. Except at the vineyard, where I was now the point man, and I still found that strange.

"We actually need to talk to you," Jordan said.

My mom sighed and offered us seats. "You can always talk to me. What's this about?"

I sat on the couch while Jordan remained standing. I looked at my mom with a frown. We'd just barged in here, but I hadn't heard from her about her chemo treatments. When I asked, she'd blow me off. As if I hadn't given up my career be there with her through all of them in the past. She continued to stress that everything was going fine.

Except she didn't look fine. She looked fragile. Her head was covered by a head scarf. Her skin sagged. Some of her glow was gone. Even with her vibrant smile. I wondered if maybe we shouldn't do this to her.

But before I could say anything, Jordan pressed forward. "We received an email from a Weston Wright, claiming to be our half-brother."

Mom's eyes widened. "What?"

"He said that he lives in Seattle, is twenty-two, and that our dad is his dad. Did you know about that?"

"That's absurd. What proof does he have of this?"

"None," I said. "Or at least, he didn't offer any in his email."

"It was around the time when you and dad were split up," Jordan pushed.

"That's true, but he never dated seriously while we were apart."

"He wouldn't have had to date seriously to have a kid."

"Jor," I muttered as Mom's face paled further.

"You're right, of course," she said softly. "But...he would have told me."

"What if he doesn't know?" I offered.

She shrugged her thin shoulders. "I really don't know, but I have no knowledge of this. Are you going to speak to your father?"

Jordan nodded. "Yeah, he's in town this weekend."

"Good. I'd talk to him before you decide what to do about this Weston. You'll want to know the truth from your dad's mouth before making a decision."

"What if he doesn't tell us the truth?" I asked.

My mom sent me a pitying look. "He wouldn't lie to you about this. What would he gain?"

I never knew the answer to that question. But I sure hoped that she was right. And that all of this would be resolved on Saturday.

29

JULIAN

I checked Jennifer's text and forced a smile.

It's going to be fine. Text me when you're done.

She was downtown with her parents at the Fourth of July festival. I'd been invited by her parents, who were none the wiser that we'd ever been fake dating, but I had to deal with my dad first and foremost.

Not that I was looking forward to it.

Just got to the course. Hopefully this doesn't take long, and I can still make the festival.

Fried food, carnival rides, and a parade, oh my! But really, you're not missing anything. Good luck with your dad!

Luck was something I was sorely in need of. Jordan and I had planned how to take this, but I had a feeling that as soon as I saw my dad, I was going to blow up. We'd waited days to have this meeting. Left the email unanswered for so long. Would it even make sense to respond to Weston's message after this? I was jittery with unspent energy and ready to get it over with.

I pulled up to the country-club entrance in my Audi. Jordan's truck was already parked out front. He was leaning against the bed of the truck. Our father wasn't here yet. Big surprise.

I parked next to him. "No sign of Dad?"

He shook his head. "He said he was on his way."

"Typical."

Jordan's face gave away nothing. I hadn't been able to get a read on him since we talked to Mom. Was he worried? Mad? Had he had it out with Annie, and that was why everything was fine? I'd talked to Jennifer about it, of course, but I couldn't get over the fact that Dad had done this. He'd done this to us. And I still didn't even know if it was true.

"Any luck on looking him up?" I asked.

Jordan shook his head. "There are a few dozen Weston Wrights online but none in Seattle. I didn't get any hits anywhere on social media. He said he was a musician, but I didn't find anyone with that name. And when I Googled, all that pulls up is some football player. Either he's lying or he's not on social media. I don't know."

"Yeah. Same," I muttered.

"I'm sending someone to look into it, but I don't know. It doesn't even look like this guy exists."

That was what I'd found, too. It was strange that all we had was this email.

Ten minutes later, our father drove into the spot on the other side of Jordan. He laughed when he saw us standing there. "Am I late again?"

I ground my teeth together. Things had been going so well with Dad. Too well maybe. We'd gone golfing after our dinner. He'd even been texting us both. Nothing serious, but enough to keep us in his life. I'd been feeling good about it. And now...this.

"Why the long faces?" he asked as he popped the trunk to get his clubs.

"We've been waiting for ten minutes," Jordan said briskly. "Where were you?"

"Lost track of time. What's the big deal?" The same Wright family smile was on his face. The one that so matched our own.

"Early is on time. On time is late," he quoted a phrase our father had used since we were kids.

He smiled. "You're right. Look at you. Old enough now to teach the teacher. I'm sorry for my tardiness. I'll work on it if it upsets you that much."

I looked at Jordan. We'd agreed that we would golf first. Talk to him afterward, but how the fuck were we supposed to do that? Jordan was already jumping down his throat, and I couldn't stay silent forever.

Our dad finally dropped the smile. He snapped the trunk closed and stepped toward us. "What's all this about? I haven't seen these looks from both of you in a long time. I thought we were making headway. Going to have a good afternoon. Maybe fireworks later."

"Maybe," Jordan agreed.

"We could have," I snapped.

Jordan narrowed his eyes in my direction. A silent reminder to keep it together. But fuck it. He might have mastered his temper, but this was beyond anything I'd ever dealt with, and we didn't need to master anything in this situation.

"What?" my dad asked. His voice shifted from nurturing father figure to business professional in a matter of seconds.

He could see the writing on the wall. He'd always been canny, even when we didn't like it. "Tell me."

Jordan looked to me, and I shrugged.

"This was your idea."

He sighed. "We got an email about you."

"About me? From whom?"

I watched him closely as I said, "Weston Wright."

He blinked. He'd heard that name before. I could see it on his face.

"You know who that is?"

"I've heard the name," he said carefully. "What did he say?"

"He said that he was our brother," Jordan said. "And that you were his father. That he lived in Seattle and was twenty-two. He claimed to not know that we existed, but that we were family."

I waited for him to deny it, to be outraged. To do all the things I expected from him. That I'd waited for with his normal bullshit. But instead, he sighed and seemed to shrink in on himself.

"I was afraid this was going to happen."

"It's true?" I gasped.

"No," he said earnestly. "It's not true. But I do know of Weston Wright."

"You do?" Jordan asked.

"Let's back up the story. Three years ago, right after you two moved here, I got a similar email from the young man. He claimed that I was his father. That I'd known his mother twenty-two years ago, and unbeknownst to me, I'd fathered a child." He ran a hand back through his hair, his face distraught. "I took the email seriously. How could I not?"

"Of course," Jordan said.

"Why would he think you were his dad?"

"I knew his mother," he said with a shrug. "He'd found old pictures of us together and assumed that I must be his dad."

I narrowed my eyes. "But you aren't?"

"Let me explain," he said, holding his hand out. "I took it as a credible reality that I might have another son. After all, around that time, I'd been separated from your mother. I'd had a few relationships. Though...nothing had ever come of it. Certainly not children."

I shuddered at that thought.

"Anyway, I reached out to his mother. She was incredibly embarrassed that Weston had contacted me. We'd known each other, and when we compared dates, it hadn't been anywhere close to the time that he was conceived."

"How close?" Jordan asked.

"A year difference," our father said. He leaned back against Jordan's truck and wiped a hand down his face. "From his mother, I found out that Wright wasn't even his last name. He had the same last name as his mother. She didn't know who the father was, and this wasn't the first time that Weston had spoken to a man she'd dated at the time."

"And what was her last name?" Jordan asked.

"Smith."

I sighed. Great. What a common name. No wonder they hadn't found a musician Weston Wright if his real name was Weston Smith. How many more of those were there?

"So, why is he messaging us now?" Jordan asked.

"Yeah. Didn't you tell him?"

"I did," he said. "We both did. I thought that he understood the circumstances. I handled it then, and I'll handle it now."

"How?" I asked.

"I'll talk to him again. I'll contact his mother." He straightened, as if realizing the purpose of all of this. "I can't have him interfering in our lives like this. It isn't fair to either of you or me."

"Or Mom," Jordan asked.

Our father's eyes rounded. "You told your mother?"

"Yes," Jordan said. "Of course we did. She was the one who insisted we talk to you before speaking to Weston."

"She must hate me. I thought we were just..." He trailed off.

It made my insides squirm to think that they might reconcile.

"To her credit, she never believed it," I offered. "She said that you would have told her if you'd known while you were married."

"Of course I would have told her," he insisted vehemently. "Can you imagine keeping a secret like that from your mom?"

Jordan and I shrugged at the same time. As if, yes, we could imagine keeping things from Mom. And we'd learned how to lie from our dad. That was for damn sure.

But...this...this felt like the truth. I didn't know if it was because I had so desperately wanted there to be an answer to this horrible question, but it all fit together. Our father was a good liar, but he hadn't been surprised by our question of him. He hadn't shied away from it at all. There hadn't been a moment of hesitation. He was good, but he wasn't *that* good. Not when we were in on his tricks.

"How do we know this is all true?" I finally asked.

"Well, I'd appreciate some trust," my dad said.

Jordan managed only a half-laugh. "Do you still have the original emails?"

He scrunched up his features. "Maybe. He sent it to the

business email, and everything from that was dumped after I was...let go. I transferred a lot over. I can go through my emails and see if I can get it for you. But you could always respond to Weston and see what he says." My dad shrugged. "I don't know what he would say. I doubt he'd admit that he'd already reached out to me and it hadn't gone his way."

"Why not?"

"Don't you see?" our dad asked. He winced before saying, "Being my son comes with privilege. I was the head of the Vancouver company. I had money to spare. I had access."

Jordan nodded. "Did he ask for money?"

"No," our dad said. "I think he actually believed he was my son."

"Then, why?"

Our dad hung his head. "I gave his mother money. She was...on hard times. We were friends at the time and reconnected for a while when I was in a dark place after you all left. He might have...discovered that I'd done that."

"Jesus, Dad," Jordan growled.

I shook my head. There it was. There it always was. The caveat.

"I try to put on a brave face for you both, but I was a mess," he said solemnly. "What do you want me to say? I'd lost the company, my wife, my kids. I'd lost everything I'd ever cared about. I hate to say it, but I wanted Weston to be my son."

I balked. "What?"

"It would have been a chance for me to start over." He sounded so desperate that my heart actually hurt for him. A feeling I'd never thought I'd have again. "You wouldn't talk to me. You wouldn't see me. Everything was gone. What else did I have? So, I wanted this new life. It wasn't real though.

It's why when Jordan called me, I hopped on the chance. I'd do anything to make this right with you. To have my real family back. I've made mistakes. I know I have, but I'm not the man I was, and I mean that."

I could see that he did. That he really truly did.

Even Jordan's face released the tension, the doubt. This was our dad, laid bare for us. The crumbled, destroyed shell of a person he'd been. He'd reaped what he'd sown, but for how long? Forever? Did he deserve an eternity of those dark days without us?

"Why don't...why don't we just play the round?" Jordan suggested. "Figure it out after that."

A glimmer of light returned to our dad's eyes. "You still want to golf?"

"Why don't we take it a day at a time?"

"Julian?" he asked me.

I swallowed and looked into the beast of my youth. And I realized he was just like all the rest of us. He'd fucked up. He'd owned up to it. Maybe we all deserved another chance here.

"I agree. Let's play."

30

JENNIFER

"Funnel cake, honey?" my mom asked.

"Yes, please."

We walked around downtown, where food trucks had taken up most of the LHUCA area. I'd been up here this morning in one of the studios, working with another portrait appointment and then a couple who wanted carnival-themed engagement shots. The portrait session had taken everything out of me—in the best way. I felt like the session was a focal point. Like I was almost done with the first round. Almost ready to show the world what I'd been working on.

I had one more shoot tonight that I was beyond excited for. Though it was a secret. I hadn't even told Julian. Thinking about it was actually a nice distraction from Julian dealing with his dad. No matter that my anxiety was being managed, I took on other people's anxiety as my own. I couldn't help it, and I didn't know how to control that. But I'd felt off all week, waiting to find out what the hell Owen Wright was going to say.

We're going to play the full round. Don't think I'll make the festival.

You're still on for fireworks, yes? Fireworks are required.

Yep. I'll be there.

What did your dad say anyway? Is Weston your brother?

I'll tell you about it later. My turn to golf.

I grumbled in frustration. *Come on, Julian. Give me something!*

"Everything all right?" my mom asked as she came back with a giant funnel cake topped with a mountain of powdered sugar.

"Yep. Julian's just texting me. He's out golfing with his dad."

"Sounds riveting," my dad said with a laugh.

He'd thrown his back out while playing golf when I was a kid and never picked up clubs again. Could hardly blame him.

"I wish that they could have come to the festival with us," my mom said.

"Me too."

Especially since the last time Julian had been around my parents, we'd been fake dating, and now, we were real dating. Not that they knew, but still. I'd lied, and I wanted them to see the truth.

"And your work?" Dad asked. "How did your shoots go this morning?"

My mom wrinkled her nose and pulled out her own phone.

"Great," I said enthusiastically to overcome my mom's behavior. "I'm almost done with my first set of portraits. Almost ready to showcase them."

"Really?" my dad asked. "How would that work?"

I opened my mouth to explain, but Mom cut in, "Have either of you gotten texts back from Chester?"

I sighed. Of course, a change in subject to my brother. "Nope. I texted him over an hour ago and nothing."

"I'm going to try to call him one more time," she said and then stepped away from us to call my brother.

I sighed. "Why is she always like that about my career?"

My dad slung an arm around my shoulders. "It's not about you. We're both proud of you."

"She isn't proud of my work."

"It's only fear. We worked so hard to get to where we are. She doesn't want to see you have to go through what we did to get ahead. She thinks pharmacy would be safer than photography."

"But I'm talented at this. I love it. Why can't she be happy about that?"

My dad shrugged. "Fear makes people act in funny ways, kiddo. She still loves you. She just doesn't know how to express her fear in any other way."

I hung my head. I knew what he meant, but it didn't make it any easier. I'd been making a living as a photographer for almost four years now, and my mom never acknowledged it as any level of success. She only seemed to like Julian because it brought me some stability. She had an aversion to Wrights, as if they hadn't earned their own work either. They'd been handed a company someone else had built. It was ridiculous. But I didn't know how to fix it, and it felt demoralizing. If only I could stand up to her and tell her how much it hurt me. My therapist had been working with me for years to get over my childhood trauma, but apparently, I was still stuck in the same cycle.

"No luck," my mom said, coming back to us. "Do you think that you could run by his place on the way home, Jennifer? I don't know if he's hurt or something. He never misses something like this."

Yep. My perfect brother. Must be injured instead of bailing on family time.

"Sure," I said. Because what else was I going to do? "You're still meeting me for fireworks tonight, right?"

"Yes, honey. Find out if Chester is coming. And Julian, too."

"I'll ask Chess. Julian already agreed," I told her. "We're going to be with the entire Wright brood. Everyone will be there."

"Well, we will have our own section," my mom said defensively.

"Of course." No point in arguing. "I'm going to check on Sutton, too."

It was the five-year anniversary of her husband Maverick passing. She had a whole new, wonderful life now, but the day still hurt in inexplicable ways. She'd opted out of all celebrations in the past, but this was the first year that she'd agreed to bring Jason and Madison to fireworks. I'd all but begged her to attend, and she'd finally acquiesced for the kids.

"Poor thing," my mom said. She hadn't liked Sutton, but she still sympathized with her losing her husband.

I smiled wanly at them and then said my good-byes. I sent off a bunch of texts to Sutton to check on her. I hadn't heard from Julian again. He must still be out on the golf course. Then I headed over to Chester's house to make sure he wasn't hurt, as per my mother.

Well, Chester's car was parked in the driveway. So, he had to be home. Another car was parked next to it that I didn't recognize. Must have a friend over, or maybe he was seeing someone and wasn't ready to tell anyone. Either way, it was annoying that he couldn't at least answer his texts.

I banged on the front door and then crossed my arms to wait for him. I didn't have to wait long before the door pulled inward.

A smiling Peter Medina answered in nothing but a pair of boxers. "Jennifer," he said. "I thought you were the pizza."

My eyes rounded. "I...am not pizza. I came to check on Chester. He's not answering his phone, and he was supposed to meet us at the Fourth of July festival."

"Chess, your sister is here," Peter said.

The way he wrapped my brother's name around his lips was almost...sensual. Not to mention that he just called him Chess, the nickname that *no one* was allowed to use. Peter... whose long-term boyfriend had left him. Peter, who we'd had Chester talk to because he'd gone through something similar. Peter, who was definitely, a hundred percent gay. And he was at my brother's house...in his boxers.

Peter pushed the door wider, and Chester appeared then. At least he was fully clothed.

But then, as if I had any room to doubt, Peter leaned forward and kissed Chester on the cheek. "Good luck."

"Uh...hi," I said.

Chester's eyes narrowed, and he pulled the door closed behind him as he stepped outside. "What are you doing here?"

"Well, Mom sent me because you didn't answer her calls. And since when did you start dating Peter?"

Chester shrugged. "Why? What does it matter?"

Suddenly, everything that had happened over graduation weekend seemed to make sense. The fights with Margaret, the half-naked ex-brothel bar, the guy inviting him into the bathtub. My brother was...gay?

"It doesn't matter," I said quickly. "I didn't realize that you were..."

He arched an eyebrow. A question hanging between us.

"Gay," he offered.

"Well, yeah. I didn't know."

"I'm actually pan," he said with a shrug. "I was out in Austin. Margaret knew. I wanted to explore my sexuality and, we decided we weren't right for each other."

"Okay," I said. "Are you out here?"

"No. Lubbock is...less forgiving for people like me. I don't know that I'm ready for that. I haven't told our parents."

"All right. I won't tell them," I said without hesitation.

He blinked. "Thanks."

"Are you and Peter...together? Are you happy?"

He smiled—a rare, completely unguarded smile. "I like him. We've been spending a lot of time together. But we're not a couple. We're not there yet."

"I'm glad that you're happy."

"I thought you'd be weird about this."

I laughed. "Why? I like Peter. I live with his sister."

"Yeah, but..."

I shrugged. "Love is love."

Then to my surprise, my brother stepped forward and wrapped his arms around me. I stiffened in shock, and then when my body loosened, I returned the hug. I hadn't hugged my brother since we were kids.

"Thanks, Jen."

"Anytime."

"Mom and Dad aren't going to be this cool."

I stepped back. "No, I suspect not. But you don't have to tell them until you're ready. I would recommend responding to their messages, so they don't show up, like I did."

He ran a hand over his five o'clock shadow. "Yeah, my bad."

I nodded at him. "You're still coming for the fireworks, right?"

"Yeah. Yeah, I'll be there. I'll let them know."

"And Peter?"

Chester looked anxiously back to the house. "I don't think I'm ready for that yet."

I put my hand on his. It was this very moment when it felt like everything shifted between me and my brother. He wasn't any more perfect than I was. He hid things from our parents. He wanted to live his real, true life but didn't want to risk their judgment. I knew exactly what that was like.

"I'm here whenever you're ready."

And I meant it.

31

JENNIFER

*M*y brand-new Canon hung around my neck as I paced my house, waiting for Julian. He'd gotten me the new camera when we returned from Mexico, and I couldn't even hold in my excitement about the newer, fancier model.

Piper and Blaire had already gone on ahead to the fireworks. They'd offered to take me with them, but I'd assured them it was unnecessary. I wanted to hear what had happened with Julian's dad. He'd been vague and unavailable all afternoon. So, I was jittery with nerves about this and my last shoot of the day.

When the doorbell finally rang, I yanked it open before Julian even removed his finger. "There you are!"

I threw my arms around him, and he laughed.

"Hey, you."

"How are you? I've been wondering how everything went all day."

"Good. Things went...good."

"Good?" I asked. "Really?"

He cringed. "Eh, I don't know. Good-ish."

"Tell me everything on the way."

His gaze followed me as I walked past him and locked the door up. Bacon meowed from the bushes, coming to twine herself around Julian's ankles.

"She likes me."

"Don't let Cado see. She's protective of Bacon," I said warily. "She still hasn't forgiven me for moving. I don't know if she ever will."

"But she's shown up for food again?"

I nodded. "Yeah. She'll eat my food, but she doesn't have to like me."

He chuckled. "Sounds like a cat."

"For real. This is why I never liked cats."

"Too bad."

I pet Bacon a few times. "We have to go. Give Cado my best."

Bacon meowed, as if in answer. Then we headed over to Milli, idling in the driveway.

"Do you really think it's wise to bring the Jag to find parking?"

"Would you rather park the SUV in a tiny parking space?"

I considered it. "No. That would suck."

"Thus Milli." He held my door open for me and then took the driver's seat. "You seem keyed up."

"I have one more shoot, and I've been waiting *all day* to hear from you."

He smirked and kissed my fingers. "Didn't realize you were waiting for me."

"I was."

"What's the shoot?"

"You'll see."

He arched an eyebrow as he pulled out of the driveway.

"Mysterious."

"So...your dad?" I prompted.

He sighed, as if he'd been hoping to avoid the question. "He says that it's not his kid. That he'd been contacted by Weston before and handled it."

My eyes rounded. "Wow. He already knew about this? Why didn't he let you know?"

"It happened after we left. He said the guy isn't even Weston Wright. He's Weston Smith. And is convinced that my dad is his dad."

"That's...wow."

"Tell me about it."

"And you think he's telling the truth?"

He shrugged his shoulders, looking defeated. "I want to believe him."

"That's not the same thing."

"I know. I know that it's stupid to put it off. My dad has lied before, but would he lie to us about something this important? I just don't know."

"What are you going to do?"

"Nothing," he said. "Well, I'm doing nothing. Jordan and I agreed not to email Weston."

"Really?"

"Yeah. He's...well, we didn't tell Dad, but we're hiring a PI and going to investigate the guy. Jor couldn't find any information on him online, and he'd rather have some concrete proof before we put it behind us."

"That sounds smart. Also very much like Jordan."

A hint of Julian came back at that. He laughed. "Yeah, tell me about it. I don't know why I didn't even think about doing something like that, but it makes perfect sense."

"Yeah," I said, thinking it through. "You don't have to talk to the guy if it's not true. And if your dad has nothing to hide, then there's no reason not to look into this."

"Except that it makes me feel shitty."

I startled at that. "Why?"

"Like I'm spying on people instead of trusting people. Even though I don't trust my dad. I felt like we were at least *working* on trusting him again. And now, we have this huge thing between us."

"You don't have to hire the PI," I said.

"But we do. I need to know the truth or else it'll always burn me up."

I nodded at that. At least he was finally talking about it. This last week, he'd been completely mentally absent.

"What do you want to do if you find out that he *is* your brother? Do you want to get to know him?"

Julian's eyes widened. "I really haven't given that much thought. I so desperately want it all not to be true." He sighed. "But also, I don't even know what I want."

I covered his hand with mine. "You might want to think about it."

"What would I even want? I really don't know. I didn't really know my cousins, and now, I love having them all around. It wouldn't be the same. But...I don't know. If it's true, it'd be really fucking weird."

I laughed unexpectedly. "It would be. I'm sure he'd be just as weirded out by all of this as you are. It would take some time for you all to adjust."

"You're good at this."

Years and years of therapy. That's what I wanted to say, but instead, I just smiled. "Thanks. Worst-case scenario-ing is kind of my forte."

"I'm more of a *best-case scenario* kind of guy," he said with a wink.

He pulled into the parking for Mackenzie Park. We were early enough that there was still enough parking for us to find a spot. As soon as the sun began to set, everything would be jam-packed for miles.

I grabbed my bag and helped him carry blankets across the grounds. The Wrights had already set up a large space at the center of the park. A slew of blankets and a dozen foldable chairs dotted the area. Other people were quickly filling in around them.

"Hey, y'all!" Nora said as we approached. She was lying across her boyfriend, August. His floppy surfer hair was half in his face as he waved at us. Her best friend, Tamara, was seated next to them, her red hair framing her face, her nose buried in a magazine.

It was nice to see the Wright section expanding as everyone drew in more and more people. For so long, the Wrights had been so insular. And now, the Abbeys were here, Emery's family was present, Chester and my parents had already set up a position nearby, and Piper, Blaire, and Peter were located not too far from them. All of the people that I loved were in one place.

Even Sutton.

Our eyes met across the distance. I dropped the blankets and went to where she sat with Annie. The kids had run off to play with Heidi's son, Holden, along with Emery's sister, Kimber's, kids, Lilyanne and Bethany.

"Hey, how are you doing?" I asked, pulling her into a hug.

She smiled up at me, only barely hiding the grief in her eyes. "It's been a long day."

"But you're here. That's progress."

She nodded. "Mav would have wanted me to still enjoy this time with my family. Jason deserves it."

I took her hand and squeezed. "He really loved you."

"He did."

Annie added her hand. "We really love you, too."

Sutton laughed, fighting back tears. "Y'all are going to make me cry again."

"No tears," I said. "Just good times with good people."

"Thank you, both of you, for caring so much. David has been a help, but having my girls here for me really makes a difference."

"Always," Annie said.

"And forever."

We hugged it out as a trio. Sutton shed a few of those tears, but it was worth it because our friend had survived. She was pieced back together in her own way with a new family and a new love of her life. She was going to be okay, but it was also okay *not* to be okay all the time. Today was one of those days.

I left them behind, pulling the camera up to my face as I snapped shot after shot of everyone together. Jensen and Emery were at the center of the group, holding their three-month-old baby, Robin. *Snap.* Heidi dug through a cooler and grabbed drinks for her and Emery, and then she turned and yelled at Holden to behave. *Snap.* Landon laughed next to her, shaking his head at his son and turning to his brother Austin. *Snap.* Austin had an arm slung lazily around his girlfriend, Julia. No drink in sight for him. *Snap.* Julia seemed to be half-listening to whatever Patrick was saying next to her. Austin punched him in the arm, and they all burst into laughter. *Snap.* Morgan appeared then, collapsing into Patrick's lap. *Snap.* Jordan arrived last. His mother on his arm as he helped her across the grounds to our little slice of heaven. She looked gaunt. *Snap.* Julian jumped from where he'd been putting together our area near Annie and Sutton.

He dashed to his mom, and they spoke. I had all three of them in the shot. *Snap.* Their mom smiled a real thing. I could see how lovely she must have been. *Snap.* Then they had her in a seat near her siblings. *Snap.*

So much life. So much vibrancy. Lubbock was its own little microcosm, and I wanted to document it all. Be here for it all. Live through it all.

For so long, I'd thought that I didn't belong. Now, with Julian finding my gaze, my family standing nearby, and my best friends at my back, I felt like I did belong here with them. With him.

I shivered at the realization and the fear that it immediately elicited. Because if I had it all, that meant I had so much more to lose. And I hadn't been joking when I said worst-case scenarios were what I was best at. Anxiety had taught me that hard lesson.

"Hey, come sit by us," Julian said, pressing a kiss to my cheek.

"Definitely."

"Do you still have that shoot?"

I grinned. "I do."

He arched an eyebrow. "It's getting late. The sun is about to set."

"It is, isn't it?"

He shrugged. "Keeping secrets."

And then the sun dipped a little bit lower. An in-between time. A time of renewal. A perfect time for photography, and I was ready.

"Now," I whispered to Julian.

"What?"

Then Patrick was on his feet, holding his hand out to Morgan, who had taken a seat on the ground before him. She laughed and let him stand her up.

"What's this about?" she asked.

But as if the tension in the area had been pulled taut, everyone gravitated toward them as I started photographing.

Patrick dropped to one knee. Morgan's jaw fell open. Her hands didn't fly to her face, and she didn't start crying. She wasn't like most of my other brides. But her eyes were wide, and she was staring down at him in disbelief.

"What are you doing?" she gasped.

Patrick retrieved a small blue box from his pocket and popped it open to reveal the glittering diamond inside. "Morgan Wright, will you marry me?"

She stood frozen in time, looking down at her boyfriend, the man she loved. I could practically feel her shaken world at the words out of his mouth. Everyone held a breath, waited. Morgan wasn't the lovey-dovey type. But Patrick was her person. She'd always liked him, and now, they were inseparably in love.

"Yes!"

The word broke the tension and the dam on her tears. She cried happy tears as he stood and slid the ring onto her finger, pulling her lips to his. The crowd around them all cheered, applause coming from the entire Fourth of July event.

Julian wrapped an arm around my waist. "Your final shoot, huh?"

I laughed and swiped at my own tears. "It was beautiful."

"You're beautiful."

Then he kissed me. Right then and there in front of everyone. I came alive in Julian's arms. In this place where I finally fit. With these people, where my skill was valued. I was finally right where I belonged.

PART V

BELONGING

32

JULIAN

*A*fter Fourth of July, time passed both more slowly and also at hyper-speed. Waiting to hear from Jordan's PI felt like it was taking a lifetime. And the delay with the distributor as they got the paperwork together only made me want to rage at the snail's pace. I'd followed up twice already and kept getting the run around about when we'd finalize everything. But otherwise, day-to-day business at the winery flew by.

Without knowing how, we were halfway through July and coming up on the Wright party. Nora had been working nonstop to make it everything it could be. She'd even called Campbell to see if he could come in for it. That was still up in the air as well since the record label was apparently on his ass about a new album. It wasn't enough to be a successful rockstar. He had to repeat the ability time and time again. I didn't envy him.

I finished off the memo I'd been working on and pushed away from my desk. I hadn't moved in hours. I needed a break.

Running a hand down my face, I shucked off my blazer

and rolled my sleeves up as I exited into the cellars. The idea to purchase West Texas Winery and make it our own Wright Vineyard had truly been Hollin's idea. And as I watched him lean over a barrel, explaining the process to a tour that had stopped in front of him, I could see why he'd wanted it so badly. He *loved* this place. He'd loved it for a decade. And I was coming to realize that it was entirely my sanctuary as well.

A flash of red hair, and then Tamara was standing in front of him. "Oh, this is a treat, ladies and gentlemen, both owners in one day."

I laughed and put on my most charming smile to cover my exhaustion. Tamara was our latest tour guide hire. She was Nora's best friend, and Nora had vouched for her. It didn't hurt that she was a knockout. Hollin had wanted to hire her before interviewing her. Bastard.

"Hey, Tamara." I nodded at the rest of the tour. "How's it going?"

"We love it here," a middle-aged white woman said.

"It's lovely," another responded.

"We're just getting out to the vineyards. Beautiful day for it," Tamara said. "Now, everyone, wave good-bye to Julian."

I laughed and waved as they headed out of the cellar doors and into the vineyard beyond.

Hollin whistled low behind me. "She might take the prize from you, Julian."

I raised an eyebrow. "For what?"

"Flirting."

"Oh Jesus, I'm not that bad."

"Not now that you're with Jennifer maybe. But, yeah, Tamara is, like, *the* flirt. She's touched me every time she's seen me."

"And you hate it?"

"She's a bit young," he said with a wince. "She grew up with Nora."

"Yeah, a little creepy. Do I need to say something?"

"No, no," he said quickly. "I can put her down gently."

I snorted. "Sure you can."

"Anyway," Hollin said, clapping me on the back, "any word on the distribution? We're ready to get going."

"No," I said with a sigh. "I don't understand. They were all for it when I met them at the gala. They made it seem like I'd hear back from them immediately, and now, it's so slow."

Hollin shrugged. "Business."

"I guess."

"Well, are you excited for the Wright party here? That's our first corporate event!"

"I am. It'll look good to have the company here. The name carries."

"That's why we named it Wright Vineyard."

"True."

"But why we're going to add Abbey vintages."

I laughed at my friend and cousin. "Absolutely. And are you bringing someone with you to the party?"

Hollin crossed his bulky arms, the tattoo sleeve visible below his rolled-up shirt. "I like to keep my options open."

"So, that's a no."

He snorted. "Whatever, dude. I like lots of hot pussy. Can't keep me down."

I shook my head. "How are we friends?"

Hollin cracked a smile. "Because I keep your life interesting."

"Fact," I said as we headed out of the cellars and into the open air.

The tour was already far enough away that they wouldn't overhear us. Alejandra appeared then.

"New tour guide is on fire. I like her. If things keep up like this, then we might even need to hire another one."

"That's good news," Hollin boasted.

"The Wright event should secure it. Any news on the distribution?" she prodded me.

"No," I said, repeating to her what I'd told Hollin. "Hopefully soon."

She cursed eloquently in Spanish. "I hate that they have all this control. But if we have to wait, then we have to wait."

"I reached out to them again today. We'll see what they say about the delay."

"Keep us up-to-date," she said with a nod and then returned to work.

Hollin clapped me on the back. "I believe in you. You got this. You're business-savvy. You'll make it all work."

"Thanks, Hollin."

He trailed off after Alejandra. He'd thought he was giving me a compliment, and I'd forced myself to take it as one. But it felt like a chain around my neck. Jordan was so proud of me. Hollin believed in me. I couldn't fuck up. I had to make this right. I needed to get back in there and talk to the distributors again. George had made it seem like a done deal. Why wouldn't I know by now?

I cursed and headed back to my desk. I pulled up my computer to get his number but saw that an email was waiting from the company.

Fucking finally.

I clicked to open it and stared at the message. It wasn't even from George himself. It was written from his secretary with him CC'ed on the email.

Dear Julian,

Thank you so much for reaching out about the distribution contract. At this time, we're unable to offer you...

My jaw dropped as I finished off the letter. A form letter. They'd sent a form rejection of our application for distribution. It didn't even list *reasons*.

What the actual fuck was this shit? I couldn't believe it. I'd been put through the hoops to get to this position. Yes, we were a new winery. Yes, we were a risk. Yes, there were reasons to deny us. But none of that had come up when I had my meetings with them. They knew Jensen. They were familiar with the Wright brand. They knew the likelihood that we'd stumble and fall was small since we had the capital to keep it afloat.

If they'd said any of those reasons, I could have put it aside and worked on it again in a year when we had more time and energy and money under our belt. But that wasn't it. This was straight garbage.

Without thinking, I dialed George's number. He'd given it to me on a business card, saying it was his personal line. I hadn't used it because so far, everything had been working out.

"Hello?" George said.

"George, hi. It's Julian Wright."

"Julian, so good to hear from you," he said as amicably as he'd been at the gala last month.

"I just received a form letter from the company, rejecting Wright Vineyard's application for distribution."

"Ah," he drawled. "I thought that might be it."

"What is going on?"

"It just isn't the right fit."

I blinked. "What does that mean?"

"Nothing personal. Purely business, son. I wanted to work with you, but when we looked at the information provided and compared it to what else was out there, we had to say no."

"So, it's because we're new?"

"No, it's not that."

"Is there a real reason for not taking us?" I snapped. I winced at my tone, but desperation took over. My charm had dissolved. This felt impossible.

"Sorry, son. Try again in a few years." He even sounded sincere. "We'll reconsider at a later date."

And the line went dead.

He'd hung up on me.

I flung the phone across the room, and it shattered against the wall with a satisfying crunch. I regretted it almost as soon as I was done with my burst of anger. Now, I'd have to replace the damn thing, too. I didn't have time for that. For anything.

What was I going to do? The question filtered through my mind on repeat.

They'd turned us down, given me no real answer for why, and then discarded us. Just that easily. This could sink the vineyard. Having a distribution agreement was the easiest way to make money in this business. Now, we could only sell on-site. We couldn't get into stores or sell online or...anything. We were confined to this one place and time. A huge hindrance to the business.

And I couldn't tell Hollin and Alejandra. They'd been so anticipating it. Hollin *believed* in me. I could go to Jordan. I squeezed my eyes shut and balled my hands into fists. No, I couldn't do that either. Jordan was always my saving grace. But how the fuck was he going to fix this? And if he did, then he'd know I'd failed. He'd handed me the company, and I'd failed. He'd been bragging to Dad about it. Fuck. I didn't know what to do.

I picked up the destroyed phone and saw that it didn't even turn on. Great. Now, I couldn't even get ahold of Jen. Not that I wanted to tell her how much of a failure I was either. She thought the world of me.

Maybe I was thinking too much of myself right now, but this had been my main focus for months. And now, it was gone. There was nothing I could do.

I ground my teeth together. Realizing there *was* something I could do.

But my phone was dead.

I'd have to go in person.

I ran a hand back through my hair and hated myself for what I was about to do. But Ashleigh Sinclair could make this right.

33

JENNIFER

"Hey, Blaire. Have you heard if Julian is still going to the game today?"

Blaire popped her head out of her room, dressed in her red Tacos uniform, her long black hair in a ponytail on the top of her head. "As far as I know. Thank God we do not have to have Chase Sinclair again as his replacement."

"Bad?"

"I did not know hot boys could be that uncoordinated."

I laughed. "Didn't he play football?"

"Oh, he can run. But he cannot dribble or pass or shoot. He kept going offsides. I'm not sure he actually knew the rules." Blaire shook her head. "A disgrace."

"Huh. Okay."

"Why? Problems in paradise?"

"No. I don't think so. I mean, I hope not." I flushed, thinking about the worst-case scenario of why Julian hadn't returned any of my texts for almost twenty-four hours. "He hasn't responded on his cell. Could you text him?"

"Sure. Sure. Let me shoot one off to the group to see if they've heard from him."

I nodded and headed back into my room. I changed into shorts and a tank top for the game, snagging a *Blaire Blush* baseball cap. She'd foisted one off on me since I never wore hats. I thought I looked stupid in them, but if Blaire said it looked good, who was I to argue?

I checked my phone again. Nothing. Seriously, I was starting to look desperate. How many unanswered messages were too many? Because I was definitely almost there. Or maybe already there.

"Hollin says he was at work. Should be at the game," Blaire yelled across the hall.

"Oh. Okay," I whispered.

So, he'd been at work but not messaged me. That was... odd. Worrisome.

I glanced at my stash of Xanax. Usually, I didn't need anything like that for games, but my brain was firing over-time, telling me all the ways that Julian was tired of me. Over us. I'd been a fun flirtation, some nice sex, a trip to Mexico. Now, it was time to move on to bigger and better.

But Julian wasn't like that. At least, the small part of my brain not currently overrun by my anxiety was saying that. We'd kissed in front of his whole family. Things had been looking good...looking up. Why did my brain have to *do* this?

"Fuck it," I muttered.

I popped a half-Xanax into my mouth.

Then I did another thing that I'd been waiting on. I pulled up my Instagram. The post was already in Draft. It was the portrait I'd done of Campbell, maybe the best picture of my entire life. And underneath it was the caption: *Portrait series #1.* I'd been wavering on when to post it, if I should even do it. But it was now or never, right?

I pressed *Share* and closed my phone.

"Ready?" Blaire asked.

"Yep. Let's go."

Piper joined us in the living room, and we piled into her Jeep before we were on our way to the soccer fields. The top and sides were off of the Jeep. Piper and Blaire sang along to the latest Halsey song at the top of their lungs. They both had great voices. I was surprised I'd never really heard them sing before.

We arrived to the fields early, but neither of Julian's cars was there. Hollin was hopping out of his truck right as Piper parked. He came around to the side to grab his bag, and his hulking bulk got right up in her space.

She cursed under her breath. "Hollin, personal space exists."

"Oh, don't act like you don't like it, Medina."

"You wish."

He smirked. A primal thing that made Piper's back stiffen. "You know, if you ever need to get that stick out of your ass, I could always help."

She glared at him as she slammed the car door. "Fuck you, Abbey."

He winked. "We'll see."

Steam rose from the top of her head. She was so pissed at him. I thought she might launch herself across the small space and claw his eyes out. Blaire and I were both paralyzed on the other side of the Jeep, waiting to see what she'd do.

But as if realizing that he was getting to her, Piper just slung her purse onto her shoulder and brushed past him without a word. Blaire and I exchanged a look. She shrugged like she didn't know. I didn't either. Hollin sure liked pushing her buttons though. And he swaggered away onto the field like his shorts couldn't contain the junk between his legs.

"They're something," I muttered to Blaire.

"Tell me about it."

"What the hell happened?"

She shrugged. "I don't know. Nothing as far as I know."

We headed toward the fields. No sign of Julian or Jordan or any other Wrights for that matter. Isaac and Annie were already on the field, kicking the ball back and forth. Cézanne's box braids were swinging as she tried to get around her boyfriend and the goalie, Gerome. He laughed and blocked her easily, even as he pulled his locs up out of his face. Nora was sitting on the bleachers, next to her best friend, Tamara. August stood between them, smiling at both girls as if he had a very dirty dream in front of him. We were just missing Julian.

"Going to warm up," Blaire said, dropping her bag. "Julian will be here. He never misses without letting us know."

I nodded. I didn't know why I hadn't gone over to his house yesterday. It wasn't like I needed an invitation. But he also always responded to my messages. I was overthinking, overreacting, but my anxiety did that. The Xanax was keeping me calm as I waited.

"Two minutes, y'all," Isaac called. The rest of the team moved onto the field toward him. His brow furrowed as he looked around for Julian. But there was no Julian. "Where the hell is he?"

Everyone shrugged. The whistle blew to get into position for the game to start. And then they were off, playing one man down without Julian, one of their best players. What the hell?

"Here!" Julian called. He was dashing toward the field,

his soccer bag banging into his thigh. He flashed me a smile as he passed, but he didn't stop. "Sorry."

"Get your ass out here, Wright," Isaac called from his midfield position.

"Yep. Yep," he said, sliding into his cleats and stuffing shin guards into his socks. "My bad."

And then he was jogging in place while he waited for the ref to let him on. He hadn't even said a word to me. Just one slightly manic smile. And he had been late. Julian Wright was never late.

I sank into a seat next to Piper. She was lathering sunscreen onto her tan skin, a hat atop her head to block her face. She offered the bottle to me. "*Mi abuelita* always says, 'Better safe than sorry.' "

"Thanks. I burn like a lobster."

"What's with your boy?"

"What's with yours?" I countered.

She arched an eyebrow. "Bradley and I are off-again."

"We both know that's not who I meant."

She huffed. "Hollin can go fuck himself."

I smirked. "You know he likes to see your reaction."

"Yeah, whatever." She eyed me again. "And Julian? I saw that deflection."

"No idea, honestly. He hasn't returned my messages since yesterday, and he's never late, but here he is."

"Late."

I nodded.

"Well, boy needs to get his shit together. If he hurts my friend, I'll cut him."

I saw something savage cross her face and didn't doubt her for a second. But the thought of Julian hurting me made my insides twist.

"Maybe it's a misunderstanding."

She shot me a look that said I couldn't be that naive. And she was right. My anxiety never let me think the best of someone.

So, I sat and watched the game. Blaire was a force to be reckoned with. Her feet were quick, and her shots were on fire today. August kept getting in her way, not passing the ball, but somehow, she made up for him. Hollin made a few incredible stops, and Gerome saved more balls than I'd ever seen. In fact, this might be the first match that I'd seen an even competition with the other team.

And it was the wrong day for that to be the case. Because Julian was off his game. Completely off of his game. I'd never seen him flub so many passes and seemingly trip over his own feet. He usually had mad ball skills, toying with the other team. Today, two times in a row, the ball had been stolen from him by a tiny girl about Nora's size. She was good, but she wasn't better than Julian on a good day.

I frowned at the display. "Something's wrong."

"Yeah, your boy *sucks*." Piper laughed when I frowned at her. "I mean, arguably, I know nothing about soccer, but he looks *bad* out there."

He did. And the team couldn't recover from him screwing up. At the end of the day, we lost, and it was hard to place the blame anywhere else.

Everyone trudged off the field, exhausted and dejected. Isaac tried for a pep talk, but no one was really listening. They downed their water bottles and changed out of their cleats.

Blaire plopped onto the seat next to Piper. "Well, that blew."

"Better luck next time," Piper said.

I patted Blaire on the shoulder. "Sorry."

She laughed and shrugged it off. "No big deal." She was looking down at her phone.

Then she gasped.

"What?" Piper and I asked together.

"You posted the Campbell picture!" she almost shrieked.

"Uh, yeah. So?"

She whipped it around to me. "Cosmere fans got ahold of it. It's viral. You already have over a million likes."

My vision blurred, and I took the phone from her to look at it. Thousands of comments. A million likes. On *one* image.

"Oh my God," I gasped.

"Congratulations!" Blaire said, throwing her arms around me. "I knew it!"

"This is so great, Jen," Piper said.

I handed the phone back. "Wow. Like...wow. What do I do?"

"First off, don't read the comments. Second, actually, why don't I handle your social media for you for a while?" Blaire said.

"Good idea."

"You look like you're in shock."

"I am."

"This is good!" Blaire said.

"What's good?" Julian asked, appearing next to us.

Blaire gave him the rundown, and his eyes widened.

"Holy shit," he breathed.

"I know," I whispered. "I don't know what to do about it."

"Nothing. Leave it to me," Blaire said, holding her hand out for my phone. I passed it to her. "I got this."

Blaire and Piper leaned into my phone as Blaire did her thing. I trusted her to handle this since she was a viral phenomenon and I was clearly...not.

I turned to my boyfriend. He'd dropped into the seat

with his head buried into his bag, trying not to let everyone see how rattled he was.

"Hey," I said.

He smiled at me. "Hey. I'm so proud of you."

"Thanks. It's kind of...surreal."

"I could see that."

I bit my lip. "Are you okay?"

"Just a game," he said with a shrug.

But there was something else. I knew it.

"I haven't heard from you since yesterday." My voice felt small, but the fact that I was even bringing it up was a huge step. I'd never held my own like this before.

His face looked pained, and he jumped to his feet. "Fuck, I'm sorry. My phone died yesterday. I have to get another one, and I didn't have time today."

"Oh," I said softly. Such an easy explanation. "I just thought...you'd find a way to reach me."

He ran a hand back through his hair. "Yeah. That's entirely my fault. I've been swamped with work, and I haven't looked up. I actually forgot about the game today. What with the Wright event tonight at the vineyard, it's been nuts."

"Right. Of course."

"Hey, hey," he said, taking my hands in his and bringing them to his lips. "I'm really sorry. I should have thought about how it would look to not respond. Why don't we go and get me a new phone right now?"

"But don't you have work for the event tonight?"

He blew out a heavy breath. "Yeah. I really do."

"Then don't worry about it. You can get one tomorrow."

"You're sure?"

"Yeah. I have to get dressed for the party anyway. I'll see you there."

He opened his mouth like he wanted to say more. His eyes had gone distant. Like there was something else eating at him.

"Julian, are you really okay?"

Just as fast as the question was out of my mouth, the look disappeared from his face. "Yeah. Yes. Totally. It's been a rough week. I'll see you tonight."

"Okay. You might need a break after this."

He laughed. "Take me back to Cabo, will you?"

"Anytime."

He pressed a kiss into my hair. "See you tonight, Dreamsicle."

"Oh my God, that nickname," I said, flushing from head to toe.

"I do it just to see you blush."

"Everything makes me blush."

He winked at me. "Don't I know it?"

And then I watched my boyfriend walk away. Something worried at me though. Like this conversation wasn't over. Like there was more that he wasn't saying. But I didn't know what it could possibly be.

34

JENNIFER

*N*ora was a magician. There was no other explanation for the dream world that she had created inside the barn at Wright Vineyard. It hardly even looked rustic after she was done with it. Long white drapes covered most of the exposed walls. Chandeliers hung all around the room. Circular tables lined the perimeter with elegant floral arrangements set amid wrought iron candelabras and purple velour runners. An enormous *WC*—for Wright Construction—was next to the stage, draped in vines and flowers, a perfect backdrop for pictures. Everything was lush and over the top.

"You are a little genius," I told her as I stared in awe. I couldn't even bring my camera up to my face to see it all through the lens.

"Thanks. I've been working day and night. I even had August freaking build the *WC* because I couldn't find anything that matched my vision."

"He built that himself?"

"Yeah. His dad is a carpenter, and they put it together. I'm so blessed."

"Is he here?"

She pointed across the barn to where he stood next to Tamara. She was in a slinky dress for the evening, her red hair a pile on top of her head. She had her hand resting on August's sleeve.

"They seem...close," I said carefully.

She laughed. "We're all close. We all grew up together, went to college together, graduated together. He actually dated Tamara in high school. He and I didn't get together until college."

"Really?"

My *worst-case scenario* alarm went off at the intimacy between them. How could they all remain friends? How could she not suspect them? I reeled myself back in. This was my own insecurity screaming at me. If Nora didn't have any, then why should I worry for her? Besides the fact that my anxiety didn't give a shit.

"Yep. The guys are backstage if you want to say hi."

"I do. But I'm going to get some detail shots of your work first."

She beamed. "That's so exciting!"

I smiled at her and then went back to documenting all the little touches she'd put into transforming the room into something good enough for a Wright Construction summer event. Then I dropped the camera around my neck and moved through the backstage entrance.

The first person I saw was Campbell Abbey. My image of him had gone mega viral. Like, I still didn't know the count on comments and likes. It had been shared everywhere with and without my name attached. Blaire said I had a few magazine requests to purchase rights to it for an article. She was vetting them for me. I was glad to have her at my side as a manager because, otherwise, I'd be so overwhelmed that I'd collapse.

"Jennifer!" he crowed, wrapping me in a hug.

I was so shocked that I didn't even move. "Hey."

"Your picture!"

I laughed. "I know. What the hell, right?"

"I love it. It was a great experience. Actually, I pitched to the record label that you should take the cover photo for the next album."

My body turned to jelly. My legs buckled, and then I was falling, stumbling. Campbell put an arm out to steady me.

"Hey, hey, whoa!" he said with a laugh.

"You're serious?"

"Yeah, dude. They were into it. They think you have a special eye."

I might die happy. I was going to take the picture for the cover of Cosmere's next album. The record label wanted me. They thought I was special. Holy fucking shit!

"You can say something."

I opened and closed my mouth. "I don't know what to say."

"Say yes."

I laughed. "Yes! Of course I want to do that."

"Excellent. I'll get you in touch with them. I'm pumped about this."

Campbell was practically bubbling with excitement. I'd seen him in a lot of elements in the few months that I'd known him—which I couldn't even believe that I could say —but here he was, in another world. As if embracing my passion ignited his own.

"Thank you so much, Campbell," I said honestly.

"Art is the reason we live and not just survive."

Something got stuck in my throat, and I could only nod

at that assessment. He was right. I wasn't used to other people acknowledging that.

Campbell's face turned serious. "Excuse me for a second."

Then he headed away from me. I followed his direction and found Blaire on her phone. She was stunning in a gauzy dress that only she could pull off. Campbell stopped in front of her and cleared his throat.

I saw the word that she said to him from here. *No.*

He reached for her as she made to leave, but she used those excellent soccer skills to evade him. I sighed in confusion at the pair of them as he followed her out the side door. I wasn't blind. I could see that something had to have happened with them at some point. Why else would they be so strange? But I'd never worked up the courage to ask Blaire. I didn't want her to shut down, and honestly, it wasn't my business.

"What are you looking at?" Julian asked, coming up behind me.

I jumped. "Oh God, you surprised me."

He laughed. "Sorry. You seemed intense."

"It was nothing." I waved off everything I'd seen as I turned to my boyfriend. He seemed more put together than he had at the soccer game this afternoon, but there were nerves underneath all of that charm and style. I wasn't sure if it was just the party or something else. I'd never seen him like this. "Are you ready for the event?"

"As I'll ever be."

"Nora really knocked it out of the park."

"Yeah. I can't wait for my cousins to see the place." He beamed with pride at the thought. It erased whatever was festering underneath for that second, and he was here with me again.

Owen Wright stood with Jordan, talking animatedly.

"You invited your dad?" I asked skeptically.

"Jor did," he said with a shrug.

"I can't believe he has the gall. Did he run it by Morgan?"

Julian nodded. "Yeah. She said it was fine, but if he got out of line, she'd kick his ass herself."

I laughed because that was so Morgan. "Makes sense."

"Showtime, ladies and gents," Hollin called to everyone standing backstage. "Let's get this show on the road."

"He's really taken to this, hasn't he?" I asked with a laugh, clutching my camera.

"He has." Julian touched my arm. "Guess that's our cue."

We stepped back out to the barn in time to see the doors thrown wide and guests streamed in. Wright Construction held two annual parties for their staff. One in the summer and the other a Christmas party. They decked the place out, hired caterers, and had an open bar to celebrate the employees who put in the work day in and day out. It was a long-standing tradition, and this was the first year that the summer party had ever been off premises.

I set up near the fancy *WC* that August had created and spent a steady hour taking pictures for the employees. It was practically a photo booth with how much everyone wanted their picture taken. It was a good sign for the company. They were cared for and appreciated enough to want to stand in front of the logo.

Eventually, much of the party had settled into the round tables, and food was brought out. There was a lull in my job. Something I would never take for granted. I headed away from the crowd, snapping a shot of Jensen and Emery rocking a sleeping Robin as I passed. Their table was packed full of Wrights. Heidi and Landon sat together, Holden noticeably absent. Austin and Julia were bickering and pointing at each other, as per usual. Patrick sat next to them, shaking his head. Morgan was nowhere to be seen, probably prepping for her big speech with David. Sutton was at a table, her children absent as well, with the rest of the girls— Annie, Piper, and a withdrawn Blaire.

I bypassed them all and leaned against the barn door. I nodded to our security. Zach was a friend of Hollin's, even more giant with more tattoos, a beard, and a *don't fuck with me* grin. They drove motorcycles together on their day off.

"Hey, Zach."

"Jennifer," he said, nodding back. As pleasant as his gruff voice got.

I pulled out a protein bar to keep my energy up. I'd been offered an area in the back room to eat, but I didn't like to be off of the floor. I'd have plenty of time to eat later.

"Full event," I muttered.

He nodded. "Yep."

And that was about the extent of Zach's communication skills.

We stood there in silence while the rest of the party ate. People were finishing soon after and heading back out onto the dance floor. I needed to get moving again, but I stood a second longer to watch it all at a distance. I wouldn't be able to actually see it close up. Not through my camera lens. Not without the social anxiety pressing in on me about the fact that I'd have to get into that large group of people.

I pulled the camera up to my face and scanned the room with it, getting a feel for where I should go next.

And then someone straggled in late to the party. He wasn't even dressed for the event, which was cocktail attire. This guy wore distressed jeans and a flannel button-up. His dark hair was long and shaggy, tumbling into his eyes. He swept it away, revealing the deep, dark eyes underneath. Eyes that looked...oddly familiar.

He paced a second and then turned, jumping slightly, as if surprised to see me.

"Are you here for the Wright Construction event?" I asked. He blinked at me in a way that said what I already knew—he wasn't here for that. "The vineyard is closed to the public tonight for a private event."

"Oh. Uh, no. I'm here to talk to Jordan or Julian Wright. Do you know them?"

My eyebrows shot up. "You need to speak to the owners?"

"The owners," he said softly. "Yeah, I do. Could you point them out to me?"

"I..." I stared at him a second longer in confusion. I wanted to ask him more, but when I opened my mouth to do so, Julian was at my side.

"Hey, what's going on?"

"Julian," I breathed in relief. "This guy was looking for you."

Julian held his hand out with that same charming smile. "I'm Julian Wright. How can I help you?"

The man shook his hand. "Uh, hey." He slid a hand back through his hair, brushing the curling ends off his forehead as he blew out a breath. "I'm Weston Wright."

35

JULIAN

*W*eston. Wright.

I froze at those words, my eyes widening. For one of the few times in my life, I had nothing to say. I had no idea where to even begin.

Because Weston hadn't included a picture in that original email. That might have been enough to convince me that he might be who he said he was. We didn't look identical. Not by a long shot. Not like me and Jor. But we had the same stature, the same dark hair and eyes, the same presence. That was all I could describe it as.

"Sorry about this," Weston said immediately. "I didn't mean to barge in on your party. I didn't know that this would be going on."

"What are you doing here?" I managed to get out.

"Well, I sent you and your brother an email a few weeks ago."

"We received it."

Weston startled at those words. He looked so young. He was only twenty-two, fresh out of college. He was Nora's age, for Christ's sake. I was seven years older, and I'd never felt so *old.* I remembered being so uncertain at his age. How had he worked up the nerve to come to Lubbock?

"You didn't respond," Weston accused.

And it was an accusation. He looked hurt. As if he couldn't think of a single reason that I wouldn't want to respond to that email.

"Maybe we should take this outside," Jennifer suggested. Her gaze was on the crowd of Wright Construction employees. They hadn't yet noticed us, but it was a big enough disruption that they soon might.

"I can't believe that you didn't respond," Weston said.

What was I supposed to say? That I didn't believe him? I didn't *want* to believe him? Fuck.

"And you thought the best response was to fly to Lubbock?" I asked in confusion.

"Julian," Jennifer whispered. She nodded to him, as if to say, *Look, he's hurt.*

But I didn't know how I was supposed to take this. Dad had said that he wasn't our brother. Mom had had no clue about it. We'd agreed to ignore the email. Jordan had that PI out there, but we hadn't heard anything back yet. Now, Weston was standing right in front of me. Right when the rest of my world was a fucking nightmare.

I blew out a heavy breath. "Sorry, I'm just shocked."

Weston nodded stiffly. "I didn't fly out here. A friend needed someone to play keys at a few shows across the southwest. I've been out of Seattle for two weeks, touring California, Arizona, New Mexico, and Texas. Abilene was our last stop. I was supposed to be on a plane home, but I was two hours from here." He held his hands up helplessly. "I couldn't do leave. So, I rented a car and drove into Lubbock. I just got here."

Jennifer gaped next to me. Her hands shook on her

camera. I wanted to wrap her up and protect her from this. I wanted her to shield me from what was coming. Because I didn't know how to handle this. My charm couldn't fix this.

"I think Jennifer's right," I forced out. "We need to move this outside or into the back room. This is a private event."

Weston nodded, deflating at the words. "Sure. Sure."

I wanted to know what the hell he'd expected to happen. How he'd even known that we'd *be* here. It had been a huge risk to just show up here.

We were heading toward the door when Jordan pushed his way through the crowd, angling straight for me. "Julian."

I stopped at the door at the tone of his voice. He wasn't exactly mad, but I could hear the tightly held control. The sound of him wanting desperately to punch something but not giving in to the temptation. The fact that I could even hear the threat in his voice was a bad sign.

"What's going on?" I asked. "Is something wrong?"

"I've been texting you. What the hell have you been doing?"

"My phone is broken," I told him. "I meant to go today—"

"Forget it," he said gruffly. "Look at what arrived."

He shoved his phone into my hand. A wave of déjà vu washed over me. The last time this had happened, my world had been turned upside down. Ashleigh had been trying to sabotage the winery, and I'd had to break off our two-year relationship. A part of me didn't want to look, didn't want to know. But I couldn't walk away. Not with Jordan's anger barely holding on to a thread.

The email was from Jordan's PI. I read the email with cold dread coursing through me. Pictures were included at the bottom. One showed my dad's arm around Weston Wright. Another with him talking to Weston and...his brother? Twin brother? Christ, they looked identical, except for the hair and clothes. Weston's was longer, almost shaggy. The other guy had it cropped short. Weston wore what I could only describe as rocker chic. Something Campbell would be seen in. His brother was in a blazer, something I'd wear. But they were undeniably twins.

Looks like you were right. After I completed my investigation, I can confirm as best I can that your dad seems to have two boys, one being Weston, who emailed you. Doesn't look like he's on social, as you suspected. The other is Whitton Wright. I can't confirm biologically, but he treats them like kids, and they have the last names. Also, there's one more thing.

I scrolled to the next picture of a teenage girl in cutoff jean shorts and a crop top. Her long black hair nearly reached her waist. She was a dead ringer for Sutton, even a decade younger.

Looks like there's a daughter, too. Harley Wright, age seventeen, upcoming high school senior. Didn't dig too much on her, but she has the same last name. So, I'd guess that's as much as you need to know.

The email went on with more pictures and more explanations of his methods. I didn't need it all. I didn't need any of it. I had everything I needed to know right here.

Our dad had other kids. *Three* other kids. Weston and Whitton being twins would have made sense. That was the same time frame that our parents had split up. It could have been an accident. Something we'd hate him for hiding from us, but at least he'd provided for them. Or something.

But Harley.

She was five years younger than her brothers. She was still in high school. Our parents had been together then. I'd been twelve. Jordan had been fourteen, a freshman in high school. Dad had still come to all of my soccer games. He'd attended everything Jordan had at school and in debate and all that. And he'd also cheated on Mom.

He'd cheated on Mom.

He had this other family.

These two boys and a little girl.

In Seattle.

He'd had them this whole time.

And he was still seeing them.

Still around them enough to have our PI take pictures of him with them.

And he'd *lied* about it.

He'd cheated on Mom and lied about it.

We'd asked him point-blank if Weston was his kid, and he'd looked us in the face and *lied*.

He'd fucking lied.

"What is it?" Jennifer asked softly, as if she could see I was about to explode.

"You have a brother and sister," I said to Weston.

Jordan jumped when he realized who was standing in front of us. "What are you doing here?"

"This is Jordan," I said by way of introduction. "Jordan, our brother Weston."

Jordan stared in confusion. "But what are you doing here?"

"He had a gig in Abilene and drove over because we hadn't written back."

"Why do you suddenly believe me? And how do you know about Whitt and Harley?" Weston asked, equally confused.

"I hired a private investigator," Jordan explained.

"What?" Weston squawked. "What for?"

"We didn't believe you," I said.

"Oh," Weston said. "I, uh...why not?"

"Our dad said that you didn't exist," Jordan said indignantly.

"What?" he asked again. "He didn't say that. I saw him two weeks ago!"

"Yeah. So, you can see why we didn't want to take you at your word."

"But you hired a PI anyway?" Weston asked.

"Always better to get the truth," Jordan said. "And now... we know."

Weston blinked. "You're ruthless."

"That would be our father," I drawled. "And I think it's time that he's in on this family bonding."

"Wait...he's here?" Weston asked.

"He's here," Jordan confirmed.

"Why? What did he tell you he was doing?"

Weston crossed his arms. "He...he works in Vancouver, like, every other weekend. He sits on boards and stuff. He was going to be up there. That's why I figured it would be good to see you. I didn't even know you were all still talking. He told us that he was divorced."

"He is," Jordan agreed. "But he doesn't live in Vancouver anymore."

I shrugged. "Or maybe he does. Why don't we finally find out what's a lie and what's the truth?"

Then the three of us turned as one as Owen Wright— our father, resident liar—materialized out of the crowd to stand before us with terrified, wide eyes.

36

JENNIFER

"West?" Owen said.

My stomach turned over at the sound of that voice. I'd been a silent witness to everything that had happened. I'd been rooted to the spot, unable to move or think or breathe. I certainly couldn't walk away as it all came out. All the bullshit and lying that Owen had gotten away with for more than two decades.

He had another family. Three kids and a mistress at the very least. He'd told Jordan and Julian that it wasn't true. He'd spun some believable tale, thinking the boys would sweep it under the rug. But the problem with lying was that, eventually, the truth always came out.

"Dad," Weston said, his voice uncertain.

"What are you doing here?"

"I keep getting that question," he said. "I think by now it's obvious."

"You lied," Jordan snarled. "You lied about everything."

"I didn't."

Julian shook his head. There was fire in his eyes. "Don't try to deny it. We hired a PI, and now, we know the truth."

Owen Wright paled to translucent paper. His veins were visible. His skin leeched of color. "You hired a PI?" he said, as if it were inconceivable.

"I did," Jordan said. "And I'm fucking glad I did since you're a lying bastard."

"Jordan—"

"I trusted you! I put my neck out for you. I told Julian that we should give you another chance. And you spit on that."

People were definitely watching now. We were a spectacle. Something I hated, but I wasn't the center of it. I was standing in the spotlight as they tore into Owen Wright. Who fucking deserved it as far as I was concerned.

Wrights got to their feet. Jensen took a few steps forward, Austin and Landon at his back. As if they'd step in if necessary. Morgan's eyes were storm clouds as she crossed her arms and stared daggers into the back of Owen's head. This had been another chance for her, too. She'd believed Jordan when he asked for Owen to come here. That he wasn't going to cause more trouble.

Owen was a tornado. You always thought you were fine one block over until it twisted in your direction and bowled your house down to the foundation.

"How could you look us in the eye and say that Weston wasn't our brother?" Julian asked. His calm was lethal, the eye of the storm. "How could you lie when we came to you for the truth?"

"Julian, it wasn't..."

"You told them I wasn't their brother?" Weston asked.

"I..."

"Yes, and he didn't mention that you had a twin or a sister either," Julian added.

Owen gulped. "You know about Whitt and Harley?"

"Private investigators are thorough, it turns out," Jordan drawled, crossing his arms.

"We could have forgiven you if you'd told the truth," Julian said. "I *wanted* to believe you."

"We both did," Jordan said.

"But you cheated on Mom. You said you loved her, and you had a family behind her back."

"Boys, this is...it's all a misunderstanding," Owen said, trying to spin the situation. But his days of spinning were over. There was no out for him here. And as he looked between his three sons, he saw no remedy to his solution. It was over. It was all over.

Jensen dropped a heavy hand onto Owen's shoulder. Austin took up the other side.

"It's time for you to leave," Jensen said as calm and collected as ever. But he wasn't a man to be fucked with. Not on a good day, and Jensen never forgave people who hurt his family.

"Jensen," Owen said, straightening. "Surely, there's no need for that."

Jensen looked at him flatly. "On Morgan's orders, you were allowed to attend this event as long as you didn't cause trouble. To be honest, I voted against it. Said you weren't worth it. It's disappointing to be proven right."

Then Zach was inside, pushing through the lot of them. He actually looked eager. It had to be boring to stand outside the door all night with nothing to do. Now, he got to throw someone out. Excellent.

Jensen handed him off to Zach, and then Owen was dragged toward the boys.

"Please, let me explain."

"There's nothing left to explain," Julian said with sorrow in his voice.

"You've done enough damage," Jordan growled.

Weston crossed his arms and looked away. As if he couldn't even look at his dad. Was that because disappointment was too keen or because he hadn't expected it from his dad? He'd obviously had questions if he'd emailed Julian and Jordan to begin with.

Suddenly, a voice cleared over a microphone at the other end of the room. Morgan stood on the stage, drawing all eyes toward her and away from the commotion at the back of the room.

"Hello, and thank you for showing up for our annual summer event. It's a great pleasure to see all of you here and enjoying the evening. I don't want to take up too much of your time, but I'm supposed to give a speech, so here I am."

Some people laughed softly, and just like that, Morgan had broken the tension. Everyone stayed focused on her while she gave her short speech and then announced a special treat—Campbell Abbey would be performing an acoustic set. That won everyone over as they cheered, and Campbell walked out with an acoustic guitar around his neck.

"Outside," Jordan ordered.

And no one argued as Weston and Julian trailed after him. Jensen and Austin nodded their way and then went back to their table. I wanted to go after them, but Campbell was playing, and clearly, I needed to be taking pictures of this. I wavered to see the three brothers together, wanting to be there for Julian. But I could also see that he needed a minute. Beyond the immediate anger, he had a much bigger family than he'd ever known, and he was going to need to figure it all out. So, I left the boys outside and went back to photographing Campbell. Annie and Sutton slid to my side. Piper and Blaire not far behind them.

"What the hell was all of that?" Annie asked.

I opened and closed my eyes. "That's Weston."

She gaped. "Oh shit. I need to go talk to Jordan."

I grabbed her arm. "I think...we should give them a minute."

"What am I missing?" Piper asked. "Should that name mean something to us?"

Sutton sighed. "It appears that Owen has another kid, and no one knew about it."

Piper gasped. Blaire went pale.

"They're all mad that he didn't tell them?" Blaire asked softly.

"That he lied about it. Plus, it's three kids, not just one."

"What?" Sutton breathed.

I explained about the PI and the three kids. It'd all be out in the open soon enough. No reason to hide it any longer. They all looked shaken and horrified by this news.

"Fuck," Annie said. Her eyes went to the door, tracking her boyfriend.

I went back to work, shooting the rest of the party and trying not to think about the people who were still absent from the room. Julian and Jordan never walked back in through the front door.

I opted for a break and headed into the backstage after Campbell finished his short set. I startled when I saw Jordan and Julian were back there, seated around a circular table, with a half-empty bottle of bourbon between them.

Campbell laughed when he saw them. "Hey, pour me a glass."

Jordan tipped the bottle to his lips and took a swig, passing it to Julian, who did the same.

Campbell shook his head. "One of those nights, huh?"

"You have no idea," Jordan muttered.

Campbell laughed, unaware of what had happened, and headed into the dressing room.

I took a breath and then sank into a seat next to them. "Hey, how are you holding up?"

Julian held the bottle up to me in cheers. "Today can fuck right off."

"I'm sorry about your dad. What happened with Weston?"

"He felt terrible and apologized a dozen times for barging in," Jordan said. "He didn't know about the party."

"How'd he even know to come to the winery?"

Jordan rolled his eyes. "That damn interview Julian did for the opening."

"Hey, you all thought it was a good idea at the time," he slurred slightly.

How much of that bourbon had he already had?

"Hindsight," Jordan grumbled. "Anyway, when he looked us up, that comes up on the Google search, and it said we were open tonight. We hadn't posted that we were closed for a private event. We'd just canceled tours and such."

"Wow," I whispered. "I can't believe he's really your brother. You looked all over for him online."

"Yeah, he's not on social media," Jordan said. "He said that the musician work he does is backing band for tours. So, it's not like he's...Campbell."

"I didn't know people could be offline," Jennifer said.

"Apparently," Jordan said, reaching for the bottle. "And apparently our dad can have a son that no one knows about."

"And a twin and another sister," Julian said, dropping his head back. "Our dad is a real son of a bitch."

"Yeah," Jordan said with a sigh. "He really is."

"So, what's the plan? What are you going to do?"

Julian shrugged. "We have to tell Mom."

"Ugh," I groaned.

"And we're meeting Weston for breakfast tomorrow to talk," Jordan added.

"Really? Do you want to get to know them?"

"That's what we need to figure out." Julian downed the rest of the bottle in long gulps.

"Whoa, whoa, whoa," Jordan said, snatching the bottle back. "You don't have my tolerance, little bro."

Julian dipped his head back and flipped him off. "I've had a night. I can indulge."

Jordan shot me a pained look. This was hitting Julian way harder than Jordan. Even though Jordan had been the optimistic one about Owen's repentance. He'd been the one to convince Julian to give him another chance. But Jordan was hardened, and Julian wasn't. Jordan had always protected him, and now, he'd pushed him right into the thick of things.

"Maybe you should get him home," Jordan suggested.

"I'm fine," he muttered, pointedly taking back the bottle and finishing it.

Jordan winced. Alcoholism ran in their family. None of them liked to talk about it, but it wasn't a good sign for Julian.

"Hey, come on. Let's get going."

"You have to work still," he mumbled.

"I got everything I need," I assured him.

Jordan got an arm under Julian and helped him out of the chair. Together, we hauled him out the back way and toward his Audi. I fished in his pocket for the keys, unlocking the behemoth. I'd never driven the thing, but I'd come over with my roommates, so I didn't have Bertha here.

Once Jordan got Julian into the passenger seat, I waved

him good-bye and pulled out of the parking lot in halting, nervous sputters. The SUV was twice as big as my car, and the last thing I wanted was to wreck his car as I drove him home. Julian spun the radio on and rolled the window down to let in the hot, dusty summer air. Rap music blasted through the speakers, but I didn't turn it down. He was drunk and hurting and probably needed a shower and a good, long nap. If he had to face his brother tomorrow, face telling his mom, he deserved to do whatever he wanted to cope tonight.

I thought that I might have to carry him through the house once we got there, but he jumped out of the SUV on his own and stepped inside without a word. I dumped the keys onto a table next to the garage door and followed him. I found him in the kitchen.

"Julian," I said.

"Hmm," he said as he popped the top on the unopened whiskey and poured himself a full glass. "Want some?"

"No thanks."

I didn't know how to help or what I could do. But drinking was probably not the answer.

"Do you want to talk about what happened?"

"You know, I really don't." Then he drank it back like a shot.

"Do you think getting black-out drunk will make things better?"

"Nope," he said, smacking his lips. "I really don't."

"Okay."

He dropped the glass into the sink and carried the bottle with him to the couch. "But I think it'll make me forget that tonight happened—at least for a few hours." He patted the couch next to him. "Come. Sit."

I dropped the camera on the nearby table, kicked off my

shoes, and curled up onto the couch next to him. He turned on the television and wrapped an arm around me. I wanted to believe that things would be better in the morning, but I'd never seen Julian like this before.

I worried that what had happened with his dad had broken him in some fundamental way, and I wasn't sure who he was going to be in the morning.

37

JENNIFER

*T*he next morning, I woke to the sound of Julian vomiting in the toilet.

"Ugh," I groaned, rolling over and covering my ears with a pillow. Not that it did much to hide the sound of his retching.

He deserved it after he'd had so much to drink that he'd passed out. I'd never seen him drink like that, and I hoped that I never saw it again. It was a new level of terrible.

The toilet flushed, and Julian came back into the room, flopping down on the bed. "Sorry," he muttered, covering his eyes. "Might have had too much to drink last night."

"Might?" I said with a laugh.

"I'm never drinking again."

I shook my head. "Lies."

"Yeah, but, not anytime soon. Or like that."

"You wanted to forget."

He gave me a thumbs-up. "Success."

I chuckled and dropped out of bed. "I'll find you some Tylenol."

"You're the best."

I rolled my eyes at him as I headed out of the bedroom. I poured him a glass of water and knocked out two Tylenol from the bottle. I carried them back into the bedroom for him.

"Thank you," he said, downing them and falling back.

"Eggs and toast?" I suggested.

He groaned and shook his head. "Food is a bad idea."

"Don't you have breakfast plans with Weston still?"

"Fuck," he spat into the pillow. "Fuck, fuck, fuck."

"Shower," I said, pointing to the bathroom. "And then some toast."

He grumbled but heaved his body off of the bed and into the shower. I made myself some toast, eating it as I buttered his toast. He came into the living room with downcast eyes, a hand still clutching his head.

I slid the plate across to him on the kitchen island.

"Thanks."

He took a small bite of the toast, trying to calm his rumbling stomach and ease the hangover that was thick on him. He didn't say anything, just ate each piece of toast in tiny little bites. I didn't have any idea how he was going to meet Weston in the state he was in.

After he finished, he cleared his plate, washed it off, and deposited it into the dishwasher. "Thanks for taking care of me."

"No problem," I said easily.

"Last night was..." He shook his head. "I don't know. I don't want to think about it."

"It's fine. You can have a bad night after what you went through."

He smiled softly at me and then winced. "It seems I'm entitled to a bad morning as well."

I laughed at him. "When's your meeting? I left my car at home. Should I call someone to get me?"

"No, I'll take you."

"You should take a cab."

He sighed. "Is it that bad?"

"Yeah," I said with a smile.

He was still gorgeous to me, but he looked rough from the alcohol. Dark circles under his eyes, pale skin, and his hair was all mussed from the shower. He did not look like he was ready to tackle everything he needed to get through today.

"All right. If you say so. I'll grab an Uber or something."

I slid my phone out of my purse and texted Annie to see if she was free. She responded almost immediately, saying that she'd be there ASAP. That she had to get to the hospital and it was on her way.

"Annie is going to get me."

He blew out a breath. "Well, that's good at least. Now, if my headache would cease to exist, that'd be great, too."

"Poor baby," I said with a laugh, kissing his cheek.

I headed back into the bedroom to change back into my dress from last night, leaving Julian's T-shirt on his bed. I picked up my purse, cursing myself for not taking my meds while Julian had showered. Now, I'd have to wait until I got home. I really preferred taking it first thing when I woke up. Oh well.

"Maybe we could pretend we haven't woken up and go back to bed for the rest of the day," Julian suggested.

I dropped my bag onto the side table and ran a hand back through my messy bob. "As much as I'd like that, you have things to do today."

"Yeah. I don't want to though."

"Tough," I teased.

He stepped forward, like he was going to draw me to him, but then the front door burst open. We stumbled apart in confusion as Ashleigh Sinclair strode in.

"Hey, baby," she crooned. "I think I figured out our little distribution problem. Why are you not returning my calls?"

I gaped at her. She was in some white skirt suit with an actual silk scarf tied around her neck and four-inch nude high heels. Her hair and makeup were done up, as if for an event. She looked flawless as she carried a black leather folder before her.

"Ashleigh," Julian said, his voice dipped with warning.

She smirked at him. "Don't you look charming in this little...number?" She gestured up and down at him, still in basketball shorts and a worn-out T-shirt. "We're going to need to get you cleaned up, so we can make the meeting with the distributors."

I looked back and forth between them in confusion. "What is going on?"

Ashleigh sighed heavily and turned to me. "Oh, you're still here?"

"Still here? I'm his girlfriend. What are *you* doing here?"

Ashleigh shot me a look of straight pity. "He didn't tell you?"

"Tell me what?"

"Ashleigh, this isn't the time," Julian said.

I whirled on him. "Tell me what?"

Julian held his aching head. "There was a...problem with the distributors. So, I asked Ashleigh for her help because she knows them."

"When?" I snapped.

"Uh...Friday night."

I saw red at those words. I stumbled back a step from him. The man I'd spent all night and morning taking care of. And now, he was telling me that the night that he'd refused to take my calls or answer my texts was the night he had been with his ex-girlfriend.

"And you never thought to mention that when I was trying to get ahold of you that night?"

"My phone is really broken," he said hastily. "I don't have it."

"Is *that* why you aren't answering my calls?" Ashleigh said.

"And the next day at the soccer game?" I accused. "Or the vineyard party?"

"There's an easy explanation for why he didn't tell you," Ashleigh said with a viperous smile.

"Stay out of this," Julian said, wincing all the time.

"Oh no, I think she's right," I said, glancing at Ashleigh. "For once, we're actually in agreement. There's clearly a reason you didn't tell me."

"I didn't tell anyone," he said. "The distributors came back with some bullshit excuse for why they wouldn't work with Wright Vineyard. I panicked and went to Ashleigh to try to figure out if we could fix it. It had nothing to do with her."

"Didn't it? Isn't that why you didn't tell me? Why you didn't go to me?"

"Why would he go to you?" Ashleigh scoffed. "What do you know about business? What contacts do you have?"

My breath came out uneven as the first working of a panic attack clouded my vision and wobbled through my body. I didn't want this to happen. I didn't want my body to take over for me, but I was helpless to stop it. And I'd forgotten to take my anxiety meds this morning. Oh fuck...

I scrambled through my bag, seemingly uncaring that they were both watching me have a freak-out. I shook a pill out into my hand and downed it dry. I didn't even care at that point. I couldn't care. Not when my entire body threatened to shut down as reality washed over me.

Julian had hidden this from me. He'd lied to me about it. He'd gone to his ex-girlfriend, who he'd claimed to hate. And yet, he'd chosen *her* over me. Her. Over me.

What had I been thinking all this time? That things with Julian were just too perfect. If something looked too good to be true, it probably was. I'd been living in this dream world. Julian and I were happy, and nothing could break that. Everything was fine. I belonged here. Finally right here, where I'd always wanted to be. I'd been dreaming, and now, I was awake. The bubble had burst. The dream world was gone. Only reality invaded my mind as I stared at what could have been and saw only what was.

"This isn't what it looks like," Julian insisted.

"It's exactly what it looks like."

"Jesus," Ashleigh said. "Don't you see that she has a problem? She's taking pills right in front of your face now, and you're not wondering why?"

I swallowed harder, glaring at her.

But it was Julian who, just for a fraction of a second, went from concerned to confused. "What pills *are* you taking?"

My voice turned steely. "Oh my God, as if that's anyone's business."

"See," Ashleigh said, "I told you she was doing drugs."

I gasped at the words and stared at her in shock. "I'm *what*?"

"When I saw you at the charity gala, you were doing cocaine in the bathroom. I saw you all sweaty, pupils dilated, wiping your nose. I've seen the addict behavior before."

I shook my head. "You are out of your goddamn mind. You will say *anything* to try to get Julian back."

"I don't have to say anything but the truth."

And then I saw the moment in front of me. Julian wavered at Ashleigh's words. He didn't even see her for the slimy bitch that she was. That she was trying to tear us apart by accusing me of bullshit. He didn't even see what was standing right in front of him. I was furious with him about hiding the distribution issue and going to Ashleigh, but that look...that look broke me.

"Fine. Believe what you want," I said. I snatched up my purse and stormed past them both and out of the house.

Annie pulled into the driveway when I stepped outside. Thank God I'd texted her earlier, or I'd have been walking home. My hands were shaking as the side effects of my panic attack lingered on the periphery.

Julian dashed out after me. He was in no position to run, but our argument must have put his hangover on hold.

"Jen! Jen, wait," he called, reaching for me.

"I don't have anything to say to you," I told him.

"Please, I don't know what she's talking about. I don't know or care about any of it. I don't want you to walk away. I'm sorry. I'm so sorry."

"You lied and hid and second-guessed me and made me second-guess myself. Tell me, Julian, how are you any different than your dad right now?"

He whipped back as shock hit him full on. He opened and closed his mouth. Then it all cleared in his face as he saw exactly what I'd said. "I...I'm not. I'm not him." He reached for me again, snagging my hand and pulling it to him. "Jen, please."

And I wanted so badly to give in to him. Julian Wright was the boy I'd pined after. Who I'd always said that I wasn't good enough for. But standing here, after all the bullshit I'd walked through, I was realizing that maybe I'd been wrong all along. Maybe he wasn't good enough for me.

I'd spent my life tiptoeing around the word *no*. I hated saying it. I *couldn't* say it. I wasn't capable of it. I was a pushover, and I complied with what everyone else wanted. I'd never found my own voice. But if this summer had taught me anything, it was that I had to stick up for myself to get what I wanted and to get the respect I deserved. In my friendships, in my career, and now, in my relationship.

"No," I said softly.

"What?"

"No," I said more forcefully. I extracted my hand. "No, no, no, no, no. And no."

"No what?"

"No to everything. No, I'm not going to just get over this. No, I'm not going to stay and listen to you try to dig yourself out of the grave that you dug yourself. No, I don't owe you an explanation. So, just no, Julian. *No.*"

He stared at me, slack-jawed. He'd never seen me like this before. And that was okay because I'd never seen me like this before either. I kind of liked me like this, to be honest.

So, I stepped back and left him standing in the driveway. I got into the passenger side, and Annie had wide eyes.

"How much did you hear?" I asked as she pulled away.

"Uh...everything." She touched my hand. "Are you okay?"

"No."

The word rolled off of my tongue again as the realization of what I'd done finally sank in. Then I started crying and didn't stop for a long, long time.

38

JULIAN

*J*ennifer had left.

       She'd left with Annie and not even looked back.

I'd done this.

My head felt like someone had split it in two with an ax. My stomach wasn't doing much better. Every nerve in my body was on high alert. I was hungover as fuck. And yet, it was my heart that hurt the worst.

Worst of all because I had done this to myself. I'd driven Jen to make this decision. I'd never heard her speak like she had just spoken to me. And I'd deserved every word of it. Fuck.

And I couldn't even go after her. One, I shouldn't drive right now. She had been right about that. Two, I had that fucking breakfast with Jordan and Weston. I'd already been deeply not looking forward to it. Now, I wanted nothing less. And finally, she didn't want me to. She'd made that clear. I had to give her space even if it was the last thing I wanted to do.

I headed back inside to find Ashleigh sitting at the

kitchen island on her phone with the leather notebook in front of her, as if nothing had happened.

"You should leave," I spat.

She held one finger up as she finished her text. I thought about taking her phone out of her hand and throwing it into the yard.

She looked up. "Sorry, what, babe?"

"I am not your babe. We are not together. You have *no* right to barge into my house ever. *Ever.*"

She just smiled. "Well, I tried calling you."

"As I told you Friday, my phone is broken."

"Still? That's so irresponsible."

I took a deep inhale. "Get out of my house, Ashleigh."

"Okay, but first, let's talk about the distribution meeting. I talked to George and explained the situation. So, we have another meeting with him today via Zoom. Let's get you into a suit and get this wrapped up."

I stared at her as if she'd sprouted an antenna. "Did you not hear a word I just said? I want you out of here."

"Julian, baby," she said, stepping up to me, "what's important right now is the business. We can discuss what we're going to do after we figure out this distribution issue. Together, we're such a powerful team."

"You know what, Ashleigh? I just realized something. Something I should have figured out a long time ago."

"Hmm?"

"If I have to work with you to get this settled, then it isn't worth it."

Her mouth popped open. "How dare you!"

"I want you out of my house. For all I know, you told George not to give me the contract and made yourself the only option."

Her cheeks colored. "I wouldn't..."

"Yes, you would," I said flatly. "You have, and you would. You'd do anything, and in my own fear, I forgot that. I just wanted this so bad. But it's not worth my integrity or my girlfriend."

"You're really going to side with a drug addict over me?"

I took a deep breath. "I don't know what those pills were, but Jen is nothing of the sort. I would have noticed if my girlfriend was on drugs."

"But at the gala—"

"Enough!" I snapped. "Enough. This is enough. I'm done, Ashleigh. I was done months ago, and you need to move on. Just move on and stop ruining my life."

Tears came to her eyes as she closed up her notebook and tucked it under her arm. "I can't move on from you."

"Too bad. You'll have to find a way. Now, kindly get the fuck out of my house."

She swallowed. For a second, she looked like she was going to try to argue with me. But there must have been something in my eyes, something resolute, because it made her finally turn and walk toward the door.

"I still love you, you know," Ashleigh whispered as she pulled it open.

"I don't think you know what that word means," I told her.

She nodded once, her jaw clenched, and then exited my house.

I wanted to not move another muscle until this hangover was gone, or better yet, get rid of this fucking hangover and find a punching bag to channel this energy into, but I didn't have the luxury. Not for either option. I had this fucking breakfast.

I didn't even have time to care about my clothes as I called an Uber to come get me. I left on the clothes I was wearing, threw on a hat, and headed to Stacked, a hole-in-the-wall breakfast joint.

When I arrived, it was bustling. Way more people than I'd thought would be there. I didn't know how Jordan expected us to have this conversation in public. Let alone somewhere *this* public. God, I wanted to reschedule. It was too bad Weston was leaving on the first plane out of Lubbock to head home and deal with his own family problems.

"What happened to you?" Jordan asked when I walked up to the entrance of the restaurant.

"Why?"

"You're wearing basketball shorts in public."

"Yeah?"

"Julian, you're obsessed with your clothes."

"Yeah." I shrugged. At least my headache was finally taken care of, thanks to the Tylenol. But I still felt terrible.

"You're wearing a baseball cap," Jordan said. He flicked the brim.

"Yeah, I get it. I look like shit. I'm hungover, and Jen just broke up with me."

Jordan reared back. "Jennifer Gibson...broke up with *you*?"

"That's what I just said."

"How? Why? Fuck, Julian, I'm speechless."

"Tell me about it. I'm a fucking idiot. That's why she did it."

Jordan arched an eyebrow. "What happened?"

I nodded away from the restaurant and laid it all out as we walked. The bullshit with the distributor, the yo-yo they'd strung me on, how I'd gone to Ashleigh, that Ashleigh had then shown up at my house this morning—all of it. Jordan listened without judgment, and when it was all out, he just sighed.

"Well, yeah, you kind of earned that."

I ran a hand down my face. "I know. But...but is she right?"

"About Dad?"

I nodded. I couldn't help it. I'd always *wanted* to be like dad. I'd worshipped the ground he walked on, but it was always Jordan who was more like Dad, who had gotten his praise and appreciation, who had wanted to run the business. And I was always more like Mom. I resented it. It was why it'd all hurt so bad when he turned out as terrible as he did because he hadn't just ruined himself as a father; he'd ruined himself as my role model and idol. Now, the last thing I wanted was to be like him...after what he had done.

"Am I like Dad?"

"Yes," he said without question, and I winced. "But so am I. Do you know the reason that I invited Dad back into our lives?"

"No," I admitted. "I thought you wanted to move on."

"Well, yeah, I did. But the other thing is that I'd talked to Mom, and she'd made me see that I wasn't just the bad parts of my father. He isn't one-dimensional, and neither are we. I'm not just his anger and pride and fear. You're not just the guy who hid something from his girlfriend. We're both the good parts of him, too. The guy who loved completely, who showed up to all of our events, who wanted the best for us. And I wanted a relationship with that man."

"But we just got the bad out of him all over again."

Jordan nodded. "We did. All over again. So, yeah, you're like Dad. The good and the bad. He helped raise us, so that's the hand we were dealt. It doesn't *define* you though unless you let it."

I sighed in a small measure of relief. "Thanks, Jor. Now, what the hell am I going to do?"

"Well, first, we're going to look into the distributor. If Ashleigh was working against us on this, then we can go after her legally. We still have all the shit from this winter. I wish you'd come to me with this earlier. I could have seen if Wright Construction had any contacts."

"I should have. I just...didn't want to let you down."

Jordan smiled and patted my back. "You couldn't let me down, Julian. I'm so proud of your work. You love that job. That's all I want for you."

"It felt like I had all this pressure on my shoulders."

"You did. Pressure is good but not if you're going to ignore the people who care about you. We're here to help and carry the burden." He shrugged. "It's a hard lesson to learn."

He wasn't wrong. I hated learning this. Hated that I'd been stupid enough to go back to Ashleigh after everything.

"What do I do about Jen?"

Jordan shrugged. "Mom told me once to grovel. Flowers and chocolates are always a good choice."

I laughed. "No way does that work."

"Worked with Annie."

"Bullshit. She'd already forgiven you."

Jordan rolled his eyes. "Whatever, ass."

Weston pulled in, in his rental car and waved at the pair of us, where we stood away from the rest of the crowd. We were going to have to finish this up now and have that long-overdue conversation with our half-brother. Seeing Weston's tentative smile made me understand that we might be losing our dad in this, but maybe we'd be gaining so much more.

"Do you think she'll forgive me?" I asked before Weston reached us.

"Give her time. Jen loves you. She'll come around."

My heart leaped at those words. Words we hadn't even come close to saying. I hadn't even let myself think about them. I'd been too worried about scaring her away. And now, I'd fucked it up, and it was all I could think about. I loved her, and I'd never told her.

I was going to make this right.

One way or another, I was going to fix this.

I had to.

39

JENNIFER

"Okay. Just lie on the couch, and I'll see if Piper and Blaire have emergency ice cream," Annie said, depositing me in the living room.

I flopped back onto the couch. Tears still leaked down my cheeks. I hadn't been able to stop crying since Annie had picked me up. Yes, I'd stood up for myself. Yes, I'd done the right thing. But now, I felt *terrible*.

My heart had been flattened. Shattered. Thrown on the ground and stomped on. Everything was too much, too fast, and I couldn't make it stop. The ice cream Annie was looking for wouldn't do a damn thing to make this better. I popped a full Xanax instead. Maybe I could drift away into oblivion and not have to think about it.

"Pipes, some help!" Annie called as Piper stepped into the room with wide eyes.

"What is happening?" Piper asked in shock.

"Found it!" Annie said, holding up the ice cream triumphantly.

She and Piper headed into the living room, and Annie

opened up a container of Americone Dream for me. She passed me the spoon, but I still couldn't stop crying.

Piper looked horrified. "What did that boy *do* to you?"

Annie sat next to me and brushed my hair back. "Hey, it's going to be okay."

"What's all the commotion?" Blaire asked, stepping out of her room in matching pink shorts and sports bra combo. She got one look at Jennifer and dashed to the couch. "Whoa! What's going on?"

"She just broke up with Julian," Annie informed her.

Piper and Blaire both gasped at the same time. Their eyes were huge as they took me in, disbelief warring with concern.

"I don't...I don't know if we broke up," I whispered.

"You told him no after that shit he pulled, and then you walked away. The message was clear."

I pulled my arms into my stomach. "I don't want to break up with him."

"I know," Annie said softly. "I know you don't."

"Maybe he'll just..." I hiccupped. "Maybe he'll send me flowers and tacos, and everything will be better."

Annie's look was so positively pitying that I had to close my eyes. It had worked for Annie. Of course it wouldn't work for me. I wasn't Annie. I stood up to Julian in the way that Annie would. I'd found my voice for the first time, but I was already regretting it. I didn't want it to be over with Julian. I was mad at him for what had happened, what he'd done, but this couldn't be the end. Could it?

"I'm so sorry, Jennifer. I really have to get to the hospital. Fuck." She looked to my roommates. "Can y'all handle it from here?"

"We've got her," Piper said authoritatively.

Blaire nodded. "Of course."

Annie squeezed my arm. "I'm texting Sutton to see if she can come over, too."

"No, it's okay," I murmured. "I'll text her later."

"You're sure?"

I nodded. She sighed and then left.

Piper and Blaire filled in for her, doing all the right things and peppering me with all the right questions. I just lay on the couch like a lump as tears fell. I hadn't known I had this many tears. I hadn't cried like this in years. Not since my last breakup when the guy had called me crazy for my anxiety. But those tears had been different. They had been self-loathing. This was defeat.

I'd had everything I wanted, and it had all crumbled to dust.

"Hey, your phone is ringing," Piper said. "Can I dig into your bag and get it?"

"Sure," I muttered, swiping at my face.

"If it's Julian, can I answer and cuss him out?" Blaire asked.

Piper shook her head. "Oh no, I can handle him."

"He doesn't have a phone," I said.

"What do you mean?" Blaire asked.

"He broke it and hasn't had time to get a new one."

"Who doesn't have time to get a new phone?" Piper asked skeptically. Then she finally grabbed my phone out of my bag. "Uh, it says *Mom*."

"Crap," I said. "I...I have to answer it." Piper handed me the phone. I sniffed and tried to clear my throat before answering, "Hello?"

"Hi, honey. Dad is almost finished cooking, and Chester is already here. You're late."

I clenched my jaw. Crap, I'd forgotten about Sunday brunch. Mom was trying to make it a thing so that we saw each other every weekend after church. Chester and I didn't go, but Mom still did. She hadn't asked if I was coming. She'd just accused me of being late. I wanted to tell her that I wasn't coming. But I'd used up my no today against Julian. I didn't have it in me to say it to my mom. Her disdain would be so much worse.

"Sorry. I got caught up. I'm on my way."

She huffed softly. "We'll save you a seat."

"Thanks."

Piper and Blaire looked at me with wide eyes when I hung up. "You're going to meet your folks?" Piper asked.

"Yeah, I forgot."

"Is that a good idea?" Blaire asked.

"Probably not, but I still have to go."

They both protested as I heaved myself to my feet and went into my room to change. I just ignored them. They didn't know my family situation. That staying home would be worse than getting it over with.

I put on a modest yellow dress and did something to my hair. I didn't look in the mirror. I didn't want to know what I looked like. I couldn't seem to care.

"Jen," Piper said, "are you sure?"

I sighed. "No. I'm really not."

"Can I drive you at least?" she asked.

"Nah, I'm okay to drive." I glanced down at the cat food bag and sighed even heavier. I'd forgotten to feed them when I got home. Things had been...bad. I needed to do it.

I took the cat food outside with me and dumped it into their bowls. Before I could even call their names, Bacon walked right up to me, purring and running her body along my legs.

"Hey, Bakey," I said, dropping back on my heels so I could pet her.

Tears came again as my cat comforted me. She probably just wanted her food, but right now, it felt like she loved me. And I could use one more person loving me.

Then to my surprise, Avocado slunk out of the bushes. I nearly startled at her presence, but I stayed perfectly still. This was the closest she'd come to me since I'd moved her. She hadn't even looked at me when I called her name.

Now, here she was, staring right at me. I didn't want her to run off, so I actually held my breath. Avocado sniffed the air as she went to her food bowl. She smelled it, and I thought she'd go back to ignoring me. But she turned away from it and came to press her body against mine. Not running it along me, like Bacon had been, just pushing into me. As if to say that she was here. She knew something was wrong, and she would be here for me.

I tentatively put my hand out and ran it down her ginger fur. She didn't purr. Only met me with her bright stare. I got two full pets in before she trotted off back into the bushes. But that was enough. I was forgiven.

A weight fell off of my shoulders. I hadn't known how much I was holding it all in, waiting for my cat to not hate me anymore. But if Avocado could forgive me after traumatizing her...maybe I could find a way to go on.

I hauled myself back to my feet and got into Bertha. I slammed my hand on the air-conditioning unit, trying to force it to turn on. Something went *clunk* on the inside, and I screamed at it with every horrible word I had in my vocabulary. But it was no use. Something was finally broken in Bertha, just like inside of me. We were the same now.

I rolled all of the windows down and already started to sweat in the Texas heat. I'd have to do something about the AC. There was no way I would survive the rest of July and August like this. I might have to have Blaire sell Campbell's image to a few magazines so that I could cover the costs. Just another fucking thing.

I pulled up in front of my parents' house. It was the same place they'd had since I was in elementary school. Cluttered with memories, a wall covered in crosses—as was so popular in Lubbock—and all the half-finished projects my father had said that he was going to get to and never did. It was a house, but it had never felt like home.

"I'm here," I called as I entered.

Mom was seated on the couch. Chester on a chair nearby. Mom raised an eyebrow at my appearance. Chester even startled. Great.

"Hi, kiddo!" my dad called from the kitchen. He was a pancake connoisseur. Something about his short time in the Army. My parents otherwise had a pretty traditional marriage. Mom cooked and cleaned and balanced the budget, and Dad worked. Even though she'd *always* had a job to help make ends meet.

"Hi, Dad."

"What happened?" my mom asked, coming to her feet.

"Nothing," I lied.

Chester blew out a breath. "Your eyes are all puffy, sis."

"Thanks, Chess," I practically growled.

He looked at me in surprise, as if it was the first time he'd seen me with teeth. Which, to be fair, it probably was.

"Have you been crying?" Mom asked. She wrapped an arm around my shoulders. "Tell me everything."

I sank into the couch and sighed. I didn't want to do this. And yet there, in the house that wasn't a home, with family that felt too familiar and yet so distant, and Chester's reassuring nod, I let loose. I shouldn't, but it was so fresh, and I couldn't stop.

"I broke up with Julian," I said as I started crying again.

My mom gasped. "*You* broke up with him?"

"Yeah. I mean, I guess."

"He didn't break up with you?" she asked.

"That's what she said, Mom," Chester broke in. "What happened, Jen?"

"I don't know. It just...it didn't work out. God, I hate to tell you this, but it was fake."

"What do you mean, dear?" Mom asked.

"When I brought Julian to graduation, we weren't dating. I hate lying to you, and I can't hold it in any longer. We were fake dating so that I wouldn't have to go alone."

They both stared at me in shock.

"Well...that's..." my mom said.

"But it was real after," I said quickly. "It was real, and we were together. But then he hid something from me and lied about it. I might have forgiven that, but then he saw my anxiety medication and assumed I was on drugs. Well, his ex assumed. I don't know if I'm even explaining all of this. But I either had to tell him about my anxiety before I was ready or give it up. And I didn't want him to be okay with me because I'd told him about my mental health."

"Well, you shouldn't tell him about the anxiety," my mom said quickly.

"Why not?" Chester said. "If he had known, then you might not have even had this argument."

"It still would have happened," I whispered. "The lying and hiding at least."

"You don't discuss your mental health, Chester. You know that. There are things that you never discuss in public."

"This wasn't public. This was her boyfriend."

"All these issues people keep dragging into the spotlight —race, money, mental problems, sexual orientation, religion. I don't need to know about this, and neither does anyone else. Keep it to yourself. Let me live my life."

Chester bristled. "What does that have to do with Jennifer and her boyfriend? Her anxiety is part of who she is. If he wanted to be with her, then he needed to love that part of her, too."

"I just think everything needs to go back to the way it was."

He arched an eyebrow. Mom couldn't see that he was mad, but I could from here. "Back to the way it was for *whom*?" he snarled. "White, cis, hetero people? I'm sorry, but I can't see how going back to the past, when things were worse for people who weren't straight white dudes, is *better* than helping everyone."

"Since when did you become so political?" my mom asked, her hackles raised.

"If civil rights and basic common decency are political, then fine, Mom, I'm political."

"Y'all," I whispered, "don't fight."

I could see the train running off the tracks, but there was nothing I could do to stop it. This was who our mother was. Who she had always been and raised us to be. She didn't know that by saying things, she'd be slapping her favorite child in the face.

"For someone who *is* a straight white man, I don't see how it matters to you."

He rose to his feet. His hands were shaking, like mine did when I was going to explode. "I don't know how to tell you that you should care about other people," he said, lethally calm.

"I care about other people," she gasped.

"And for the record, I'm not straight. I'm pan. And I have

a boyfriend named Peter. My life isn't political. It's just living. And so is Jennifer's."

My mom's jaw dropped. "You're...pan? What does that mean?"

"I like everyone, Mom. I don't care about their gender identity or their sex. I fall in love with the person."

She nodded in shock. "And you have a...boyfriend."

"Peter," he said, his voice softening on the word. "Peter Medina."

"I...well, this is a lot to take in, Chester. When did you decide?"

"I've always known. Jennifer knows. So, I'd appreciate it if you put your feelings about the matter on hold and listen to us. Listen to Jen when she says that she's hurting because of her anxiety. I wasn't ready to tell you about my sexual orientation, and she has every right to hide her mental illness, but she doesn't *have* to just because you think it's more socially acceptable."

Dad walked out then with a plate of pancakes. "Brunch is ready. Is it too late to invite Peter over?" He'd clearly heard everything.

Mom gaped at him.

Chester just smiled at Dad. "You want him to come for brunch?"

"My son has a boyfriend that I haven't met. It's time to remedy that. Connie, will you help me set the table?"

She nodded, glad to have something to do.

Chester clapped me on the back. "Sorry to steal your thunder."

"By all means," I said, still blinking away my own surprise. "I didn't think you wanted them to know."

"Well, Mom crossed the line, and I never should have let you take the brunt of her for all these years."

"Thanks, Chess."

He pulled me into another hug. "What are you going to do about Julian? Anxiety is a part of you. If you had a broken foot, would you take pain meds and hide it from him, for fear that he'd judge you for it? The stigma is bull-shit, Jen. You know it is. So, are you going to tell him the truth about who you are?"

When he put it like that, it was amazing that I'd hidden it at all. Anxiety was part of me. Why was I ashamed of that? Because my mom didn't like to discuss it? Because some douche ex had called me crazy? Would Julian judge me for it? That was my fear.

And there was only one way to find out.

40

JULIAN

*H*ollin and Alejandra sat in front of me for a meeting I'd called, wearing equal looks of amusement I'd waited a couple days to do it—to inform them about the distribution problem. I'd wanted to deal with all of my personal issues first.

Breakfast with Weston had gone really great. I'd been shocked that as soon as we'd gotten him out of the winery and into a normal setting, he'd shucked off that fear and unease. He'd been a completely different, totally awesome person. He played keyboard in a few different bands, subbing in when it was necessary, and worked at a small indie record label in Seattle in his downtime. He also did IT work when he needed the money. It was what his degree was in, but his passion was in music. He reminded me so much of Campbell when he talked about it. Despite our differences with our dad, I could see that he was someone I wanted to get to know.

Whitt and Harley were another story. Whitt hadn't wanted him to try to talk to us. Harley had actually been the one to discover we existed. She was an upcoming senior in high school and a bit of a genius. She'd pieced together our existence, but she was dealing with the rage of being right. It'd take time.

Then we'd had to tell Mom. She'd taken it better than I had. She hadn't been surprised even, just disappointed, and had gone to bed early. I hated it for her, but it was what it was.

"Wright, come the fuck on. We have work to do," Hollin said impatiently.

I took a deep breath. "We didn't get the distribution contract."

"Ugh, okay," Hollin said.

Alejandra lazily dropped her head sideways to look at Hollin. She held her hand out. "Pony up, Abbey."

"Fuck," he grumbled. He dug out his wallet and dropped a twenty into her hand.

I looked between them. "What is going on?"

"Oh, we never thought you'd get it," Alejandra said.

"I did!" Hollin said.

"*Pobrecito,*" she crooned, patting his cheek. *Poor baby.*

"Wait, what? If you didn't think that I was going to get it, why were we going for it? Why did I just stress myself out for weeks?"

"Like, normal people can't get that their first year open," Hollin said. But he gestured to me. "But you're a Wright. If anyone could do it, you could."

"Yeah. You have contacts and currency," Alejandra explained.

"But, hey," Hollin said, coming to his feet, "this means, you're just like everyone else."

"And I'm twenty bucks richer," Alejandra said. "So, thanks for that."

They headed out of my office, ribbing each other over

the bet. Meanwhile, I was stuck in my seat. I'd worked so hard for this, only to find out it was basically impossible. But they had been right on some level, too, weren't they? I could have gotten the contract. If I'd played Ashleigh's game, then Alejandra would have paid up to Hollin. I did have the contacts and currency. But it was still frustrating.

Hollin popped his head back inside. "Hey, how are you holding up?"

I shrugged. "It's been a rough week."

"You and Jennifer?"

I shook my head. "She hasn't returned any of my calls or texts."

"Bummer."

"Yeah, I guess I earned it."

"You think?" Hollin asked, flopping back into the seat and kicking his boots up onto my desk. "What makes you say that?"

"I went to Ashleigh about the distribution issue and hid it from...everyone."

Hollin whistled. "Well, fuck."

"She was going to fix it, too. You were probably right that I could have gotten it."

"Damn. But you'd have sacrificed your dignity in the meantime. And Jennifer, who we all know you're head over heels for."

"I am," I agreed with a sigh.

"And anyway, you know Ashleigh sabotaged the deal in the first place to make you come to her. Isn't that her MO?"

"Yeah. She didn't admit to that, but yeah, I got so caught up that I didn't see it."

"That's why you need to come to me, bro." Hollin patted his chest with his tatted arm and grinned. "I'll keep you on the straight and narrow."

I laughed. "Why do I feel like *straight and narrow* doesn't mean the same thing to you as it does to me?"

"Eh," he said with a shrug. "So, how are you going to win Jennifer back? I have some big ideas."

"Oh God, do I even want to know?"

Hollin grinned wolfishly. "It'll make a splash at least."

"Nah, I think I'll give her some time. We have to work together still, especially since we got the contract for Morgan and Patrick's wedding."

"For reals?" he asked. "They're getting married here?"

"Yeah. Nora had them sign the paperwork. A Wright wedding with the Wright CEO at a Wright Vineyard."

"Y'all are fucking obsessed with your name. It's a little weird."

I snorted at him. "Says the guy who insisted we use it."

"Yeah, because we need money, and people associate y'all with money. But we're serving Abbey wine because I know what I'm fucking doing."

"So true," I said with a shake of my head. "But if she doesn't return my messages by this weekend, I'll go to her place, try to grovel."

"Good idea. Buy flowers. Girls love that shit."

"How would you even know with a three-date rule?"

He scoffed. "I told you, that's not what it fucking is."

I chuckled, and it felt good to laugh a little with Hollin. That the world wasn't ending even though this weekend had been shit. I needed to figure out how to approach Jennifer. I couldn't—*wouldn't*—let her go.

Hollin's phone rang noisily in the office. "It's my dad." He answered, "Sup?" Then he straightened up, dropping his boots to the ground. "What happened? Yeah, I'm with Julian now. Let me put you on speaker."

I glanced at him as he put the phone down on my desk on speakerphone.

"Hey, Julian. It's Uncle Gregg."

"What's going on?"

"I just got off the phone with your aunt Lori. She's with your mom, and she had a fall. She passed out, and they took her by ambulance to the hospital."

"What?" I gasped, jumping to my feet.

"I wanted to let you know. If you and Hollin want to get to the hospital, we'll meet you there," he said. "I'm going to call your brother next."

"I'll be there."

He told us the hospital, and then Hollin and I raced for the parking lot. We hopped in his truck and peeled out. I shot off a text to Alejandra to let her know why we'd left. Gregg was contacting Jordan, so all I had to do was worry as we drove across town to the hospital.

My mom had looked fragile for weeks. I had assumed it was the chemo. That she was going to recover like normal. I'd been so embroiled in my own issues that I hadn't had time for her like I had the last time we did this. Then we'd told her about Dad. Fuck, of course she was going to take it hard. She'd put on a show for me and Jor.

Hollin didn't try to reassure me on the way. He knew what could happen. What I had to lose.

So, he parked in the visitor lot, and we dashed inside. We met Jordan in the lobby. He'd been a lot closer, working at Wright Construction downtown.

"You made it," Jordan said with relief.

"Have you heard anything?" I asked.

"Just got here. Guess we'll find out together." Jordan looked grim. "I texted Annie to see if she'd meet us. I'd feel better, having her assessment."

We passed through the double doors and then found Mom's room. The door was slightly ajar when we knocked. Aunt Lori opened the door with a sad smile.

"Hey, guys," she said, brushing back her short bleached-blonde hair.

"How's she doing?" I asked.

"She's stable, but they're monitoring her. Why don't you go in and see her?"

I pushed past her without a second thought and found my mom lying in a bed, hooked up to beeping equipment, and looking as thin and rundown as I'd ever seen her.

"Mom."

"Julian," she said with a smile. "Did Lori worry you enough to come by?"

Jordan appeared in the door, too.

"Both of my boys."

"Hey, Mom. How are you feeling?"

"I'm fine," she said. She even laughed. "It's all a big misunderstanding."

"A misunderstanding? You passed out and came to in a hospital."

"Lori overreacted. I don't need to be in here."

I frowned, and Jordan exchanged a look with me. I didn't believe her. She didn't look *fine*. She looked worse than when we'd seen her on Sunday. That was only a couple days ago, and she'd taken a downturn.

"Is this because of Dad?" I asked the question I hadn't wanted to.

"What? No. Your father is...no longer my concern."

"He said he was trying to reconcile with you."

She laughed. "Is *that* what he said? What a fiction. No, he apologized and asked me about the cancer. He was polite but nothing more. It's clear he's moved on. And you know what? I finally have, too."

Jordan and I both looked at her in shock. Our mom had loved our dad far longer than she should have. She had loved him still, even when she divorced him and moved away and started a new life. To have moved on was a huge thing for her.

"I still love him, but I'm not in love with him," she said to our shocked faces. "It's for the better. Maybe I can start dating again."

I groaned, and Jordan looked green.

"Not to interrupt," Annie said, entering, "but that sounds like a good idea to me."

"Oh, Annie," Mom said. She was beaming. She *loved* Annie. "Jordan didn't pull you from the ER, did he?"

"He did, but that's okay."

"Are you going to let me out of here?"

Annie pulled her chart up on an iPad and laughed. "I think we'll listen to whatever the oncologist said. It looks like your vitals are still not where he wants them to be. He said to keep you overnight."

"I know. But I don't think it's necessary."

Annie smiled a careful, doctoral smile. "Well, the doctor says it's necessary. So, here we are."

My mom rolled her eyes. "All right. Fine. I'm here already. What's one night?"

Annie kissed Jordan. "I should really get back though. They're going to need me the minute they realize I'm gone."

"Okay, babe. Love you."

"Love you, too," she said and then headed out the door.

"I'll be right back," I said, dashing after Annie. "Hey, Annie!"

She sighed and turned to face me. "How can I help you, Julian?"

I ran a hand back through my hair. "Could you...tell Jennifer about this?"

She furrowed her brow. "Is your phone still not operational?"

"No. It works. She just won't respond to me."

"And you don't deserve that?"

I winced. "Uh, I do, but I just...I want her to know. I'm not asking for more...yet."

"You Wright men," she said with a huff.

"Please, Annie. I fucked up, but I want to fix things. You of all people should understand."

She wavered for a second and then nodded. "Fine, Julian. But she doesn't owe you anything."

"Of course."

She got out her phone and texted. "There."

"Thanks, Annie."

She shook her head. A small smile came to her lips. "Good luck."

Then she disappeared. And I needed every ounce of that luck if I was going to fix this with Jen.

41

JENNIFER

"Hi, I'm here to see Helena Wright," I said to the nurses' desk. "Can I be buzzed through?"

"Sure thing, honey," the nurse said.

The buzzer went off, and I yanked the door open.

"Thanks," I threw out as I rushed forward.

Annie's text had sent me into a frenzy. I hadn't been responding to Julian's messages. I wanted to, but I needed to decide what I was going to do about it all. He'd said he was sorry and that he wanted to fix things. But saying those things were not actions. And I didn't know how to reconcile what he'd done with what I wanted from him. Not to mention, plucking up the courage that Chester'd had with our mom.

Anxiety was a part of who I was. It wasn't *who* I was, but it was a defining point of my person. Did I risk Julian seeing me differently by divulging that? Did I risk everything by being my real self?

All I knew was that when I'd found out his mom was in the hospital, I had to get to him. I had to get to him right now. I was mad at him, but I wasn't callous.

I stopped in front of the door for Helena's room. My hand rose, but I didn't knock. I was half-worried that I would be interrupting and half-worried that I would have no idea what to say. Welcome back, anxiety.

I took a deep breath and then knocked.

"Come in!" a voice called.

I turned the knob and found myself face-to-face with a room full of people. Julian and Jordan sat at their mom's bedside with Hollin and Nora also there along with their dad and aunt. I'd met them all at some point, but I was blanking on their names. Mostly because I was now accosted with the sight of everyone staring at me.

"Hey," I said with a small wave. "I just, uh, came to check on you."

"Jennifer, I'm glad you're here," Helena said with a smile.

"Are you...are you doing all right?"

"Fine," she said, staring at her sons. "They're keeping me overnight, but I'm fine."

"That's such a relief. I'm glad to hear that. I was worried."

Julian shot to his feet. "Can we talk?"

I eyed the room. Everyone tried to look anywhere but at me. I swallowed. Eesh. Then I nodded, backing out of the room.

I heard his mom and Hollin make fun of him from the open door and almost smiled a little at it. Clearly, everyone knew what was going on with us.

"Hey." Julian pulled the door closed behind him, silencing the spatter of laughter. "Sorry about all of this. I'm glad that you came."

"I wanted to make sure she was okay. And you too."

He grinned. "I appreciate it. My mom does, too."

"You could have texted yourself."

"I wasn't sure you were taking my texts."

"And whose fault is that?" I snapped.

He clenched his jaw and nodded. "Mine. A hundred percent. All my fault."

I sagged at those words. "No, it's mine, too."

"Not at all, Jennifer. I fucked this up. I hid the stuff with Ashleigh. I'm sorry I went to her at all. I'm sorry that I asked about your pills. I don't deserve you even being here."

"Well, those things were pretty bad."

He laughed softly. "Yeah. I'm an idiot." He gestured down the hall. "There's a waiting room with chairs and a vending machine if you want."

I nodded and walked side by side with him down the hallway and to the nice waiting room. It was thankfully empty. Julian paid for two waters and passed one to me. I was glad to have something to do with my hands.

He took a good sip and then sank into the couch next to me. "I want to apologize. Again."

"It's okay."

"It's really not okay. I just...I had all this pressure on my shoulders. I thought I had to make the impossible happen. That everyone would think less of me for not doing it all. I was wrong. No one cared, but I learned that only after failing. And I told Ashleigh that if I had to work with her to get this, then it wasn't worth it. I think—hope—that she finally got the picture. I won't entertain any of her bullshit anymore."

"That must have been hard."

"It wasn't," he said easily. "You know, I was still harboring this deep wound from Ashleigh. I kept letting her dig back under my skin. There was a hole where she'd hurt me. But then *you* happened."

"Me?" I whispered.

"You. I realized that the two years with Ashleigh was nothing. They were a lie. Nothing could ever compare to what I have with you."

"Julian..."

He laughed softly. "I know. Too much, too fast, right?"

"It's everything I ever wanted to hear," I admitted. "I wanted this so bad that I deluded myself into thinking you wanted it, too."

"I do! I do want this. I want you."

"But I wasn't honest with you either."

He furrowed his brow. "What do you mean?"

I took a deep breath. I could do this. I could get all of this out. I was making this decision, and it was the right one. No matter what his reaction.

"I have an anxiety disorder," I told him. "It's relatively severe, and I've been medicated daily since high school. I also have severe social anxiety, and I get debilitating panic attacks. So, I have emergency Xanax as well as a sleeping pill to help with the anxiety-induced insomnia."

Julian didn't even blink. He met my gaze evenly. "Okay."

"Okay? That's it?"

"Well, I mean, I thought you were just shy. I've always thought you were shy, especially in crowds."

"I am," I said with a shrug. "I am shy, but a lot of it is a medical issue that I've been dealing with my entire life. I've been in therapy for almost as long. It's why I'm pretty good at breaking down other people's problems and finding a solution. Not that I'm great at that with my own problems."

"This all makes perfect sense."

I flinched. "It does?"

"Yes, I think it explains a lot of your behavior. I thought you just...didn't want to be with me. That you weren't as into me as I was into you. But in reality, you were dealing with this mental illness all on your own."

"I...I was," I said. He'd articulated it so clearly.

Julian sat for a minute in contemplation before asking softly, "Why didn't you tell me?"

I hung my head. The question I'd been dreading.

"Not that you were obligated to," he said quickly. "It's your mental health. I want you to feel the best about what you're going through. I just...I don't know why or even how you were able to keep it from me."

"Well," I began, swallowing hard, "I didn't know how you'd react."

"React?" He honestly looked confused.

I took a deep breath and let it out carefully. "My last real boyfriend found out about it. This was a couple years ago. And he...he called me crazy."

Julian winced. "Fuck."

"Yeah. He said I was crazy, and that was why he didn't want to be with me. It ended poorly. Not to mention, my mom has always kind of ingrained in me that I should keep this to myself. But I'm tired of hiding this big part of myself."

"Jen," Julian said, cautiously taking my hand, "I would never judge you for this. Anxiety is a real illness. And I'm so sorry that anyone made you feel like you were less for having it."

Tears rushed to my eyes. The words I'd always wanted to hear and feared I never would.

"Thank you," I whispered.

He leaned forward, cupping my jaw in his hands, and kissed me tenderly. "You're a gem, a revelation. You are the best thing that has ever happened to me. This changes absolutely nothing with me. It only makes me see the perfectly wonderful, vibrant woman that I'm in love with more clearly."

I gasped against his mouth, my eyes shooting open. "Love?"

"Yes. Jennifer, I love you."

My throat closed up, and I thought I was really going to start crying now. "Julian, oh my God," I whispered. I rested my forehead against his. "I love you, too."

"God, it's good to hear that."

I laughed through my tears. "It really is."

"And again, I'm sorry. I won't repeat the mistakes I did to upset you. I want to work to be the man who deserves you."

"You already are." I kissed him again. "You already are."

He pulled me into his arms and kissed me long and deep. "God, I thought I'd lost you."

"I know. I thought so, too. But I never wanted this to happen."

"Me neither." He kissed me again before pulling me to my feet and lacing our fingers together. "You're mine."

"All yours."

"That's what I like to hear."

So, I kissed him again, glad that I'd found the power of my own truth. The power of being exactly who I was and having a man who loved me for that person and nothing else.

Julian Wright saw the pieces of me, jagged edges and all, and he loved me anyway. Just as I loved him.

EPILOGUE
SIX MONTHS LATER

"That's a wrap!" Campbell called to everyone backstage.

The Wright Vineyard workers cheered at the end of the longest night since harvest. Julian shook hands with the band, rubbing elbows with the record representatives who had come to see the kickoff to Cosmere's world tour. The fact that it was in the middle of nowhere in Lubbock, Texas hadn't been their first choice, but it sure as hell helped the vineyard.

Campbell pushed through his admirers to find me and threw his sweaty arms around me. I laughed and hugged him back.

"Congratulations! I cannot believe that you're about to go out on tour and I won't see you for months."

Campbell grinned. "We'll miss you, Gibson. But I have a surprise for you."

"Oh?"

He dropped a CD case into my hand. "Signed by the whole band."

"Oh my God," I whispered as I stared down at *my* photograph under the plastic case. "I'm definitely getting this framed."

He laughed. "You made it happen."

"We made it happen," I told him.

He winked at me and then dove back into the fray.

Julian returned a minute later to my side. "Ready to go home?"

"I'm so jittery. I can't believe this all happened. And look what Campbell gave me."

Julian looked at it. "You're such a fangirl."

"I so am."

He laughed and wrapped an arm around my waist. "Let's get out of here."

"Oh, sultry voice," I teased. "Someone has a lot of energy."

"You just said you're jittery."

But he took my hand and tugged me out of the back entrance to the barn. We waved at Jordan and Annie as we passed. Piper was standing against a wall, and Hollin was saying something that made her back stiffen. She looked like she always did when he talked to her, like she was *this* close to stabbing him with something sharp. Blaire wasn't here at all. She'd already bailed with no explanation. Though I had an idea as to why.

But best of all, Julian's mom had come for the show. She'd been let out of the hospital the next day when her vitals were back on track. Then she'd spent months doing chemo with a fuzzy mind and a desperate look about her. She'd turned a corner at Christmas, and she was back to her bubbly self. Still wearing a head scarf and promising to find a new man for herself. Annie and I were more into it than the boys, of course.

"Milli or Cornelia?" Julian asked as we approached the car.

With the money from the cover album shoot and the selling of my latest portrait session, I'd finally given up on Bertha. And like I'd suggested to Julian all those months ago, I'd named my new car Cornelia. She wasn't anything fancy like Milli—a VW Jetta instead of a Jaguar—but I loved her all the same.

"Cornelia," I said. "Obviously."

He laughed and let me drive him home. I'd left food out for the cats so that I could stay the night. I'd been doing that a lot lately. Though I wasn't quite ready to move in. Maybe when my lease was up. We'd been talking about it, but he was okay with waiting. Especially since we both knew Avocado might kill us if we moved her again.

I pulled up to Julian's house, and he rushed around to help me out of the car. He shouldered my photography backpack and then dropped a kiss on my lips.

"So, you know how Campbell surprised you with the CD?"

"Yeah?" I asked as he walked backward in front of me toward the house.

"He's an asshole. I planned a surprise first."

I snorted. "He didn't know that, did he?"

"No."

"Then how is he an asshole?"

"Go with me on this one."

"Okay. What's my surprise?"

"If I told you, it wouldn't be a surprise," he said with a glint in his eyes. We reached the front door. "Close your eyes."

"What? Seriously?"

"Seriously, Jen. Close them. Cover them with your hands. No peeking."

I sighed and did what he'd said. I couldn't see his hand as it passed in front of my face, but the dark got darker, so I knew he was doing it.

"I can't see you!" I grumbled.

He laughed and unlocked the door, helping me over the first step inside and depositing me in the living room. He disappeared for a minute and then finally said, "Okay, now, open."

I opened my eyes, blinking at the bright lights. Then I gasped.

"Oh my God, Julian, what did you do?"

On the floor in front of us was the cutest, smallest, most adorable little white kitten I'd ever seen in my life.

"I got us a kitten."

"But I don't like cats," I said with a wink.

He laughed boisterously and then knelt in front of the cat. I dropped to my knees next to him, playing with the tiny thing, running my finger down her belly, letting her gnaw on my finger.

"She's so cute. Gah! What's her name?"

"All yours, Dreamsicle," he joked.

I shook my head. "You and that nickname."

"Hey, you earned it."

"Well, little one, what do you think your name is?" I asked the kitten. "Probably something to go with your two older sisters, yes?"

"Definitely. Avocado, Bacon, and..."

"Tortilla."

"Tortilla!" Julian roared, rolling over to laugh. "Oh my God, yes!"

"We can call her Tilla."

"Cado, Bakey, and Tilla. You have a full dinner now."

"Together, they make some kind of taco," I said with a shrug. "What do you think, Tilla?"

She meowed, looking up at me with the biggest blue eyes in the world.

"I think she approves."

"I approve," he said, drawing me back to him. "I approve of us. This family."

"Family?" I asked carefully.

"She's ours now."

"I like that."

He smiled. "You spend so much time here, and the other cats don't need as much love. I thought it'd be nice to have an indoor cat who only partially hates us but might some-times love us."

"That's about as good as you can get with a cat."

"You, me, and Tilla. One big, happy family."

I stared down at the kitten and sighed. "I feel like I belong here."

"You belong with me."

Our fingers interlaced, and I realized that he was right. That belonging I'd always searched for, I had now. I had it here with Julian. He knew about all my deepest, darkest secrets and accepted me for who I was. I knew about the struggles he had with his dad and his family. And we fit— not despite the issues, but because we were overcoming them together.

And now, we were a little family here. A forever, all wrapped up in one little tortilla. One day, we'd want more, have more, but for now, this was right where I belonged.

THE END

ACKNOWLEDGMENTS

Serves Me Wright was the book that I was most afraid to write. If you've been following me on this journey long, you'll know I kind of like to break hearts. Shocking, I know! And when I decided that I wanted to start with the Wrights again and have the Wright Vineyard, I worried that Julian and Jennifer wouldn't have the normal angst that I enjoy personally writing. So I dug deep. I asked myself a lot of tough questions about being introverted and anxiety and depression. I looked at the effect having a broken family would have on a good man. And then when I sat down, after all of that fear, I just fell in love with Julian and Jennifer. And I hope that you loved them as much as I did. So, I want to thank everyone who was there for me as I laid on the floor in a tantrum trying to figure out how to write nice people being nice. You're the real heroes!

ABOUT THE AUTHOR

 K.A. Linde is the *USA Today* bestselling author of more than thirty novels. She has a Masters degree in political science from the University of Georgia, was the head campaign worker for the 2012 presidential campaign at the University of North Carolina at Chapel Hill, and served as the head coach of the Duke University dance team.

She loves reading fantasy novels, binge-watching Supernatural, traveling to far off destinations, baking insane desserts, and dancing in her spare time.

She currently lives in Lubbock, Texas, with her husband and two super-adorable puppies.

Visit her online:
www.kalinde.com

Or Facebook, Instagram & Tiktok:
@authorkalinde

For exclusive content, free books,
and giveaways every month.
www.kalinde.com/subscribe